PENGUIN BOOKS

Hide and Seek

M. J. Arlidge has worked in television for the last fifteen years, specializing in high-end drama production, including prime-time crime serials *Torn*, *The Little House* and *Silent Witness*. Arlidge is also piloting original crime series for both UK and US networks. In 2015 his audiobook exclusive *Six Degrees of Assassination* was a number-one bestseller.

His debut thriller, *Eeny Meeny*, was the UK's bestselling crime debut of 2014. It was followed by the bestselling *Pop Goes the Weasel*, *The Doll's House*, *Liar Liar* and *Little Boy Blue*. *Hide and Seek* is the sixth DI Helen Grace thriller and will be followed by *Love Me Not* in 2017.

Hide and Seek

M. J. ARLIDGE

PENGUIN BOOKS

PENGUIN BOOKS

UK | USA | Canada | Ireland | Australia
India | New Zealand | South Africa

Penguin Books is part of the Penguin Random House group of companies
whose addresses can be found at global.penguinrandomhouse.com

First published by Michael Joseph 2016
Published in Penguin Books 2016

001

Copyright © M. J. Arlidge, 2016

The moral right of the author has been asserted

Set in 12/14.33 pt Garamond MT Std
Typeset by Jouve (UK), Milton Keynes
Printed in Great Britain by Clays Ltd, St Ives plc

A CIP catalogue record for this book is available from the British Library

ISBN: 978–1–405–93530–2

www.greenpenguin.co.uk

I

She moved fast, keeping her head down. The corridor was full of bodies tonight, but she bullied her way past them, never once looking back. Expletives and abuse accompanied her clumsy progress and as she turned the corner into her wing, she felt a large glob of saliva hit the back of her neck. Normally she would have turned to confront the offender – she loved cracking bones – but there was no question of that tonight.

Lock-up was only fifteen minutes away and Leah knew that if she could make it back to her cell she would be safe. She'd been lying low in the Skills Department, concealing herself in a disused storeroom, but when the bell rang for end of association, she knew she had to move. She was not superstitious by nature, but as she left her hiding place, she kissed her crucifix three times, muttering her boys' names and praying for luck. She had a feeling she would need it.

They knew. And now they were coming for her. It was just a question of where and when. Holloway Prison is a maze of narrow, ill-lit corridors, with numerous opportunities for ambush. Leah knew the terrain better than most – she'd been here five years already – but that was no guarantee of safety. Not when you were being hunted by the pack.

As she quickened her pace, Leah was suddenly overwhelmed by fear – she had the strong feeling that she would die in here, amid the filth and the misery. She could picture herself bleeding out on the floor, as her attackers circled her, their eyes full of hate . . .

'Get yourself together, girl.'

The words came out in a harsh whisper and Leah cut them off abruptly, chiding herself for her weakness and stupidity. She was in deep trouble for sure, but she was nearly home – it would be crazy to mess it up now. Taking a deep breath, she emerged from the corridor and, crossing the gantry, skipped up the stairs to Level Two. She was treading lightly, trying not to make any noise, but her steps beat out a dull metallic rhythm. Her eyes darted left and right, expecting an attack at any moment, but to her surprise the way remained clear.

In fact, nothing seemed out of the ordinary tonight. As Leah scanned her wing, she saw the same old faces, jawing and laughing before their enforced separation for the night. Everybody seemed relaxed, even happy, and Leah now felt a surge of optimism. Perhaps all her fears had been for nothing. A short dash and she would be back in her cell, safe and sound.

All she had to do now was pick her moment.

2

She felt their eyes boring into her.

It had been like this ever since her arrival. Police officers sit somewhere between grasses and child killers in the prison pecking order, objects of morbid curiosity and derision. So from the gantries, the cell doorways, the serving hatches, they watched her. Detective Inspector Helen Grace was still awaiting trial, but she'd already been convicted by her fellow prisoners, who'd labelled her a murderer and a pervert, while doling out some old-fashioned Holloway punishment. At the front of the queue were the handful of violent offenders that Helen had put away *herself* – for them getting even with the disgraced police officer was a duty as well as a pleasure.

Her only respite from the daily grind of petty insults and casual violence came during working hours – inmates knew better than to mess with the smooth running of the prison – but even here there was little cheer. Duties were apportioned by the prison staff and Helen's nominated officer – a burly sadist called Campbell – took great delight in allotting her the most unpleasant tasks. Toilets and showers, medical waste, laundry and, worst of all, canteen clear-up.

This was always a painstaking duty, but tonight it had been particularly gruelling, thanks to the mess left behind by 'Lucy'. Lucy was a woman now living as a man, who'd nevertheless serve her sentence in Holloway as she was biologically female. She loathed the place and was fighting a tortuous legal battle to be transferred to a male prison. Her fellow inmates knew this and enjoyed provoking her, refusing to call her by her chosen name: Michael. Predictably things had kicked off again tonight and in the resulting brawl serious blows had been exchanged. Lucy had later vomited while being restrained, making Helen's clean-up operation even more unpleasant.

Helen was just finishing the job, eking out the last few minutes before lock-up, when she heard someone approaching. Even without looking up, she knew who it was. The inmates were all back on their wings and, besides, the slow measured tread was unmistakable. She looked up to see Cameron Campbell approaching, leaving a steady trail of footprints behind him on her freshly mopped floor.

'You missed a bit,' Campbell said, gesturing to his footprints.

'Sorry, sir,' Helen replied. 'Won't happen again.'

'Make sure it doesn't. If there is one thing I abhor, it's . . . sloppy work.'

As he spoke, he raised his right foot, nudging the rim of Helen's bucket until it toppled over, slewing huge amounts of vomit-flecked water across the floor. Helen watched the water's progress, then turned back to Campbell, her eyes burning with anger.

'Do it again,' Campbell continued casually, brushing past Helen. 'I want this place spick and span for the Christmas festivities.'

Furious, Helen bent down to grab her mop and as she did so she felt a sharp elbow ram into her kidneys. It was so sudden and so violent that it knocked the breath from her and she fell to her knees, clutching the bucket rim for support. Campbell didn't break stride, didn't bother to look

4

back, but the girls on the gantries were clearly enjoying the show.

'Look at the pig with her nose in the trough,' one wag shouted and others soon joined in.

Helen raised her head, refusing to look broken, but all she saw was a hundred mocking faces – laughing, joking, revelling in her misfortune. In her former life, she'd been a respected police officer – she would have dealt with someone like Campbell swiftly and decisively – but now she was powerless to act. In here she was the butt of all jokes, an accident waiting to happen, a handsome trophy for any inmate brave enough to chance an attack.

She had survived thus far, but how long could her luck hold? She was surrounded on all sides by women who'd slit her throat as soon as look at her, yet the authorities seemed determined to turn a blind eye to her predicament. There was nowhere to run to, nowhere to hide, so Helen could never let her guard down, never relax.

In Holloway, danger was only a heartbeat away.

The footsteps came to a sudden halt and Leah looked up sharply. But seconds later, her cell door slammed shut and she heard the reassuring sound of the latch bolts deploying. She collapsed back on to her bed, exhausted but relieved.

Luck had been on her side tonight. She'd taken advantage of the scene in the canteen – Campbell enjoying himself at the expense of her neighbour yet again – to race back to her cell. The ten minutes that ensued, as she waited for lock-up, had been agony. But it was over now.

The Judas slit snapped open and a pair of eyes appeared. Leah had come to know the eyes that spied on her and could recognize which prison officer they belonged to. Campbell's eyes were grey and cold, Sarah Bradshaw's were a weak light green and Mark Robins's were chocolate brown and kind. The latter was doing the rounds tonight. Leah smiled to herself as she heard him working his way down the line, chivvying the girls into their cells.

Most of the women hated this part of the day. As night descended they were locked away with only themselves and their dark thoughts for company. Many had been neglected as kids, some had been abused and pretty much everybody in here had self-harmed at one time or another. The night brought back memories of abandonment and loneliness, pushing many girls over the brink. It was no wonder that most suicides happened after dark.

But Leah didn't mind being locked up. During the day, she

had enough on her plate, keeping out of harm's way, so the night was *her* time. A time when she could imagine herself elsewhere. When she could make herself believe that she was at home with her boys, Dylan and Caleb. Doing normal things. Being a good person. Being a mum.

She often cried when she thought of them, but the tears somehow made her feel warm. Like their love was with her in the room. Cheered by this, she used her time alone to plot her future, planning how she would get to be with her boys again. She was doing a life stretch and visiting orders were scarce, so she'd had to think around the problem.

She was taking a massive risk, but there was no other way. Her mum and the boys were visiting tomorrow, and while she was in the relatives' centre, she would demand to see the Governor. She had *earned* her transfer to the enhanced wing. From there perhaps she could get moved to an open prison. Was it too much to hope that she might even get early release one day?

Leah lay on the bed and pulled the blanket up to her chin. The sun was setting and this usually made her feel calm and relaxed. But she was jumpy tonight and couldn't settle. Her mind kept flitting back to the boys. To Dylan's funny little giggle when he was tickled. To the fineness of Caleb's hair. To that warm feeling she had when they both lay in bed with her in the morning.

They were only memories, increasingly distant memories, but they were all she had. So snuggling down, she lost herself in the past, hoping that sleep would come.

And as if on cue, the lights suddenly snapped out, plunging Leah into darkness.

4

Helen stood by the window and stared at the moon. It was full and beautiful, its gentle light penetrating the gloom of her cell. It revealed a ten-by-twelve-foot room, painted lime green and furnished with a bed, sink and toilet, all of them screwed to the floor. This was Helen's world now.

It was long after lock-up, but she was often to be found like this, preferring this lonely vigil to the 'comfort' of her narrow bed. The bedstead was old, the mattress lumpy, and, besides, Helen could never sleep for the noise. As soon as the lights went out, it started. Inmates calling to each other, calling to their mothers, calling to God. It was as relentless as it was predictable. When the shouting stopped, you heard the moaning. When the moaning stopped, you heard the crying. And when the crying stopped, you heard the vermin.

A large rat had run right over her on her first night, scurrying across her bed, before vanishing into the brick-work. He was one of many who felt they had the run of the place. Bluebottles circled the toilet day and night, sharing the tiny cell with the cockroaches which emerged after dark. The first few times Helen had spotted the latter scuttling across the floor, she'd stamped on them. But as each victim was quickly replaced by another, she'd given up. They were trapped in here too, so she'd decided to live and let live.

She now spent the night hours watching them go about their business, before exhaustion eventually drove her to bed. The hours after lock-up were the toughest for Helen, when the horror of her situation made itself felt. It seemed impossible, but here she was in Holloway – the prison that had been her sister's home after she murdered their parents. A few lifers still remembered Marianne, speaking approvingly of her intelligence and wit, and slightly less warmly of the violence she meted out. Her son, Robert Stonehill, had murdered three people in order to frame Helen, which is why she now spent her days in the company of liars, thieves and killers.

Retrieving a piece of chalk from the window ledge, Helen crossed the room and drew a single line on the wall next to her bed. It was one of many in a long, neat row – Helen religiously chalked off each day of incarceration. She had survived forty-six nights behind bars thus far – if she could make it through another fifty, she would have made it to her trial. It was this, and this alone, that kept her going.

Helen still hoped to prove her innocence in court, though she knew this would be tough. Robert had been thorough – planting her DNA at the murder scenes, killing on nights when Helen had no alibi and tempting her to lie to fellow officers about her personal connection to the victims. Her lies had been exposed and after that her fall from grace had been swift. With no female Category A prison in Hampshire, she'd ended up here. Her one remaining ally, DS Charlie Brooks, was working to secure her release, but what were her chances? Robert seemed to have disappeared off the face of the earth.

Every day, Helen told herself to be optimistic, to have faith in the criminal-justice system. But each night brought fresh doubts and Helen was starting to fear she'd be stuck in Holloway for ever. Was such an injustice possible? Could people really be so badly fooled?

At times like this Helen felt as if the whole world had forsaken her. She was a pariah, starved of company and bereft of sympathy. Helen had always been a private person, but even so the isolation here was crushing. There was no one she could really trust, no one she could confide in, and, as the nocturnal parade of rats and bugs proved, the only inmates willing to spend time with her now were the vermin.

5

Leah awoke, breathless and scared. She had been dreaming again. This time she was being chased down a corridor that seemed to go on for ever. In her dream, she had no idea where she was going to, nor whom she was running from. All she did know was that, despite her best efforts, she was getting slower and slower. Looking down she'd been astonished to discover that she had no legs – she was just a floating torso, clawing the air in her desperation to escape her pursuers.

She buried her face in the pillow and breathed out. Her nightmare had been so vivid that her heart was racing and a thin sheen of sweat clung to her forehead. Shrugging off these dark thoughts, she pulled the blanket up around her, determined to snatch a few hours' sleep before the day began. But as she did so, she froze. The blanket refused to move and Leah realized that the rhythmic breathing she could hear was not her own.

Someone was sitting at the end of her bed. Leah closed her eyes, praying that she could banish this dark vision, but still the sound of the breathing intruded. In, out, in, out. Leah wanted to scream but instead she remained still. She knew that what she did in the next few minutes would decide if she lived or died.

By playing dead she could buy herself some time and, turning fitfully as if in half-sleep, she tucked her right arm under her body. It was hidden now and slowly she slid her hand towards her pillow. This was where she kept her shiv – an improvised knife, made up of a razor blade and a toothbrush handle. It had saved her life on more than one occasion and she grasped gratefully for it now.

Except it wasn't there. Abandoning all caution, her fingers groped frantically, covering every inch of the cold mattress. But even as she did so, a measured voice said:

'Looking for this?'

Leah didn't want to, but she couldn't help herself, turning now to find out who had spoken. The locked cell was gloomy and swathed in shadow – she couldn't make out the figure sitting at the end of her bed, but she *could* see her trusty shiv gripped in their hand, its lethal blade winking at her in the moonlight.

6

'We've got a knife attack. Wounding with intent to kill. Who wants it?'

Detective Inspector Sanderson's voice filled the MIT office. Despite the early hour, the room was full – with some familiar faces and some new ones. There was a moment's pause – did anyone need another case? – before DC Lucas stepped forward, just pipping Edwards to the post.

'I'll take it,' she said cheerfully. 'Anything out of the ordinary?'

'Kebab shop confrontation. The perpetrator's claiming self-defence, but it looks like attempted murder to me.'

'I can't think of a better case for a vegetarian.'

Lucas's manner was playful, but the speed with which she scooped up her warrant card and bag belied her tone. Much had changed on the seventh floor since Helen Grace's incarceration. The whole team had looked up to their inspirational leader – Sanderson included – and her disgrace had affected everybody. She had been in charge of the Major Incident Team for so long that it had taken them a while to get used to the sight of somebody else in her office. Still, Sanderson was getting more comfortable in the role now and she regarded Lucas's desire to impress as evidence that progress was being made. Perhaps there was life after Helen Grace.

Sanderson felt she'd done more than enough to earn her promotion, having pushed through the complex investigation into her predecessor's criminal behaviour with rigour and tact. But it had still come as a shock when Detective Superintendent Gardam told her she was going to be the new Detective Inspector. Jonathan Gardam had been reassuring, however, urging her to reshape the team in her own image. This was partly to encourage her, but was also a deliberate attempt to repair some of the damage caused by Helen's arrest. The reputation of Hampshire Police had taken a terrible battering, following the revelation that they'd harboured a killer in their midst, and Gardam seemed determined to rectify this. He knew Sanderson was a by-the-book girl – a fact that no doubt had some bearing on her elevation.

Predictably, the one fly in the ointment was Charlie Brooks. Her loyalty to Helen was unshakable and the fact that Robert Stonehill had been in Southampton at the time of the infamous S&M murders only reinforced her belief that Helen was innocent. In reality there was not a shred of evidence to connect him with the killings, but this made no difference – Charlie was obsessed with Helen and on more than one occasion Sanderson had had to reprimand her for her lack of focus.

Scanning the room, Sanderson was depressed to see that Charlie's chair was empty. She hadn't called in sick, wasn't being deployed elsewhere today and she knew better than to go absent without leave.

Which begged the question: where was she?

7

'Take a good look and tell me if you recognize him.'

The elderly shopkeeper leant over the confectionery display and took the photo from Charlie's outstretched hand.

'What's he done?'

'Assault, battery, theft. He beat the owner of a carpet shop half to death over the contents of the till. Could happen to anyone, so, please, take your time.'

The lie was so practised that it tripped off Charlie's tongue.

'Nasty-looking bloke, isn't he?'

'You better believe it,' Charlie continued. 'We think he lives around here, so perhaps he popped in here for fags or beers?'

He perused the picture in silence. Charlie said nothing, impatient for an answer, but determined not to break his concentration. He was probably the fiftieth shop owner she'd canvassed in the last few weeks and she was beginning to feel that she was clutching at straws.

The man in the photo was real enough – Robert Stonehill – but the crime for which he was being sought was entirely fictional. There was no carpet shop owner, no assault, and Charlie knew that in fabricating a police incident she was breaking every rule in the book. Still, it allowed her to file a crime on the system, buying her some time to follow it up. It wasn't a deception that could last, she would be found out in the end, but there was nothing else for it.

A short phone conversation with Helen was enough to convince Charlie of her innocence and since then she'd been searching for evidence to help effect her release. She had scoured the Western Docks – Robert's nerve centre had been there – but the primary evidence she'd hoped to find eluded her. The main investigating team *had* found the imprint of a size 9 Vans trainer in the derelict building in which Helen was arrested, but they had dismissed it as irrelevant. Charlie, however, was convinced it belonged to Stonehill.

'What do you say? Has he been in here? He's about six foot, quiet sort of guy, ordinary clothes, but expensive trainers . . .'

Stonehill had been working at a remote branch of Wilkinson's during his killing spree, using the alias Aaron West. Charlie had worked out all possible routes from the murder sites to his nerve centre and, armed with a photo and a recent description of him, she'd been pounding the streets, targeting the mini-markets, newsagents and convenience stores. Stonehill was a canny operator, but he was still human. He had to eat.

'Sorry, love, I don't recognize him.'

'Look again. It's really import—'

'I'd like to help you, but he's not been in here.'

His tone was harder now, though his manner was not unkind. He could probably sense Charlie's desperation. Taking the photo, Charlie thanked him and left. There were three more premises on her list to check out. She could probably just about work through them before her absence gave anyone serious cause for suspicion. Whatever the consequences, however depressing this door-to-door drudgery was, there was no question of Charlie giving up.

Not while an innocent woman was behind bars.

8

'Let's get this party started.'

Sarah Bradshaw's voice rang out clear and true, as she buzzed the cell open. The bolts slid across and she yanked the heavy door towards her. Ignoring the mumbled complaints from within, she moved on, methodically unlocking each cell on the wing. She was making good progress and her charges were starting to emerge. Too groggy to argue, too strung out to resist, they shuffled out of their doorways, waiting for the order to go to breakfast. There was no aggravation, no attitude. Little wonder that roll call was Sarah's favourite part of the day.

'Get your game faces on, ladies. It's another day in paradise . . .'

Smiling to herself, Sarah opened the last cell door, before crossing the central gantry to the east side. Instinctively, she shot a look back behind her – she was the only officer on duty this morning thanks to staff shortages and knew from experience never to turn her back on her charges. To her satisfaction, however, everyone was behaving themselves. Grace was first out as usual and the others weren't far behind. The junkies, schizos and whack jobs who'd spit in your face as soon as look at you at the end of the day were quiet as church mice this morning. It was amazing what hunger could do.

Whistling tunelessly, Sarah continued on her way, swinging her keys as she went. Reaching the end of her round, she turned to survey her kingdom. And now for the first time, she noticed the gap in the line.

Everyone was present and correct, except for Leah Smith. She was housed between Helen Grace and Rosie Haynes, an inveterate shoplifter and frequent visitor to Holloway. *They* were both out on the landing, waiting patiently for instructions, but there was no sign of Leah. She was not someone who usually challenged authority so – best-case scenario – her absence from the line meant a sick or recalcitrant prisoner. Worst case, it was a code black – prison terminology for an attempted suicide.

'On the landing, Smith. Don't keep these nice ladies waiting . . .'

It was said confidently, but there was tension in Sarah's voice now. Suicides were messy and always set the other inmates off, as the inevitable lockdown ensued.

'Don't make me come in there and get you. Not if you want to eat today . . .'

Still no movement, so turning on her heel Sarah marched back to the western side of the wing. The other inmates were getting in on the act now, offering lurid suggestions for how Sarah might rouse Leah from her slumbers. Sarah ignored them, walking fast along the corridor past Baylis, past Cooke, and eventually past Grace too. Sarah had now arrived at Smith's cell and, taking a breath, she heaved the door open and stepped inside.

To her relief, all was quiet. She'd been expecting torn bed sheets, blood on the floor or even a flooded cell. But, no, Smith was lying on her bed, covered from head to toe by her blanket.

'Get your arse up, Smith, or I *will* put you on report.'

Still Leah didn't move. Fear started to puncture Sarah

Bradshaw's anger now. For some reason she couldn't put her finger on, she had the strong feeling that something was very wrong in this cell. It looked ordinary enough, neat and tidy ... but the silence inside it was strangely suffocating.

Whatever it was, Sarah suddenly had to know. So stepping forward, she took a firm hold of the corner of the blanket and, after a silent count of three, yanked it off the bed.

9

Cathy Smith peeled back the duvet to reveal Dylan and Caleb hiding underneath. She'd been trying to get the five-year-old twins up for over half an hour but they were being cheeky this morning. She'd eventually managed to get them out of their bunk beds, but they'd immediately fled, hiding first in her wardrobe, then in her bed.

This time she showed them no mercy. Having located their hiding place, she pulled the duvet off, exposing the giggling fugitives. They tried to make a break for it, but she was ready for them. She pounced, tucking one under each arm, dragging them back on to the bed. For a minute they protested, struggling and kicking then, seeing that the situation was hopeless, they turned on her, tickling her for all they were worth. Cathy protested – she was a highly ticklish grandmother – but secretly she loved every minute of it. In spite of the tough start these boys had had in life, they were extremely affectionate and loving.

They were only six months old when their mother committed murder. Three, four, five times a day, Cathy cast her mind back to that night, wondering if she might have done something differently. Perhaps if she'd refused to babysit the boys then Leah wouldn't have been at that pub, wouldn't have seen her no-good boyfriend with another girl. Had she been too soft on her? Too accepting of the mood swings, the drinking, the violent flashes of temper? Often Cathy cursed herself for her failings, laying the blame for the ensuing tragedy firmly at her own door. Other times she tried to put it down to sheer bad luck. Leah hadn't meant to kill the girl, didn't realize that she was expecting a baby . . .

So many lives destroyed in one moment of madness. The girls' parents broken by their loss, Leah serving a life sentence and Cathy bringing up two baby boys, despite the lack of a man in the house or a steady income. Each day was a struggle to meet their needs and yet . . . every day brought little surprises, moments of joy that made it all worthwhile. Cathy was exhausted, but in spite of everything she never begrudged the boys her role as their carer. After all, if she hadn't taken them on, they would have ended up in care.

Cathy was keeping the family together. One day Leah would be released and then they could all be together again. Until then she wouldn't grumble, wouldn't complain. She would do what needed to be done and make the most of their infrequent visits to Holloway. There were pictures of Leah all around the flat, but in truth nothing could replace one-to-one contact.

With an eye on the clock, Cathy pulled the boys to her, kissed them once on each cheek in turn and said: 'Breakfast, then clothes and teeth. Double quick, please.'

The boys groaned but Cathy was prepared.

'I've got Coco Pops for good boys who do as they're told. After all, we don't want to be late for Mummy, do we?'

Cathy smiled as the boys scampered off. She knew Leah depended on their brief visits. And, if she was honest, so did she.

10

Helen pushed through the crowds, searching for a place of sanctuary. She had never seen the canteen so busy – the unsettled inmates gathering together for moral support – and there was not a seat to be had anywhere. Helen was seldom invited to join anyone's table, but usually there was an out-of-the-way spot she could claim as her own. This morning, however, the prison gangs and cliques were out in force, seeking safety in numbers. Those that did catch her eye radiated hostility, even suspicion, as if Helen herself might have been responsible for her neighbour's death.

Clutching her breakfast tray, Helen made another circuit of the room. She was buffeted every step of the way, stray elbows finding their way to her ribs, but finally she got a break. Jordi, a cheerful former prostitute, caught her eye and shuffled up to allow her some room. Helen had helped the illiterate sex worker write her recent parole application – Jordi had teenage daughters whom she missed desperately – and they were now on friendly terms. Hence her act of mercy.

Helen seated herself quickly and cast an eye around the table. Babs, a seventy-year-old lifer with a dodgy hip, but a good heart, nodded at Helen, giving her tacit support to Jordi's generosity of spirit. Noelle, a boisterous drug dealer who'd always been fair to Helen, did likewise, flashing her gold teeth quickly before returning to her cornflakes.

The others at the table Helen didn't know well and she expected them to object to her sudden arrival, but their mood was subdued today. Hostilities had been suspended following the night's shocking events – Helen noted that no one was even bothering to bait Lucy this morning.

'You not eating?' Babs asked, as Helen toyed with her breakfast.

'Maybe later,' Helen replied, though in truth she couldn't face anything.

'Have something. You won't get another chance until lunchtime.'

Relenting, Helen picked up her burnt toast, but before she could take a bite, Jordi dived in.

'You hear anything last night?'

'For God's sake, Jordi,' Noelle interrupted. 'Let the woman have her chow in peace.'

'Just asking . . .'

'Nothing . . .' Helen answered, to Jordi's evident disappointment. 'I was up half the night, but even so . . .'

'Did you see anything then? When Bradshaw went in?'

Helen shook her head once more. At roll call, you stand by your cell and don't move unless you're told to. It's part of the deadening routine of prison life which you flout at your peril, but Helen now regretted her obedience. It was clear from the moment Sarah Bradshaw entered Leah's cell that something bad had happened. Helen had heard Bradshaw's half-scream, the fast, muttered expletives and then the shrill shriek of the bell, as the panicking officer punched the emergency alarm. Campbell, Robins and the rest had scrambled to assist, as lockdown kicked in. The hungry inmates were kept inside until Leah's cell had been properly sealed off, leaving Helen in the dark about what had happened.

Code black. That had been everyone's first thought, but rumours spread fast in prison and speculation had now taken a more sinister turn. People were saying that Leah Smith had been murdered.

Helen was no great friend of Leah's – her neighbour was suspicious, hostile and prone to violence – but the troubled young woman had been the first person Helen met in Holloway and she'd made an effort to show Helen the ropes. Such generosity towards a jailed police officer had surprised Helen, though she later wondered whether Leah's deep unpopularity had prompted her actions. She'd never fully got to the bottom of why Leah was so reviled. She knew a special kind of hatred was reserved for inmates who'd harmed children or babies, but Leah's unpopularity was so ingrained that Helen wondered if there was something else at play. Her lack of knowledge – both of Leah's history and of her fate – gnawed at her. Outside, she could have demanded answers. Inside, she was as clueless as the rest.

'If she *was* done in, there are plenty of suspects,' Noelle said darkly, casting an eye around the canteen.

'Easy, Noelle. Don't go throwing stones . . .' Babs warned gently.

'True though, innit? A lot of people with guilty consciences in here this morning.'

Helen listened as Noelle continued her dissection of prison politics. Jordi seemed less interested, excusing herself to hunt for more food, but Helen was keen to hear what Noelle had to say – even if most of her 'facts' were unsubstantiated rumour and speculation. Leah was a marked woman and would have been a feather in the cap for any inmate. Though she'd recently tried to get clean, she was also a habitual drug user and alcoholic, which often brought her into conflict with the authorities *and* the prison gangs. To top it off, her temper was legendary – she'd recently threatened to gouge one of the kitchen staff for short-changing her on baked beans. Such is the stuff of life and death in prison.

Noelle continued to talk, but solid information was hard to come by this morning. Babs had tapped up the 'Golden Girls' – the small coterie of pensioners seeing out their days in Holloway – but had come back empty-handed and to everyone's surprise it was Jordi, returning breathless and upset from the serving hatch, who finally broke the news to them.

'Sandra knows a girl who works in the Governor's office,' Jordi said, nodding to the burly cook at the serving hatch. 'She says an outside unit has already been called in.'

This was *not* a common-or-garden suicide then. Helen didn't say anything, but she knew that the Prisons and Probation Service would only be summoned if there was something unusual or suspicious about Leah's death.

'They're saying that she was murdered in her bed and that . . . they'd done a job on her. They sewed up her mouth. Her eyes too.'

Helen stared at Jordi, barely taking in the words.

'They *sewed* her eyelids to her bloody cheeks. That's how they found her – eyes shut, grinning from ear to ear . . .'

Noelle remained silent, as Jordi now wept. Even Babs looked shaken and she had seen more than most. Helen kept her counsel, but her mind was already turning on this macabre development. She had heard unpleasant tales of prison justice before, but this was something else. It made her feel sick to the stomach and by the looks of it she wasn't the only one – Sandra's news was doing the rounds and the atmosphere in the canteen had suddenly changed. Normally the inmates were raucous and excitable at mealtimes. But not today.

Today everybody looked terrified.

11

It was a horrific sight to behold. The tattered blanket lay on the floor where Sarah Bradshaw had dropped it and just above it on the narrow bed lay the mutilated corpse of Leah Smith.

Celia Bassett had been the Governor of Holloway Prison for over five years, but nothing had prepared her for this. Leah's face was waxy and pale, her body rigid and there was not a drop of blood anywhere. The normally restless Leah would have looked calm and at peace – were it not for the rictus grin that gripped her brutalized face.

Celia moved forward, the plastic coverings on her shoes making a strange swishing sound against the floor, and forced herself to take a closer look. She was immediately struck by the colour of the cotton thread – a pretty powder blue – and the neatness of the stitching. It wasn't a perfect job, having presumably been carried out quickly and in the dark, but it was an effective one, sealing the mouth tight and tugging it up at the corners. The eyelids had been similarly dispatched, stitched robustly to Leah's cheeks.

'At least she died with a smile on her face,' said a voice behind her, its Scottish lilt infected with sarcasm.

'Shut the fuck up, Campbell, this isn't funny.'

'Funny or not, it's not our problem now . . .'

Celia turned to reprimand her most senior officer, but he was already on his way out of the door. He'd been her acting Head of Security since the previous incumbent departed suddenly, but he couldn't have been less interested in this sudden tragedy. It made Celia's blood boil – regardless of his responsibilities, Leah Smith was a human being, for God's sake – but his weary cynicism came as no surprise to her. Holloway was due to be mothballed at the end of the year and the prison's skeleton crew of officers were already beyond exhausted, ground down by the daily stress, abuse and violence. The last thing they needed was a major incident like this, which might reflect badly on them and their chances of a decent relocation when the old prison closed its doors for the final time.

And Campbell was right of course – this *was* out of their hands now. She had already alerted the PPS and an investigator was on his way to take control of what would now be a murder enquiry. Celia knew from experience that the PPS guys were remorseless, thorough and single-minded, paying little heed to context in their desire to ascertain 'the facts'. It would disrupt prison life, raise the anxiety level of officers and prisoners alike, and perhaps reveal some extremely unpalatable truths.

Celia stared down at the corpse once more, her heart in her boots. Leah's sufferings were over. But, for the rest of them, the nightmare was just beginning.

'Why can't we see her? What's the problem?'

Cathy Smith was a patient woman, but she was beginning to lose her temper. It was never an easy journey to Holloway – two buses and a Tube to negotiate – and even when you did get there, things never ran on time. She had a number of cleaning jobs and two small boys to feed, wash and clothe – her time was precious, but nobody seemed to appreciate that. Visiting hours that were supposedly set in stone were seldom honoured and when you tried to find out what was going on you were met by vacant stares. It was as if the authorities wanted to punish the relatives too, though of course they were the innocent parties.

They had been here for over an hour already. The visitors' centre was an uninspiring place for the twins, though the presence of a small, plastic Christmas tree had cheered them a little today. It had raised their spirits after a long journey and Cathy had been touched by their excited discussion about what Santa might bring them this year. However, as soon as the boys had discovered that the generous-looking presents beneath the tree were actually hollow boxes, the complaints started up. Normally, Cathy let them play on her phone, despite the fights this caused, but it was out of juice today. Nothing seemed to be going her way, so in angry mood she'd collared the visitors' clerk for the third time, demanding information.

'I've asked for someone from the Governor's office to

come down, but to be honest I'm as much in the dark as you are at the moment. I can't get through on the phone . . .'

'Right hand doesn't know what the left is doing,' Cathy muttered as she walked away without waiting to hear more. Why did they always have to make things so bloody awkward?

She was considering what to do for the best, when she spotted Mark Robins hurrying through the centre. It was the quickest way out of the prison and he was obviously in a rush, but Cathy darted across the hall to intercept him. He had always treated both Leah and Cathy with kindness and could be relied upon to give a straight answer to a straight question.

Robins jumped as if scalded when Cathy touched his arm. The talkative officer seemed lost for words today, so Cathy jumped in.

'I can see you're in a hurry, Mr Robins, so apologies for intruding. We're here to see Leah, but we keep getting fobbed off with excuses. I don't mind waiting but it's the boys . . .'

Normally Robins would have jumped in to reassure her at this point, but still he remained silent.

'If it's not going to happen, I'd rather know,' Cathy continued quickly. 'The boys will be disappointed for sure, but I don't want to keep them here if we're not going to get in. We could always come back.'

Cathy's last words seemed to have some effect and finally Robins spoke.

'Look Cathy it's best you stay here. I'll radio up and get someone to come down and see you.'

'See me? Why would they need to see me?'

'It's best that they do this,' Mark continued quickly. 'I've got to run now, but a family liaison officer will be with you very shortly. You have my word on that.'

'A family liaison officer . . . ?'

The words died on her lips – Robins had already disengaged and was heading for the door. Cathy watched him go, gripped by a sudden fear. Robins was normally so helpful, but today he looked uncomfortable, even a little scared. What the hell was going on? What had happened to her Leah?

The boys were laughing in the background once more, playing at being Santa with his presents under the tree. But for once Cathy couldn't bring herself to look at them. Already something inside told her that it would be a bleak Christmas for them this year.

13

They marched in single file, never once breaking stride. The shocked inmates were still reacting to Leah Smith's brutal death, but the crushing routine of prison life had reasserted itself nevertheless. There were skills sessions, association time, exercise and phone calls to come, but as soon as breakfast was up, the inmates were dispatched to the shower block.

For Helen the morning shower was always a trial. She hated exposing her body to all and sundry and had had to harden herself to the insults that rained down on her, as her fellow inmates drank in her battle-scarred torso. More than this, it was the smells, sounds and sights that she found shocking – inmates being brought to clamorous orgasm by their jail girlfriends, Lucy, the protesting transsexual, being dragged kicking and screaming into the showers following another 'dirty protest' and even on occasion the amateurish, blood-soaked attempts at suicide.

But today Helen was prepared to swallow her discomfort, as she had a job to do. Finishing her shower, she made her way quickly along the stalls, peering through the steam like a clumsy voyeur. Ignoring the invitations and catcalls her behaviour provoked, Helen carried on down the line until she finally found who she was looking for. Rosie Haynes was just completing her ablutions and Helen was on to her fast, pulling her aside as she finished her shower.

'Where's the fire?' Rosie snapped, clearly irritated to have been collared by her deeply unpopular wing mate.

'There's no fire, I just wanted a word.'

Several heads turned, so Helen pulled Rosie into the stall and turned the shower back on. Almost immediately the noise levels rose again, the inmates speculating about the morning's grim events.

'What about?' Rosie replied curtly.

'Leah, of course.'

'What can I tell you? I've only heard the same rumours you have –'

'That's not what I mean. Did you see or hear anything last night?'

It was a long shot, but Helen had to ask. It was horrific to think that her neighbour had been brutally murdered and defiled while she slept close by. Rosie's cell bordered Leah's on the other side, so it was possible she knew something.

'I fell asleep sometime around three a.m. and was up just after six. Did you hear anything between those times?' Helen continued.

'Not a thing.'

'Come on, Rosie, I know you're not a great sleeper –'

'I was lucky last night. Got a solid eight hours.'

It was almost said with a note of triumph, which angered Helen.

'Have you picked up anything on the grapevine then?' she continued quickly. 'Do you know if anyone had a problem with her?'

'Are you *serious*?' Rosie spat back, raising her voice. 'That stupid bitch killed a kid. Stuck a knife right in that girl's belly. She said she didn't know she was expecting, but the word is she knew *exactly* what she was doing. To be honest I'm surprised she lasted as long as she did in here.'

'You don't mean that –'

'Don't I? You ask me, prison's too good for the likes of *her*.'

'Why you sticking up for her anyway?'

Alarmed by a new voice, Helen turned to find Chantelle, a heavily tattooed gang member, approaching.

'You know something we don't?' she continued accusingly.

'Of course not,' Helen replied. 'I'm just trying to find out what happened last night. Leah was a mum to two small boys –'

'It's just scum looking out for scum,' sneered another inmate, as she joined the fray. 'Funny how they put you two together, isn't it?'

Helen was now surrounded, a crowd of semi-naked women encircling her, but she refused to back down. Leah Smith was like many of the women in Holloway, she had complicated mental health issues and belonged in a hospital rather than a prison. But there was precious little fellow feeling today. To the other prisoners, Leah was a child killer pure and simple, who'd forfeited her right to life.

'Even if we *had* heard anything, do you think we'd tell you?' Rosie piped up again. 'Perhaps you've forgotten that you ain't got a badge any more?'

There was laughter and hollering from the group, but Helen had had enough.

'Don't you *care* that someone was murdered last night?' she said suddenly, aiming her venom directly at Rosie. 'Someone just like you.'

'Fuck off. I was nothing like that cow –'

'They picked Leah's cell. They could just as easily have picked mine. Or yours.'

For the first time, Rosie didn't have a ready comeback. Her front was exactly that – she was as scared as everyone else.

'Whoever did this got into her cell, murdered her, then vanished without a trace,' Helen continued. 'Which means none of us are safe.'

Helen turned to face the rest of her adversaries. Her words seemed to be having the desired effect. The crowd, which had been aggressively raucous moments earlier, was now silent.

'So before you go congratulating yourselves on a young woman's death, think about *that*.'

Pushing her way through the crowd, Helen made for the exit, watched every step of the way by thirty anxious inmates.

14

It hadn't taken long for the cavalry to arrive. Celia Bassett had just got back to her desk when the front gate buzzed up to say that Benjamin Proud and his team had arrived. Celia's heart sank at the news – she'd hoped to have a little time to gather herself before they descended upon her. In official parlance, Proud and his colleagues were known as Prisons and Probation Service Investigators. Among her staff, they were known as the Spanish Inquisition.

Ten minutes later, Proud was standing in her office. The formalities were dealt with – a Home Office pathologist sent to the mortuary and forensic officers dispatched to the crime scene – then Proud was quickly down to business.

'I'm going to need a timeline of Smith's movements the day before she died – what she was doing, who she associated with – and an accurate account of what happened *after* the discovery of her body. I'll also need access to her health charts, details of any counselling she was undergoing as well as her parole record.'

Proud said all this without once looking up from his file. He was not a bad specimen – broad-shouldered, imposing, with a self-assuredness that was impressive. He wasn't one of the robotic geeks they usually sent her. But this also made him dangerous. He was obviously assertive and dogged, with an aversion to bullshit. He certainly wouldn't make life easy for them, but Celia wasn't ready to be cowed. She had managed this place pretty well in the most trying of circumstances and had no intention of letting this latest incident reflect on her tenure at HMP Holloway.

Proud had now stopped talking and to her embarrassment Celia realized she was staring at him.

'Is everything ok, Miss Bassett?'

'Fine. You were saying?'

'I was asking if there were any disturbances in the prison yesterday? Anything that might be relevant to Smith's death?'

'Nothing out of the ordinary. We have a lot of volatile prisoners, so there were a couple of minor brawls –'

'I'll need details of those. Chapter and verse on who was involved and why.'

Celia nodded, though asking why fights kicked off in here was a bit like asking why the sun comes up in the morning.

'Any friends or relatives who visit her regularly?'

'Just her mum and twin boys. They're here now actually. An FLO is bringing them up.'

'I'll let you deal with them,' Proud said quickly. 'But obviously you'll pass on any important details they might have regarding her state of mind?'

'Of course,' Celia responded tartly. 'Though I think we can rule out suicide on this one.'

Proud looked unimpressed by her sarcasm, so Celia continued quickly:

'In the meantime, feel free to go wherever you need to, though I must insist you are accompanied at all times for your own safety.'

'Obviously,' Proud replied, as he rose.

He offered his hand to Celia and as she took it, he said:

'Is there anything *you'd* like to add?'

'Me?'

'Any suspicions you have about who might have done this?'

He was still holding her hand, while looking straight into her eyes. Was this some kind of test? Did he always do this?

'None at all. But if I think of anything, you'll be the first to know.'

Nodding, Proud released her hand and turned on his heel. He walked away fast, issuing instructions to a couple of colleagues — seemingly oblivious to the massive lie he'd just been told.

15

She heard her, before she saw her. Helen was marching back to her cell from the showers, deep in thought, when she heard a distinctive sound.

Squeak, squeak, squeak.

Helen looked up and was not surprised to see Wheelchair Annie moving down the corridor towards her. Instinctively, Helen cast a glance over her right shoulder. Alexis, Annie's thug-in-chief and one of Helen's former collars, appeared behind her, confirming her suspicion that this was not a chance meeting.

Annie was an MS sufferer, serving a ten-year stretch for drugs offences, human trafficking, pimping and more besides. She also happened to be the main supplier of narcotics to the prison community, thanks in part to the amount of time she spent in Holloway's infirmary. The hours of physical therapy she underwent there gave her ample time to foster the right connections and gain unfettered access to both licensed and unlicensed drugs in their stores. She was unable to move without a wheelchair, and while this should have put her at a disadvantage in prison, such was the influence and financial muscle she wielded that she was pretty much untouchable. It paid to be nice to Annie.

'Well, don't you look a pretty picture? All nice and clean.'

Helen smiled, but said nothing, keeping half an eye on Alexis. She was sixteen stone of malevolence – with a personal score to settle with Helen.

'But that's you all over isn't it?' Annie continued. 'Miss Goody Two Shoes. Pretty much everyone in this place is a customer of mine, but not you . . .'

'Drugs aren't my thing, Annie, you know that . . .'

'Body a temple, is it?' Annie replied, taking the opportunity to run her eyes over Helen's toned figure. 'Or perhaps you're just keeping yourself in shape for when you *get out*.'

This raised a mirthless laugh from Alexis. It was generally assumed that nobody was innocent in this place or would be leaving any time soon.

'Gotta keep believing,' Helen joked, maintaining a light tone.

'To which end, let me give you a piece of advice,' Annie said, wheeling herself up close. 'There's an old saying about curiosity and the cat. I suggest you heed it. It would be a shame for you to have to spend Christmas in the infirmary.'

It was said with a smile, but the look in Annie's eyes was one of malice. Clearly Helen's conversation with Rosie had not gone unnoticed.

'I'll be good,' Helen lied. 'Now, if you'll excuse me, Annie –'

Helen tried to push past, but suddenly felt her head snap back. Alexis had grabbed her by the hair and, placing a meaty hand on her shoulder, now forced her to the ground. Helen's kneecaps struck the metal gantry hard, but she immediately tried to struggle to her feet. The weighty Alexis had her pinned down, however, and all Helen could do was look up, as Wheelchair Annie wheeled herself still closer. The two women were at eye level now, though Helen was at a distinct disadvantage.

'I'm sure you'll be good as *gold*,' Annie told her calmly.

'After all, it's a while until your trial, isn't it? What is it now? Six weeks?'

'Seven,' Helen muttered.

'You see my point then?'

Helen said nothing in response, refusing to give Annie the satisfaction. Her adversary was right, though – there was time enough to deal with her, if Annie chose to do so.

'So if I were you,' Annie concluded, 'I'd keep my nose out of other people's business . . .'

She ran her finger over Helen's nose, eventually bringing it to rest on her lips.

'And your pretty mouth shut.'

'I'm so glad we found time to have this little chat. We should do it more often.'

Sanderson smiled awkwardly and shifted in her chair. This was the one part of her job that she struggled with. Detective Superintendent Jonathan Gardam had been encouraging and supportive since her promotion, but she still found him hard to read. He said all the right things, but she was never sure that he actually meant them, nor if he was impressed or displeased with her performance.

'I think it's important that we communicate effectively,' Gardam continued, leaning back in his chair. 'If I'm honest, I think it's the one area in which I failed with your predecessor.'

Sanderson looked at Gardam, but said nothing. Her new boss had never admitted any regrets in relation to Helen – he had always portrayed her as a black sheep who'd tarnished the name of the department with her reckless, obsessive behaviour.

'Don't look so shocked,' Gardam laughed, chiding Sanderson. 'I'm not a complete megalomaniac. Helen betrayed us all, but as her superior officer I should have known what she was up to –'

'I don't see how you could have. She lied to all of us.'

'Even so, to have no inkling of what she was up to –'

'She was a very private person. And a very deceitful one at that.'

'Well, thank you, Joanne, but it won't stop me beating myself up about it.'

Sanderson smiled, but felt herself blushing. He'd never used her first name before. Oblivious, Gardam carried on:

'I think she'd been indulged for too long. I know that can't fully account for what she did, but in my view she was allowed too much licence here. She fostered a culture of individuality, of risk-taking. I think she fell in love with her own myth – the hero cop who always put her body on the line. In the end, she probably believed she was untouchable, that she could do anything and not be called up on it. People speculate that she killed those people because they were blackmailing her, but I think she murdered them because she thought she *could*.'

'I guess we might never know,' Sanderson offered blandly, though she had often pondered the same question herself.

'Which is why I think teamwork is so important. This department, this station, has taken an awful battering recently and it's our duty – your duty – to help rebuild belief in the Major Incident Team. From now on our watchwords have to be integrity, solidarity, unity.'

He teased out the last word, giving it extra emphasis, before continuing:

'No more solo players. You're either part of the team or you're out. It's as simple as that.'

Sanderson nodded vigorously, although this conversation was starting to make her feel uneasy.

'Anyway, I've kept you from your duties long enough,'

Gardam said, rising. 'But I wanted to have this chat. I know you're ambitious, I know you believe in the system, so I've no doubt that you'll instil the right values into your team. It's your train set now, Joanne.'

He shook her hand and looked her in the eye.

'Don't let me down.'

17

Charlie hurried along the pavement, searching for suitable targets. Morris Road was a busy thoroughfare, linking the restaurants and bars of Bedford Place to the train station and beyond that the Western Docks. It would be a good route for someone wanting to leave the city centre and return towards the docks, as it was generally busy and you wouldn't draw attention to yourself. It had a few shops and a pub, but otherwise was fairly run-of-the-mill and nondescript.

Spotting a newsagent's, Charlie darted across the road and pushed inside. She wondered privately why they still called themselves newsagents, as she surveyed the interior. Increasingly they were more like discount alcohol shops that happened to sell newspapers too, such was the variety of cheap cider and lager on display. Charlie had no doubt that all the local fifteen-year-olds beat a path here for their booze and fags. But that wasn't why she was here, so pulling Robert Stonehill's picture from her bag, she hurried over to the owner.

He was a young Asian guy, seemingly more interested in his smartphone than minding the shop. But Charlie's warrant card got his attention and he happily accepted the photo. He was casting an eye over it now and Charlie was already scrolling forward – working out how many shops she would be able to tick off before returning to base – when he suddenly spoke.

'Yeah, I've seen this guy.'

Charlie looked up sharply.

'Couple of times. A while back now . . .'

'When?'

'August, I think. No, it was September actually . . .'

September was the right answer. Charlie suddenly felt tension rise inside her as she asked the next question:

'How sure are you?'

'Pretty sure, you know. He never said nothing. Just got his milk, his bread and handed over the cash. I thought he might have been a junkie or something. He looked right through you.'

Charlie was already looking round the shop and in the far corner of the room she spotted a CCTV camera.

'What are the chances you might have CCTV footage of him?'

'Could do. The old man likes to keep an eye on the place . . . and me,' he replied, laughing.

'Then maybe you could show me the way.'

Shrugging, the young man hopped round the counter and, having flipped the sign on the door to 'Closed', ambled off towards the back of the shop. Charlie followed him, her heart beating fast. After weeks of fruitless searching, she finally had a lead.

18

Helen walked into her cell, then stopped in her tracks. She was not alone.

She had hurried back to B-Wing, keen to gather her thoughts following her interview with Annie, but it was now clear she wouldn't get the chance. Her cell had been turned upside down – mattress on the floor, toiletries scattered, books torn from their spines. Two uniformed prison officers were working up a sweat, conducting a painstakingly thorough search. Cameron Campbell by contrast was standing in the centre of the small room, calmly surveying their efforts. He turned now, as Helen entered the room.

'Look what the cat dragged in . . .'

'I didn't realize there was a cell search today, sir,' Helen replied evenly, ignoring his taunt. 'If I'd known, I'd have skipped shower –'

'There isn't. It's just you, Grace.'

Helen stared at him, but said nothing. Every which way she turned, she seemed to excite hostility and suspicion.

'Can I ask why?' she eventually asked, just about concealing her irritation. She had few possessions and little privacy and hated this clumsy intrusion.

'No, you cannot. I am the Head of Security here and I will do whatever I feel is necessary to keep the inmates safe.'

'I see.'

'So perhaps you can cut these two some slack,' he said gesturing to his fellow officers, who were now examining the brickwork under her bed, 'and tell us where you keep it.'

'Keep what, sir?'

'The needle and thread, Grace, don't be fucking obtuse. Where is it?'

Helen couldn't help laughing, but the sound she made was ugly and bitter.

'You don't seriously think *I* had something to do with Leah's death?'

'That's exactly what I think,' Campbell replied, walking towards Helen.

'That's ridiculous,' Helen spat back, witheringly.

'Seems pretty logical to me.'

Still he advanced, so Helen took a step back. Immediately she regretted it, as she now found herself in the corner of the cell. Campbell was quick to take advantage, moving fast to box her in.

'I've worked in this place for ten years and we've never had anything like *this*.' He gestured towards Leah's cell. 'But then you turn up and within a matter of weeks . . .'

'Come off it, I liked Leah . . .'

'Nobody *liked* Leah. You trying to curry favour by getting rid of the one person more unpopular than you?'

'Of course not, that's completely crazy –'

'So maybe you did it because you *like* it?'

Helen said nothing, eyeballing Campbell. Did he really believe she was responsible or was he just taking the opportunity to make her life a misery?

'Is *that* what this is about? Do you get off on it?'

He moved in closer and Helen now felt something press against her thigh. Looking down she was alarmed to see

Campbell's truncheon digging into her. Staring directly at her, Campbell moved it upwards, over her crotch, over her stomach, over her chest, before eventually bringing it to rest on her throat.

'Victim number four, is she? Or are there others we don't know about?'

Helen cast a beseeching look at the other officers, who'd concluded their search. But they made no attempt to help her. Clearly they were used to Campbell's tactics and were not going to get involved.

'Look, I don't own a needle. And I never touched Le—'

But Helen didn't get to finish her sentence, Campbell ramming his truncheon into her windpipe and pinning her against the wall.

'Don't lie to me, Grace. You're a dirty little pervert, who loves inflicting pain and misery . . .'

Helen tried to answer back, but she couldn't breathe, let alone speak.

'A pervert who thinks she can carry on where she left off,' Campbell continued, his nose just millimetres away from Helen's now. 'But let me tell you this. I have run this prison for a good few years and we've always been tight as a drum. And that's the way it's going to stay.'

He was glaring at her now, flecks of his spittle landing on her face as he spoke.

'I *know* you did this and once I have proof, I will make sure that it doesn't happen again. Do you understand me?'

Helen nodded, though it hurt to do so, the hard wooden truncheon pressed tight against her throat.

'Good,' Campbell replied briskly, suddenly stepping away from Helen.

She slumped forward, gulping in air, even as she rubbed

her bruised throat. Campbell meanwhile gestured to the other officers to leave. He followed them to the door, but paused on the threshold, turning once more towards Helen.

'Until next time . . .'

Then he was gone, leaving Helen alone amid the carnage.

19

It was a scene of bedlam, inmates jostling each other as they crowded into the small space. Andrew Holmes had been the Chaplain at Holloway for over five years but he had never seen so many souls in his modest chapel. The converted workshop was used to hosting congregations of twenty or thirty at best, but there were over twice that many this morning.

'I was only talking to her yesterday,' an emotional Noelle was saying, raising her voice to be heard over the din.

'I know,' Andrew replied. 'It's a terrible shock when someone we know, a friend, is suddenly taken fro—'

'You don't get me. I wasn't saying anything nice to her. I called her a bitch because she wouldn't take my laundry shift.'

'And you regret that now?'

'I don't know, but still I shouldn't have said it, should I?'

Andrew smiled tightly and moved on. Noelle was a regular here, though whether she truly believed or just enjoyed the social side of the services was unclear. Certainly her 'contrition' for her various misdemeanours was skin-deep. Sold down the line by her dealer boyfriend some years back, Noelle was definitely a woman more sinned against than sinning in her own eyes.

'Is it true what they are saying about her?'

Andrew was talking to the tearful Maxine, a devout Christian with an unfortunate tendency to kleptomania, but found himself being tugged back by the insistent Noelle.

'About her getting cut up and that?'

'Noelle, I've other people to deal with. I don't know any more than yo—'

'You must know *something*. You're staff.'

'Even so. The chapel is my area of influence.'

'If you know something, you need to tell us. Don't be hiding nothing.'

Andrew was struck by the sudden neediness in Noelle's tone. She was a formidable, impressive woman, standing a good six inches taller than him and tough with it. But today she seemed nervous.

'Do they know who did it?' Noelle continued, still clutching his arm. 'Have they got anyone?'

Andrew now realized that the whole room was listening to their conversation, the inmates searching for some crumbs of reassurance. Flustered, he tugged his arm away from Noelle and smoothed down his surplice. He knew he cut a comical figure in the inmates' eyes, with his frayed dog collar and bent glasses, but he needed to appear impressive and in control today. For their sakes, if not his own.

'I promise you that the moment I hear anything you'll be the first to know,' he said, gathering himself. 'I'm aware you're all concerned for your safety and I understand why.'

Andrew was pleased to see the inmates nodding, gratified perhaps that someone was listening to their concerns.

'Once we're finished here, I'll go directly to the Governor, to try to find out more. In the meantime, I suggest we try to keep calm. I'm sure there will be a thorough investigation and that the culprit will be swiftly identified.'

More nods from the group. Clearly this was what everyone present was hoping for.

'For now though, I'd like to suggest that we pray for Leah and her family. They will need all the help they can get in the weeks ahead.'

To his surprise, all present now dropped to their knees without fuss or dissent. The call to prayer usually occasioned a partial exodus during services, but not today. So often his duties left him feeling dispirited – it was hard bringing hope to those who had already despaired of life – but now there was a pressing need for him. It was a strange silver lining, but you had to take what you could get in life.

Normally he was a lone warrior in a sea of lost souls, but this morning, for the first time in years, Andrew Holmes felt glad to be alive.

20

Charlie hardly dared to breathe. Weeks of anguish, weeks of hopeless searching came down to this moment.

She was holed up in the tiny office at the back of the shop, watching grainy black-and-white CCTV footage. Each new customer brought fresh excitement, fresh hope, only for it to turn out to be a hobbling pensioner or teenage mum. But now halfway through the footage recorded on 14 September, a young man had entered the shop. A man who at first glance looked like Robert Stonehill.

He had a Portsmouth FC cap on and kept his head down, but there was something in the physique that looked familiar. He browsed the aisles quickly, shoving cheap convenience food into the basket. Biscuits, pot noodles, milk, bread, chocolate. No care was taken – it was as if the speed of the transaction was more important than the items themselves. Frustratingly, the CCTV camera was behind the till, away from the aisles, the owner seemingly more concerned with the money in the register and the spirits behind the counter than the goods on display. It was hard to see the man's face, but he soon emerged from the aisles and hurried towards the till. Charlie sat forward in her seat.

He was clearly in a hurry. He paid for his groceries, handing over a twenty-pound note, keeping his head down all the while. But then, just as he was receiving his change, he darted a look up to his right. It was presumably a quick check to see if the store had CCTV and in doing so he had looked right down the camera lens. He turned quickly and left, but Charlie was sure of what she'd seen. The shape of the face, the eyes, the furtive expression – it was *him*.

But that wasn't all. Noticing something else, Charlie paused the footage. Framed by the doorway, she could make out the full figure. The clean-shaven face, the tight-fitting anorak and best of all a pair of Vans on his feet. For the first time, Charlie had something concrete to corroborate Helen's version of the story.

Which is why she now felt tears prick her eyes.

21

Helen looked quickly upwards as she hurried across the association yard. During the first week of her incarceration, a drone had been spotted hovering overhead. Helen had assumed it was the press trying to grab images of her. More than that, she suspected it was the work of Emilia Garanita, who was now making a name for herself in the national press, following her sensational scoop on the Robert Stonehill case. Another parasite feeding off Helen's remains.

But there was no drone today – it hadn't been seen for a few weeks now – and Helen hurried over to the far corner of the yard. She was looking for the 'Listeners', a group of inmates who offered confidential counselling services to prisoners. The authorities liked them because their subtle influence could help keep the inmates in check. Helen liked them because they were the keepers of Holloway's secrets.

She needed to find out who was responsible for Leah's death. Her task now had an added urgency – she would have sought justice for Leah anyway, but Campbell's aggressive threats increased the importance of acting without delay. So, having repaired the damage to her cell, she'd headed immediately for the association yard.

The Listeners' services were in demand this morning and Helen had to wait her turn. Eventually, Eleanor, a warm-hearted pensioner doing time for benefit fraud, became free. Helen grabbed her and the pair began to walk the perimeter fence.

'What have you heard?' Helen said, cutting to the chase.

'Nothing much.' Eleanor bridled at Helen's antagonistic tone. 'She'd obviously pissed someone off . . .'

'Come on, Eleanor. Leah had no mates here, but I know she talked to you lot. You were the only people who *would* talk to her.'

'And anything she said must remain confidential.'

'Why? She can't be hurt any more. And if you know something –'

'Why are you so interested?'

'Because she's a human being.'

'Leave it to the authorities. There'll be an investigation –'

'And what will that achieve? You've been here long enough. They don't have the resources or the personnel . . . They'll scout around for a couple of days, find nothing, then mark it down as "unexplained" . . .'

'So young, but so cynical . . .' Eleanor said, half smiling.

'This isn't funny,' Helen said, taking Eleanor by the arm, stopping her in her tracks. 'The rest of this lot might be prepared to shrug it off, but I'm not.'

Eleanor looked down at Helen's hand. Her smile slipped now, as she continued:

'And what will you do if you *do* find out something?'

'I'll take it to the relevant authorities.'

'So now you want to be a copper *and* a grass?' Eleanor asked grimly. 'You really do have a death wish, don't you?'

'I've handled worse than this.'

'You think?'

'Look, Eleanor, the longer we stand here talking, the

more people are going to think we're mates. So it's probably in everyone's interests if you just tell me what you know. I won't bother you again, I promise.'

Eleanor cast a quick look around the yard, then said:

'You didn't hear this from me, but the word is that she had been to see the Governor. That she was Bassett's stooge now.'

'She was giving her information?'

'She was trying to buy her way to the enhanced wing.'

'Who was she giving up?'

'I don't know for sure, but it doesn't take a genius to work it out. Her supply of smack dried up pretty suddenly, didn't it? And she was a fiend for that stuff.'

Images of Leah queuing for her cup of sickly green methadone reared up in Helen's mind.

'You think Annie did this?'

'Maybe. But who could say for certain? In case you hadn't noticed, Helen, this place is crawling with killers.'

For a moment, Helen was silent. Eleanor was right – there were plenty of suspects crammed within the prison's crumbling walls. Was she crazy to think she could find the culprit?

'I'd leave it well alone, if I were you,' Eleanor continued. 'That's *my* advice to you. Now are we done? As you can see, my services are rather in demand this morning . . .'

Eleanor pulled herself free of Helen and walked off towards her fellow Listeners, who were being circled by a crowd of jumpy inmates. Eleanor was right – of course she was right – yet her words hadn't affected Helen's determination one little bit. She finally had some information, a tangible suspect and that familiar fire in her belly. If she could unmask a murderer, while neutralizing Campbell in the process, then so much the better. Leah's killer had struck mercilessly and with impunity and there was no telling if – or when – they might strike again. For her own sake, and everyone else's within the prison's crumbling walls, Helen had to act.

22

Jordi watched Helen walk back across the yard. From her high vantage point, she could see the whole scene – the cluster of prisoners hugging the fences and Helen's solitary march back to their block. Normally this would have cheered her – she loved the fact that Helen wasn't intimidated by *anyone* – but today her friend's isolation made her feel sad. She looked so tiny and vulnerable from up here, as if you could reach down and squash her.

Jordi clung to the bars and watched Helen until she disappeared from view. She should be out there with her – normally Jordi was the first one out of her cell during association time – but she couldn't face anyone today. Not now that her heart was breaking.

The letter lay on the floor where she'd dropped it. It was short, impersonal, and its message was crushing. Her appeal had been refused. There would be no date with the parole board now. No opportunity to argue for her liberty. No chance to see her kids again.

Suzanne and Chloe were growing up fast, clumsy teenagers with quick tempers and a difficult past. They had been in care for nearly ten years and every time Jordi thought of them it made her cry. She had given birth to them, brought them up for five years, doing the best she could – then they had been taken from her. Thrust into the care system, facing who knows what danger, hardship and heartache. They wrote to her, spoke on the phone from time to time, trying to keep her up to speed with their lives. But she could tell they were holding things back and that scared her. Not just because of the dangers and temptations they faced, but because they were confronting these without her. She couldn't help them, couldn't comfort them. They had each other, but everyone needs their mum sometimes. In her darker hours, Jordi wondered if they would turn their back on her one day. Could they ever just . . . forget about her?

Crossing the room, Jordi tore the letter in two and threw it in the bin. Her parole application had been word perfect – thanks to Helen – but what good had it done? Every six months or so people encouraged her to try again. Do-gooders with law degrees, giving her false hope. Their reasoning always made sense – after all, she was the innocent party in her crime. She and Eric had had a decent thing going at first. Jordi would walk the streets, luring punters into a side street, where Eric would rob them. Easy pickings and for a while things were good, until that awful night. She could still picture the punter fighting back, threatening to do them both in. And she remembered Eric stamping on the guy's head, again and again, as she screamed and tried to pull him off. She'd told the jury the truth – that they hadn't set out to kill him – but it had made no difference to them or the judge. She and Eric both got life for murder, with little chance of parole. This didn't stop her trying, not while her girls needed her, but it made the comedown all the worse. In prison it is the hope that kills you, not despair.

The truth was that Jordi was never getting out of this place. She would never be a proper mum to her little girls. That was something she was going to have to live with. But on days like these she wondered if she had the strength.

23

'I was about to give up on you. You should have been here an hour ago!'

Emilia Garanita kept her volume down, but spat the words out. She was battling a number of tight deadlines and the copy wouldn't write itself. Especially not while she was sat in this café, watching the Polish builders flirt with the teenage mums. Sarah Bradshaw ignored her, settling down in the seat opposite and wiping her brow with her sleeve. She looked breathless, sweaty and unhappy.

'Where have you been anyway?' Emilia enquired, softening her tone. It had taken several weeks to cultivate Bradshaw. She would be stupid to undo all that good work by coming on too strong now.

'Staff training,' Sarah said, not looking up from the table. 'Couldn't get out of it.'

Emilia had the strong sense that the prison officer was lying to her, though as yet she wasn't sure why. She decided not to push it – she had other fish to fry right now. Checking that the counter girls were occupied, Emilia slid a smartphone across the table. Sarah snatched it up clumsily, stowing it in her jacket pocket.

'It's an unregistered phone with only one number in it. So it can never come back to you. The phone number can't be linked directly to me either.'

Sarah nodded, but said nothing.

'And this is for you.' Emilia slid a fat envelope across the table. 'There's plenty more where that came from – if you get me what I need.'

'Thank you,' Sarah muttered, stowing the envelope with her phone.

'Of course, if you do get caught, we never met.'

'Sure.'

'Good, then don't let me keep you,' Emilia concluded, keen to get cracking on her *Evening Standard* piece. 'After all, time is money.'

Sarah nodded awkwardly and hurried away. Emilia watched her go with a mixture of amusement and concern. There was a lot riding on this – Emilia had taken a risk jacking in her job in Southampton – and Sarah was not the most reassuring of accomplices. On the other hand, few would suspect such a gauche character, so perhaps she wasn't such a bad choice after all. Emilia hoped she'd picked right.

If she *had*, and things went to plan, then her gamble was about to pay off big time.

24

Helen moved fast along the corridor, in the direction of the library. She wanted to be alone for a while, to probe the narrative that was taking shape in her mind. So far she only had rumour and innuendo to go on, but it *did* make sense. Annie had been Leah's supplier – of heroin, weed and God knows what else – and Leah had been off the gear lately. Moreover, Annie had suffered a big setback recently – the prison authorities uncovering a big stash of drugs under a false panel in one of her associates' cell.

Annie of course was untouched by this discovery, but her sidekick was currently doing thirty days in Seg – the dreaded Segregation unit – and Annie had been hit hard in the pocket. She was unlikely to take such a setback lying down and if Leah was responsible – grassing up her supplier to curry favour with the Governor – then she would surely be made to pay for it.

Helen was pondering how best to proceed with her investigation, when a noise made her look up. Alexis was standing in the corridor in front of her. She was leaning against the wall, but she was looking directly at Helen, a thin smile spread across her face. What alarmed Helen even more was the fact that her right hand was hidden from view, tucked into the pocket of her hoodie. Helen had put Alexis away for a string of vicious, racially motivated assaults a few years back and the sixteen-stone thug had neither forgotten nor forgiven.

Turning quickly, Helen retraced her steps towards the association yard, but another of Annie's sidekicks now came into view, blocking her chance of retreat. Helen now cut right, towards the open wings of A-Block. It wasn't her block but if she could get there, she would be safe. There would be too many witnesses for Annie's thugs to try anything.

Alexis and her friend were already in hot pursuit, so Helen now broke into a sprint, eating up the yards between the ill-lit corridor and the safety of the neighbouring wing. Her pursuers gave chase, but Helen was fitter than them and had too much of a head start. The access doors were soon upon her and Helen burst through them, breathing a massive sigh of relief as she did so.

Now out on the gantry, she scanned the block for fellow inmates, keen to strike up a conversation with someone, *anyone*. But to her horror, the wing was completely deserted. She had never seen it like this before and she now realized that this was exactly where they'd *wanted* her to go.

Kicking herself for her stupidity, she sprinted along the gantry, but as she did so another of Annie's girls appeared, blocking her route forward. She heard the wing doors swing open behind her – Alexis and her friend – so immediately looked over the railing to the gantry below. It was a good twenty foot down to the suicide net, but if she landed right, she could probably make it away . . .

Except Annie had two of her gang stationed there too, anticipating this move.

Straightening up, Helen turned to face the sneering Alexis. There was no doubt about it, she was trapped. And there was nothing to do now but fight for her life.

25

'We have to reopen the investigation.'

Charlie's voice was firm, despite the churning in her stomach. She and Sanderson were locked in the latter's office, the black-and-white image of Robert Stonehill flickering on the laptop screen in front of them.

'Are you saying that as a police officer or as Helen's friend?'

'Don't patronize me.'

'It's a valid question.'

'No, it isn't. Every step of the way, people have been happy to dismiss Helen's account of what happened, but look at that face. And look at the date on the timeline. This is September the 14th – the day before the first murder – and here is Robert Stonehill taking a direct route from the Torture Rooms back towards the Western Docks.'

'We know Stonehill was in Southampton around this time. This is not news.'

'But look at his behaviour. If he was here by chance, why is he acting so furtively? He sees the CCTV camera and virtually runs out of the shop.'

'You're reading an awful lot into a few seconds of footage.'

'Look at the shoes. A fresh Vans footprint was found in his base at the docks –'

'Helen's base at the docks.'

'A fresh Vans footprint size nine – a man's size – was found there and here *he* is wearing the same brand –'

'Jesus Christ, Charlie, do you know how many Vans trainers are sold in the UK each year?'

Charlie stared at her boss for a moment, trying desperately to contain her temper. She could tell that many of her colleagues had half an eye on their exchange and she had to resist slapping Sanderson, however tempting that might be.

'You're a good cop, Joanne,' she continued in more emollient tone. 'Doesn't it strike you as odd that Robert Stonehill was working in Wilkinson's for three months, but goes missing the day that Helen is arrested? She chased him out of the store and down to the docks, which is what he wanted all along. Because he wanted to frame her –'

'Do you realize how crazy that sounds? We have no independent evidence that this "chase" ever took place – no CCTV, no witnesses –'

'So why did Helen have mud on her boots when she was picked up? She ran across an allotment for God's sake in her pursuit of him –'

'So now you're basing your case on mud?'

For the first time, Charlie hesitated. Put like that, it did sound stupid. She opened her mouth to respond, but Sanderson nipped in first.

'This is all circumstantial. Whereas we have bona fide evidence linking Helen to the murder scenes, not to mention her own admission that she lied to her colleagues, to her friends . . .'

Sanderson stressed the last word, while looking straight at Charlie.

'So while I appreciate your loyalty to a former colleague, it is time to let this go. Consider this an official warning. Helen deceived all of us and now she is going to have to answer for her actions in court. The evidence has been assessed, her trial date has been set . . .'

Sanderson paused, before delivering the coup de grâce:

'And this investigation is closed.'

26

Helen waited until they were almost upon her before she struck. Alexis and her friend had closed in fast, scenting blood, but Helen had held up her hands in surrender. Alexis looked at her with contempt, opening her mouth to unleash a volley of abuse. But she never got the chance. Moving with lightning speed, Helen rammed her fist into Alexis's mouth, sending her spiralling backwards.

Instantly her accomplice attacked, launching a hefty fist in Helen's direction. Helen ducked the blow deftly, spinning to knee her attacker hard in the stomach. Winded, her assailant reached into her pocket and Helen took advantage of this split-second delay to drive her hard into the metal railing behind. They crashed into it and, as the woman collapsed to the floor, Helen moved off quickly in the direction she'd just come from.

But suddenly she was pitching head first on to the gantry. Her forehead struck it hard and, dazed, she turned to find Alexis holding on to her ankle. Helen kicked out savagely, desperately trying to free herself, but already it was too late. The women descended upon her from all angles now and Helen found herself being dragged into an empty cell. She screamed for help, but the door was slammed shut, cutting off her cry. She was alone with her attackers now.

'You like a little pain, don't you,' Alexis drawled, spitting blood at her.

Helen had knocked out both of Alexis's front teeth but

this didn't make her feel any better, especially as her adversary now drew a weapon from her pocket. Helen's heart sank – it was a long sock stuffed full of bulky batteries – a common prison weapon capable of inflicting terrible injuries in the right hands. Alexis swung it round and round, gathering speed all the while, as several pairs of hands pinned Helen down. Then suddenly and without warning, Alexis brought it crashing down on Helen's kneecap.

Helen howled in agony but seconds later she felt it land again, slamming into her stomach. The breath was punched from her and immediately Helen retched. Alexis's arm was raised again and this time as she struck Helen yanked an arm free, successfully deflecting the blow. But no sooner had she done so than she felt a crushing blow to the back of the head. Clearly Alexis was not the only one who was armed.

Helen's head was spinning. The blows rained down from all sides now, but she was unable to move her arms or legs to stop them. She was losing consciousness fast, the whole scene playing out in a hideous blur. She couldn't hear properly, she had double vision and there was nothing to do now but surrender to the attack.

Her resistance was at an end.

27

'Who would do such a thing?'

Cathy Smith had been speechless at first, but now she was finding her voice.

'Who would do that to my Leah?'

'We don't know, but I promise you we *will* get to the bottom of it.'

'She was a good girl, she didn't get into fights,' Cathy continued, barely hearing Celia Bassett's interjection. 'And she was always trying to help you lot.'

'I appreciate that, which is why you have my word that we will find her killer. We have a team working on this already –'

'It's definitely her? You've seen her with your own eyes?'

'I was summoned to her cell straight away and yes, it's her. I'm very sorry.'

Cathy hung her head, running her hands over her weary face. Through the glass of the door, Celia could see Leah's boys being entertained by her PA. They were clearly unaware of the tragedy and Celia immediately wondered how Cathy would break it to them.

'Who found her?'

Celia turned back to find Cathy staring right at her.

'One of the female officers. Sarah Bradshaw – I think you know her.'

Cathy nodded weakly, then said:

'And where is she now?'

'In . . . in the mortuary.'

'I want to see her.'

'And you will.'

'I want to see her now. I won't believe it until I do.'

'I'm not sure that's a good idea with the boys here and, besides, the pathologist is still doing his . . . is still inspecting her, so for the time being –'

'She should never have been here.'

Cathy was staring at Celia with naked hostility. The latter said nothing – she'd heard this complaint *a lot* in her time.

'She should have been in a hospital. She was isolated, depressed . . .'

'I appreciate that –'

'Do you? Have you seen the state of her arms? How she cut herself?'

Celia had seen Leah's arms and though they were depressing, they were not unusual. Though she'd never admit it publicly, self-harm was rife in Holloway.

'The other inmates were out to get her, have been from the start. You knew that and yet you did nothing.'

'That's not true, Cathy. We intervened many times on her behalf.'

'And what good did that do? As soon as your back was turned, they were at it again.'

There was an element of truth in this, but unless something 'serious' happened, Celia's hands were tied.

'She begged to be moved. You said she *would* be moved.'

'I didn't, Cathy,' Celia corrected her, privately thanking her lucky stars that there was no record of her conversations with Leah.

'You *did*. I know it and you know it. And though I

may never be able to prove it, her death is on your conscience.'

Cathy rose abruptly and moved towards the door. Celia rose too, just in time to see the grief-stricken mother turn back and spit at her:

'Her blood is on your hands.'

28

Leah's naked body looked wan under the industrial lights. The prison mortuary was old and run down, slowly going to seed as plans were made to mothball the prison permanently. It was hardly the ideal place to carry out a post-mortem, but Benjamin Proud knew speed was of the essence, so he'd decided against moving her to another facility. Prison murders were tough to solve – evidence vanished swiftly, inmates refused to talk and even prison officers were reluctant to help. Benjamin wanted to gather the evidence as quickly as possible – his best hope of apprehending the killer was to catch them while they were still trying to conceal their involvement in this brutal crime.

Leah lay on the slab in front of him, her body a road map of trauma, neglect and self-hatred. Numerous tattoos, even more razor blade scars and a litany of scabbed needle marks – these in addition to the nicotine-stained fingers, cracked nails and profuse body hair. This was not a woman who'd thought much of herself or who'd found much succour in life. Leah had been surviving, not living, for years now but the final indignity had been saved for the end. Benjamin shuddered as he took in Leah's face. Her mouth and eyes had been opened for examination, but the bloody suture holes remained as grim decoration.

'Not a pretty sight, is she?'

Benjamin turned to find Dr Asim Khan approaching. Putting on his professional face, Benjamin replied:

'What have you got?'

'Not much so far. I've taken bloods for analysis and swabbed her mouth and fingernails. I've also taken hair samples from her head and armpits . . .'

Benjamin ran his eye over Leah's upper body, as Khan continued:

'. . . obviously if they throw up anything, I'll feed it straight back in. In the meantime, I've done my first sweep of the body. There's no defensive cuts or bruising to the hands, though her nails are broken, so you'll need to check with the forensics team – there may be nail fragments at the crime scene.'

Benjamin made a note of this, then replied:

'Cause of death?'

'Unknown.'

'Seriously?'

'I've only done a surface pass, but there's no obvious wounds or bruising. Furthermore, there are no ligature marks, no facial discolouring, nor any appearance of vomit in the windpipe.'

'Please don't tell me it was natural causes . . .'

'The internal exam should tell us more.'

'Let's hope so.'

Benjamin immediately regretted his sarcasm. Khan was doing his best in very difficult circumstances. This case was unnerving him though – he had investigated many prison deaths over the years, but nothing quite like this.

'Was the sewing done pre- or post-mortem?' he continued.

'Post, I'd say, judging by the lack of bleeding.'

'So our perpetrator enters her cell, kills her and then calmly hangs around to sew her up?'

'That's a pretty fair assumption and believe me that's just the start . . .'

Benjamin stared at Khan, bracing himself for more bad news. He didn't like the expression on the pathologist's face.

'On first sight, it appeared only the eyes and mouth had been mutilated, but actually it was a much more thorough job than that.'

Khan now directed his attention to the victim's lower torso. As Benjamin's eyes crawled over Leah's body, Khan concluded grimly:

'Our killer really went to town on this one.'

29

'They did a nice job on you, didn't they?'

Helen turned her head towards the voice and immediately regretted it. Everything hurt and any movement, however minimal, caused her agony. Moreover, her vision was blurred and though she could see three shapes standing in front of her, she couldn't make out who – or what – they were.

All she wanted to do was close her eyes and sleep, but willing herself to be strong, she squinted at the shapes and slowly her vision normalized. As it did so, she was surprised to find Jordi, Noelle and Babs standing in front of her.

'How you feeling?' Babs continued gently. 'Is there any part of you that *doesn't* hurt?'

Helen was lying in a comfortable bed in the prison infirmary, though how she'd got there she had no idea. She felt too sick to speak, so shrugged a response to Babs's questions. The truth was that, though she was pleasantly surprised to be alive, she felt terrible.

'I should have seen this coming. Annie's been on the warpath all morning,' Babs carried on ruefully. 'Thank God *one* of us had her eye on the ball.'

She gestured in Noelle's direction. Helen followed her eye line and was surprised to see the burly drug dealer blush.

'I was coming back from chapel, when I saw Annie's crew gathering together,' Noelle muttered. 'They only move in a pack when they're up to something. So I followed them and when I saw what they was up to . . .'

'She chased them all the way back to B-Wing, giving a few of them a taste of their own medicine,' Babs added approvingly. 'Then she and Jordi carried you to the infirmary. Better than waiting for the screws to do anything, believe you me . . .'

Helen suddenly felt tears prick her eyes. She wanted to thank both women but couldn't find the words. So she held out her hand instead, which was grasped eagerly by a guilt-stricken Jordi.

'Sorry, babe,' Jordi said, her voice catching. 'Too caught up in my own shit, when I should have been looking out for *you*.'

Helen waved the thought away. She didn't want Jordi blaming herself – this beating was her fault and hers alone.

'How do I look?' Helen eventually croaked, keen to move the conversation on. 'Is it bad?'

'Not really,' Noelle responded quickly. 'A few stitches, a couple of bandages and you'll have to keep those ice packs on for a while, but other than that . . .'

Helen managed a smile, though she suspected Noelle was lying. She couldn't shake the pounding in her head, the raging fire in her kneecaps, nor the dull ache in her side. Helen suspected she'd sustained a couple of cracked ribs during the assault.

'Anyway, to help you along the road to recovery,' Jordi jumped in, 'we've brought you a few treats.'

'Broke open our piggy banks,' Noelle confided.

From within their hoodies, the three women now produced chocolate bars, magazines, a bottle of Ribena and best of all, four packets of cigarettes. A treasure trove by Holloway standards.

'This must have cost you a fortune . . .' Helen protested.

'Cleaned us out, but we wouldn't have it any other way,' Jordi concluded.

They piled the booty on to Helen's bed and for a moment Helen was speechless. These women had so little – £15 a week to buy all their toiletries, food and writing materials – and they had blown all of it on her.

'I don't know what to say,' Helen eventually managed.

'Then don't say anything. Let's get you checked out and safely back to your cell,' Babs replied soberly, gesturing to the nurse. 'This place is Annie's territory – you don't want to stay here a minute longer than necessary.'

'Is a cell likely to be any safer?' Helen replied, Leah's death still fresh in her mind.

'Maybe, maybe not. But here's a little tip for you,' Babs continued, leaning in close. 'A ten-pence piece makes a good screwdriver. Loosen your bed screws and ram it up against the door. Nobody's coming in then.'

Babs straightened up as the nurse arrived, winking at Helen as she did so. Not for the first time today, Helen felt grateful for their support. She had few allies in Holloway, yet in her hour of need these three good women had come to her aid, which moved her more than she could say. No question, life never fails to surprise you. You really do find kindness in the strangest places.

30

'You should have seen her, Steve. She just stood there and told me – *ordered me* – to drop the case. Helen was good to her – she bloody promoted her, for God's sake – and now she's been stabbed in the back.'

Charlie was pacing back and forth in the kitchen. She'd been home for over an hour, but her temper showed no sign of cooling. On more than one occasion she'd caught Steve shooting anxious looks at the ceiling, fearing that she'd wake Jessica.

'So what are you going to do?'

'I don't know, but she's crazy if she thinks I'm giving this up. Our boss – her friend – is rotting in prison –'

'But what more *can* you do? If what Helen says is true, Stonehill will be well clear of here by now. He's got what he wanted –'

'*If* what she says is true?' Charlie cut in, failing to conceal her irritation.

Steve paused for a moment and then continued in a measured tone:

'Look, Charlie, I'm fond of Helen, you know I am. But you're risking a lot here purely on the strength of her word . . .'

'She's telling the truth.'

'You can't *know* that and you'd be mad to sacrifice your career on a point of principle. You and Sanderson have been at each other's throats for months now. Are you sure this isn't just another excuse for a fight?'

'Have you listened to anything I've said –'

'I've heard plenty, believe me.'

'Then I'd expect better of you. I'd expect you to *support* me.'

For a moment, Steve seemed lost for words. Then he looked up and Charlie saw real anger in his expression.

'You have no right to say that to me.'

His voice was suddenly loud and harsh.

'I've backed you every step of the way. Even when I had doubts. So don't you *dare* accuse me of not supporting you.'

Jessica was stirring upstairs. Shaking his head, Steve marched to the door.

'Steve –'

'I love you, Charlie. But don't push it.'

He spat the words out, his body visibly shaking, then he marched away up the stairs. Charlie watched him go, feeling guilty and foolish. Steve was right – she had no cause to take it out on him. He would come round, but Charlie knew she would have to work hard to recover lost ground. She cursed herself. Her day had started so promisingly, but it was ending with a resounding slap in the face. Her best-laid plans were now in ruins.

31

Where had she gone wrong? What had she done to deserve *this*?

Cathy Smith sat on a battered chair in the relatives' room, lost in thought. Dylan and Caleb were playing with some toy cars, laughing and scrapping, but Cathy was immune to their happiness today. Her daughter – her only child – was dead.

It didn't seem possible. How could it be that so much love, so much effort, so much worry could be expended on someone, only for them to vanish from your life? She would never laugh with Leah again, never nag her, never talk to her. She was gone.

Was this all somehow *her fault*? She hadn't given Leah the greatest start in life, despite her best efforts. No father to care for her, no siblings to fight her corner – just the two of them, struggling to make ends meet. She should have persuaded her to stay on at school, to make something of herself, but Leah was determined to follow her mates. She said she would get a job, contribute to the family budget, but her so-called friends were layabouts, only concerned with scoring drugs and booze. And as soon as she met *him*, that was it. She had tried to warn her daughter – could see what he was the moment she set eyes on him – but Leah wouldn't be told of course. She was too like her mother.

History had repeated itself, but this time with a tragic twist. That girl, her baby and now Leah dead too. Some might call it justice, an evening up of the score, but if they could look into Cathy's heart right now, they wouldn't dare.

What was she going to say to the boys? She had worked so hard to make sure that Leah was part of their thoughts, part of their life. What should she do now? They would have very few actual memories of their mother – they were only babies when she was convicted. Anything they did 'remember' would have to be prompted by her, from the souvenirs of a precious life now thrown away.

The future suddenly stretched in front of Cathy, long, bleak and full of uncertainty. They would get by, but what would happen to the boys when she was gone? Who would care for them? There was no one. Just their grandmother, failing in health and sick at heart, hoping against hope that she would hang on long enough to see them right. This, then, was the boys' bitter inheritance.

32

Helen lay on the bed, drifting in and out of consciousness. Despite Babs's fierce protestations, the nurse had insisted on keeping Helen under observation for a couple more hours, until the powerful sedatives had worn off. It was the right call – she was still dizzy and unsteady on her feet – but it made her feel uneasy. Her head was filled with visions of Annie's cronies returning to finish the job.

Part of her craved sleep, the other half was desperate to stay awake. Gradually Helen felt her body giving in, exhaustion finally taking its toll. It felt good, closing her eyes and shutting out the world. Banishing all thoughts of Leah, Annie, of her own wretched position in the prison that had tormented her sister for many years.

What had it been like for Marianne? Had she found herself in situations like this, where you had to front up or be swallowed alive? Marianne's default response to hostility had always been violence – she'd taken someone's eye out in this place – but was she defending herself or was *she* the aggressor? Marianne was not naturally a bully, but this place had clearly done something terrible to her.

Helen was well away now – losing herself in weird, disquieting dreams of her sister fighting her way through the filth and the misery – when suddenly she felt her body tense up. She wasn't sure why at first – she raised her heavy eyelids but could only see the nurse doing her paperwork in her office, the other patients sleeping nearby . . .

But then she heard a sound. Footsteps. Padding softly in her direction. Helen willed herself to rise from her bed. She was weak, her defences were down and she was at their mercy. But still, she couldn't die, not here . . .

She could sense their presence, only a few feet from her now. They kept coming towards her and as Helen forced her eyes open, she glimpsed something dark, gripped in a fist, coming right at her . . .

Helen thrust out a hand, grabbing her attacker's wrist. To her surprise, her assailant yelped. And now, as Helen's vision stabilized, she saw Sarah Bradshaw trying to free herself from her grip. But Helen had no intention of letting go.

'What are you doing?' Helen rasped.

'Let me go.'

'Tell me.'

Even as she said it, her eyes locked on to the object in Sarah's hand. It was not a knife or an iron bar – it was a smartphone.

'Who?'

'Let go of me or I'll have you on report.'

But instead of letting go, Helen twisted her skin hard. Sarah swallowed a fierce expletive, shaking her arm furiously.

'Tell me who or I swear I'll break your wrist,' Helen continued.

'Garanita. Emilia Garanita,' Sarah exhaled weakly, shooting a nervous look towards the nurses' station.

Helen released her grip, exhausted by her efforts. Sarah backed off, swearing quietly and rubbing her wrist.

'Oh no, you don't,' Helen said, raising herself awkwardly to a sitting position. 'I'm not finished with you yet.'

'Yes, you are, you crazy bit—'

'Do you want a picture or not? That *is* what you came for, right?'

Sarah hesitated, uncertain how to proceed.

'I know I'm not looking my best,' Helen continued, gesturing to her bruises and her stitching. 'But I guess that's the point.'

Shooting another look at the nurse, Sarah scuttled forward, raising the phone to Helen's eye line. As she did so, Helen lurched towards her, putting her hand over the phone and pulling Sarah in close.

'Here's the deal, Sarah. I won't get you fired and I'll even let you take your photo, but I want something in return.'

Alarmed, Sarah stared at Helen, before whispering weakly:

'What do you want?'

Helen moved in closer still, until she was virtually nose-to-nose with the whimpering prison officer.

'I want information, Sarah. And you're going to give it to me.'

33

The door swung open and Jordi marched into the room. Immediately, two huge women bore down on her, but Wheelchair Annie stopped them with a wave of her hand. Keeping a close eye on her bodyguards, Jordi continued her progress towards Annie, her eyes burning with anger.

'You had no right to do that . . .'

'Do what?' Annie said innocently, placing her copy of *The Count of Monte Cristo* on the bunk nearby.

'You could have killed her, for God's sake –'

'I don't know what you're talking about, Jordi,' Annie continued, casting a glance over Jordi's shoulder to check that she was alone. 'Please don't tell me you've been drinking agai—'

'If you know nothing, then why's your Rottweiler missing two teeth?'

Jordi gestured towards Alexis. Immediately, the vast woman took a step forward, but was checked once more by Annie. Her control of these women appeared to be total.

'Fall down the stairs, did she? Maybe she had an accident brushing her tee—'

'What have you come to say, Jordi?' Annie interrupted, her mood suddenly souring.

'Leave Helen alone. She's a good person –'

'She's a copper –'

'She's a good person, who doesn't cause any problems –'

'That depends on your point of view, doesn't it? She likes

to stick her nose in where it's not wanted, messing with the smooth running of the prison –'

'Messing with your business, you mean –'

'And she needs to be *encouraged* to curb her natural instincts. There's no place in here for a vigilante cop –'

'And Leah? What the hell had she done to you? She's got kids, for God's sake, little kids . . .'

'Breaks my heart,' Annie replied, with no visible sign of emotion. 'But then it's a cruel world, isn't it?'

Annie stared at Jordi, challenging her to say more. Surrounded by her gang, she looked an intimidating sight, but Jordi wasn't quite finished yet.

'Helen is a decent girl –'

'Never thought I'd see the day when you were pals with a cop . . .'

'You and your girlfriends are out of line –'

'No, you're out of line, Jordi,' Annie suddenly shouted. 'And if you've any sense you'll find yourself another playmate. I've done right by you since you've been here. Every time you've needed a fix, I've sorted you out –'

'At four times the street price –'

'Supply and demand, Jordi. You demand, I supply. But that can very easily change.'

Annie let the words hang in the air, before she continued.

'Due to recent events, my stocks are a bit low and some unfortunate souls are going to have to go without. I could scratch *your* name off my list. But maybe you've kicked the habit, gone clean . . .'

The final phrase was laced with sarcasm and though she hated herself for it, Jordi could feel her resolve fading. She should continue to fight Helen's corner, but Annie had her over a barrel, knowing full well she would never beat her addiction. Once more, Jordi felt tears threatening – when had she become such a spineless fuck-up?

She was defeated, but Annie wasn't finished yet. Moving in, she took hold of Jordi's arms and pulled her in close, whispering her final warning:

'I'm your friend, Jordi. Your only friend. So do yourself a favour. Keep your opinions to yourself . . . and stay away from Grace.'

34

'Tell me what it looked like.'

Sarah Bradshaw glanced anxiously towards the nurses' station, clearly wanting to be anywhere but here. As if sensing this, Nurse Evans finally looked up from her papers – evidently surprised by the presence of a prison officer in the infirmary so late in the day. Bradshaw smiled awkwardly at her and after a moment's hesitation, the nurse resumed her paperwork.

'What do you mean?' Sarah muttered, still refusing to look at Helen.

'Leah's room. When you found her, what did it look like?'

'It looked . . . normal. She was lying on the bed with the blanket over her. She looked peaceful.'

'Any blood on the floor? Or the walls?'

'No.'

'Any signs of a struggle?'

'No.'

'Any bruising on her, signs of torn clothing?'

'No, not that I saw. She looked the same as usual, apart from . . .'

Sarah tailed off, clearly ambushed by the memory. Helen watched her closely. Judging by her expression, the rumours of Leah's mutilation were all true.

'Tell me.'

'Please, I've already been through this once . . .'

'Then do it again.'

Sarah finally looked up and, clocking the smartphone gripped tight in Helen's hand, continued in a low voice:

'They'd sewn her up.'

'They?'

'He . . . she . . . it . . . whatever.'

'What had they done? What did you see?'

'They . . . they'd sewn her eyelids down, to her cheeks. They'd sewn her mouth shut too, but also . . .'

'Yes?'

'They'd done the same with her vagina and . . . every other bit too.'

'What do you mean?' Helen replied, swallowing down her revulsion.

'Her nose, her ears, her arse, they'd all been filled in. There wasn't a bit of her they hadn't done a job on.'

'Filled with what?'

'I don't know for sure. It looked liked Vaseline or something. It was spilling out of her ears, her bum . . . They'd stuffed her good and proper.'

Sarah shook her head and finally turned to look at Helen.

'Why did they have to do *that*? They could have just . . .'

Sarah trailed off, the exhaustion and emotion of the day finally overcoming her. She dropped her head and sobbed quietly now and Helen found herself laying a comforting hand on her shoulder. Out of the corner of her eye, Helen noticed Nurse Evans raise her head once more, then lower it again. Clearly she felt this was none of her business and Helen was grateful for her discretion.

'Have the forensics team picked up anything from the scene?'

Sarah shook her head, but didn't look up.

'No fingerprints, clothing fibres, anything that helps point them towards who did this?'

'Not that I know of,' Sarah replied quietly. 'But they probably wouldn't tell me anyway.'

'Ok, I need to see the pathology report.'

'Are you serious? I haven't got access to tha—'

'I need to see it and you're going to get it for me. I'm sure you've got friends in the Governor's office.'

Sarah looked aghast, clearly wanting to tell Helen to take a running jump. But the fight had already been knocked out of her and she hung her head and stared at the floor once more. Helen didn't enjoy turning the screw like this, but the brief details she'd been given about Leah's death had alarmed her. This didn't sound like any prison murder she'd ever come across. It felt like something far worse.

'Get the report for me and I'll play nice,' Helen continued. 'If not, I will have your job. You may think I'm down and out here, Sarah, but I still have friends in the Force and the Prison Service, who take a dim view of corrupt officers . . .'

'All right, all right, I'll see what I can do.'

'I'm very glad to hear it,' Helen responded, handing the smartphone back to Sarah and settling back on the bed.

'Now, how about that photo then?'

35

It was late and Emilia Garanita was tired. She had been holed up in Costa Coffee all day and the novelty of her surroundings was beginning to wear off. She had no office now that she was freelance, so had to take advantage of free wi-fi where she could find it. This place was central, quiet and friendly, but she was on her sixth coffee of the day and was beginning to feel wired *and* stale. She longed to leave her weird cocoon and drink in some cold, night air – she had only been living in London for a few weeks and she still loved walking the streets after dark, taking in the sights and sounds. Holloway was a strange part of the capital – trendy and expensive in some parts, but deprived and dangerous in others. Emilia enjoyed skirting this line, straying off the main paths, in search of something interesting.

She had plenty of time to explore as she knew few people in London. In some ways it had been a rash decision to come here, but when opportunity knocks you have to respond. So she'd decided to throw caution to the wind and cash in on her brief notoriety as the journalist who broke the Helen Grace story. Walking into the editor's office at the *Southampton Evening News* and laying her resignation letter on his desk had been supremely satisfying. He had never appreciated – or paid – her enough. But even so, jumping into the unknown was unnerving and she'd been pleased that a few of the national newspapers had bought articles from her. She'd had pieces in the *Mail*, *Telegraph*, even the *Guardian*, trading on her knowledge of Helen and her interest in serial killings, and was doing fine. She was breaking even – no more than that, at this stage – but who knew what the future might hold?

Something was going on at Holloway. Sarah Bradshaw had looked anxious and distracted when they met and a couple of phone calls to contacts she'd fostered in the visitors' centre at Holloway had convinced Emilia that something was amiss. Hard info was difficult to come by as yet, but clearly something had rattled the staff. Later in the day, it had been confirmed by Holloway's own press officer that there had been a death in custody and that the Prison and Probation Service were investigating the circumstances – but Emilia was sure this wasn't the whole story.

Emilia had considered texting Sarah but ultimately thought better of it, not wanting to confuse the issue. Sarah was there to do a job for her, but once it was done, Emilia would be on her case. It would cost more cash, but if there was something interesting going on she needed to know about it.

She had just pulled up her personal bank account to check that she had the requisite cash to pay for more information, when her phone pinged. Snatching it up, she was pleased to see that it was Sarah sending her a text, with a photo attached. Emilia read the few words – 'prison beating, Grace injured' – then opened the photo.

Immediately her hand went to her mouth and she looked up quickly to see if her audible gasp had turned any heads. Shielding the screen from view, Emilia looked at the image, amazed by what she was seeing. A very sorry-looking, very bruised Helen Grace. She realized now that she had had no cause to doubt Sarah's competency – this was *perfect*.

Emilia was already pulling up her most recent article – about the treatment of coppers behind bars – in readiness to attach the photo. It would cause some grief within the prison, but if Sarah kept her cool, nobody would link it to her. And as for Emilia, well, this was ideal – a compelling article and yet more evidence if it was needed that only *she* had the inside track on this story. There really was no doubt about it – Helen Grace was the gift that kept on giving.

36

Celia Bassett shut the door and locked herself inside. She had sent her PA home, switched off her phone and told the night staff that she was not to be disturbed. Dr Khan's report lay on her desk in a plain, blue folder. He had completed his examinations a couple of hours ago and breaking with protocol had written up his report on site. Celia's own PA had run off copies for Proud, Khan and herself. The look on her face suggested she'd read it while doing so and that the contents did not make for easy reading.

Celia had sent her home partly out of concern for her welfare and partly out of a desire for privacy – she needed a little space and time to try and gather her thoughts after the most traumatic day of her career. She had seen gruesome, depressing sights in her time as a prison governor, but none that had unnerved her as much as Leah's death. Everything about it just felt wrong.

'There's no point worrying about phantoms,' her dad always used to say. He was a solid Yorkshireman who believed in hard graft, a cool head and persistent application. Celia had inherited many traits from her dad. Whenever there was an unpleasant task to grapple with, she liked to meet it head on, without hesitation or procrastination. 'Bad news doesn't improve with age' was another of her late father's maxims.

She opened the file and skimmed the particulars of identity, age and so on. These she already knew. She paused longer on the summary of the injuries – shocking in their detail – but didn't linger on the photos. Instead she hurried on to Dr Khan's wider conclusions.

She was reading fast, hoovering up the unpleasant details of a body ravaged by the trials of life, but as she turned the final page she came to an abrupt halt. At first, she didn't believe it. She turned away, then looked back to the report, but it was no better on second reading. Now it hit the desk, as Celia slumped back into her chair.

It couldn't be true, could it? But there it was. Written in black and white in the report. Celia stared at the offending pages in shock. She had meant to read it, then head home to grab some sleep, but she was going nowhere now. Nor would she be getting any sleep. The situation was far worse than she could possibly have imagined.

37

Mark Robins was clearly shocked by the state of Helen's face, but trying his best to conceal it.

'Let's get you back to your cell. I'd say you could do with a little beauty sleep.'

It was not said unkindly, so Helen took his arm and manoeuvred herself off the bed. She had finally been passed fit to return to her cell, after much cajoling of the nurses, but the latter had insisted a prison officer accompany her. Sarah Bradshaw was otherwise employed and Campbell was hardly likely to come to her aid, so Helen had not been surprised to find Robins in attendance.

'Little steps,' he continued softly. 'We don't want you falling flat on your face . . . again.'

Helen ignored his gentle jibe, concentrating instead on putting one foot in front of the other. Each step was pure agony – the pain arrowing up from her kneecaps to her hips – but she was pleasantly surprised to find that her legs could bear her weight. Slowly the faltering couple made it to the door, then out into the corridor beyond.

Lock-up was long since past and the prison was now shrouded in darkness. Helen shuddered inwardly as she limped along the gantry, though a small part of her was glad that the prison walkways were deserted tonight. She hoped to be a bit more mobile by morning, but knew she cut a sorry figure now. Any signs of weakness were seized upon in prison, so she was glad to be invisible. Her enemies within Holloway didn't need any encouragement.

Robins distracted Helen from her injuries as best he could, chatting amiably as they stumbled along the gantry together. Helen had never really spent any time with Robins and she was surprised to find that in person he was thoughtful and kind. He had deep-brown eyes and a pleasing face and in other situations Helen might have found him attractive. But he was part of a regime that delighted in tormenting her, and though she suspected he wasn't by nature sadistic himself, his acquiescence let others abuse their position, forever damning him in Helen's eyes. He was, however, pleasant enough company tonight, gallantly insisting that Helen hold on to his arm as they proceeded along the gantry at a snail's pace.

As they neared B-Wing, Robins suddenly changed the subject, abandoning their small talk.

'I don't suppose you want to tell me how this accident happened?'

He had avoided asking the question until now and Helen wondered if he'd been deliberately biding his time, winning her trust before asking about the attack.

'I guess you wouldn't believe me if I said I'd fallen down the stairs.'

'No.'

'Then I think it's probably best I say nothing.'

Robins nodded, then continued:

'You know you don't have to suffer in silence. I'm sure you probably have a low opinion of the system here, but it can work for you, if you know how to play it.'

'I thought I was the prime suspect? Public enemy number one?'

'Only in Campbell's eyes.'

Robins let his words hang in the air as they shuffled along B-Wing towards Helen's cell. Thirty seconds later, they had made it to her doorway. Robins held it open for her, but as she made to enter, he stopped her once more.

'There are plenty of people you can speak to, if you need help. The nurses, the Chaplain obviously. And me too. We're not all bad eggs in here.'

He placed his hand on her arm in a friendly gesture of support, then stepped back to allow her to proceed. Helen nodded her thanks, uncertain how to respond, then walked into her cell. With a final farewell, Robins pushed the door firmly shut behind her, the latch bolts deploying with a satisfying clunk.

Sitting down on the bed, Helen looked around her cell. She had grown used to it over the last few weeks, but it seemed unfamiliar and threatening tonight. The truth was that she was scared – unnerved by Leah's savage murder and the brutal events of the day. She was gripped by the feeling that her ordeal was just beginning and that more blood would be shed before it reached its conclusion. Though she tried to remain optimistic, to hope for the best, she saw only bleak days ahead of her. The clouds were thick tonight, the moon well-hidden, and Helen, like every other inmate in Holloway, was lost in the darkness.

38

It was late now and the prison was quiet. The night shift had begun and the inmates were safely locked in for the night. All except one. Leah Smith was undertaking a journey few thought she would ever make. She was leaving Holloway for good.

Her mother stood in the windswept courtyard waiting for her daughter. Cathy had found a friend to take the boys for a few hours, while she carried out this unpleasant but important duty. The boys had protested bitterly – they didn't want to be separated from their grandmother and could tell that something was wrong. But Cathy had insisted, packing them off with promises of treats. There was no way they could be here to witness this.

A firm of local undertakers had been called and they were on hand as the coffin arrived on a prison trolley. It lurched as it descended the ramp to the cobbled floor of the courtyard and for one heart-stopping moment Cathy thought the coffin would tumble to the ground. But the undertakers were experienced, they knew Holloway's terrain and eased the trolley over the stones towards the awaiting hearse.

Numb. That's how Cathy felt as she watched its progress. Could it really be that her daughter, her flesh and blood, was in that plain, wooden box? But even now, as she looked on in a catatonic daze, something new and unpleasant started to intrude on her consciousness.

People were shouting.

She didn't know where the cries were coming from at first, but then she saw them. Faces pressed to the windows, staring down at the spectacle below. Some had opened their windows despite the freezing temperature and were now making their feelings plain. A few were shouting goodbye or even celebrating her 'escape' from Holloway, but the majority of the catcallers were doing nothing so pleasant. Cries of 'scab', 'grass' and 'bitch' accompanied Leah on her journey towards the gaping mouth of the hearse.

Cathy refused to look up, refused to react. Her heart was breaking inside but she would not give them the pleasure of seeing her cry. For herself as much as for Leah she would preserve her dignity, while privately cursing their black hearts. She stood there, stock still and silent, as Leah came to rest in the back of the long, black car. The undertaker crossed over to Cathy quickly and, muttering a few words of condolence, shook her hand before returning to the hearse.

Cathy stood back to make way for it, as it drove past her and out of the prison gates. Still the abuse rained down – Leah was leaving Holloway, heckled all the way. Within these prison walls, there was no forgiveness. Even in death.

39

Helen turned away from the window, unable to watch. She'd assumed the inmates would turn out for Leah's departure and had expected some abuse. But not the torrent of bile that had poured down on Leah's poor mother. Even now, she was still standing there, unsure where to go or what to do. It is always the families that suffer the most.

Helen returned to her bed, her head full of disquieting thoughts. She'd assumed that Annie's gang had attacked Leah – the stitched-up mouth a warning to other grasses – but now she wasn't so sure. It wasn't just the sexualized nature of the attack – mutilating her genitals and stuffing every orifice – that gave her pause for thought. It was the care that had been taken. Annie's thugs were brutal and effective, but clumsy with it. Moreover, the careful draping of the blanket over the body suggested some deeper motivation than mere revenge. Did the 'tenderness' of the killing and the hiding of the body from view betoken some kind of affection for Leah? Having killed her, did the killer want to draw a veil over their deeds? Or was the murderer trying to construct a sick tableau that contained a hidden meaning? The truth was that her death felt more like a ritual killing than simple prison justice.

Nobody was saying it, but Helen could sense others were thinking the same thing. Leah's death was perverse and unusual and had left inmates feeling vulnerable and scared, Helen included. Rising from the bed, she lifted up her mattress and ferreted around for her small canvas bag. This was where Helen kept her valuables – if you could call them that. Stamps, phone cards, cigarettes, even buttons and pens – the strangest things become currency within prison. The closest thing she had to a ten-pence piece was a metal button, so she pulled this out and dropped to her knees.

Thankfully it fitted snugly into the head of the screws that secured the bed to the floor and Helen began to twist. Gently at first, for fear of snapping the button, but then with more force as the screw refused to yield. The screws had been painted over, presumably to make attempts to remove them more difficult, so abandoning the first screw, she moved on to the next. This time Helen couldn't even get the button into the screw head – the paint was too thick and would take an age to wear down. So she moved on to the third and, when that resisted, the fourth.

She twisted, yanked and turned for all she was worth, but it refused to budge. Helen had been relying on Babs's tip – it was her insurance policy against suffering the same fate as her neighbour – but now her attempt had failed, Helen felt unsettled. She did not scare easily, but her cell was swathed in darkness, she had no weapon with which to protect herself and there was a killer on the loose.

There would be no sleep tonight.

40

He was waiting for her.

Sanderson had arrived at the station on the dot of eight, only to find Jonathan Gardam already in her office, admiring the framed certificates on the wall. They were few, in comparison to her predecessor's haul, but she had felt the need to put them up anyway, to prove to herself that she belonged here. Sanderson didn't welcome Gardam's intrusion, but swallowed down her irritation and adopted her cheeriest tone in greeting him.

'You've beaten me to it, sir.'

'Don't worry, I'm not checking up on you,' Gardam said, turning to her with an easy smile. 'But I did want a quiet word. I hear you've been having more trouble with DS Brooks.'

Sanderson smiled awkwardly. How the hell did these things get out so quickly? It was probably just the station grapevine, but he wouldn't put it above Gardam to have a mole in her team. He was that kind of operator.

'She's been doing some follow-up on the DI Grace investigation. She felt that there were some lines of enquiry that had been overlooked.'

'And what do *you* think?'

'I think . . . that that investigation is closed and I told her so last night.'

Gardam nodded, but said nothing. Sanderson felt she should say something more to fill the silence, so continued:

'I sent her home, but I'm expecting her back this morning. We have a very heavy caseload at the momen—'

'Do you think that's wise?'

'I . . . I wasn't sure what else I could do,' Sanderson replied, wrong-footed by his blunt interjection.

'This is your team now,' Gardam responded, staring directly at her. 'Any mistakes, any insubordination, reflects directly upon you. In my considerable experience, shit flows upwards.'

Sanderson knew this was true – the number of station chiefs who'd been forced to resign by anxious politicians and police commissioners was proof of that. But how this applied to her situation was unclear. Charlie's actions, though misguided, demonstrated loyalty, determination and considerable ingenuity. Sanderson was hoping that by squashing the matter quickly, she might do everyone a favour.

'I understand that, but I'm not sure this really constitutes a disciplinary matter. I've spoken to her and I'm hoping we can leave it at that. DS Brooks is a talented, experienced officer –'

'I know you two go way back,' Gardam continued, his smile dipping slightly, 'but you must be careful that this doesn't blind you to her faults.'

Sanderson nodded, unnerved by the subtext of Gardam's words. Despite everything, she still respected Charlie.

'Well, sir, if you really feel that disciplinary action is nec—'

'I'm not talking about that, Joanne. It takes months and can be messy –'

'Right. So what exactly are you suggesting I do?'

'I'm suggesting that you regain control of your team. If a face doesn't fit, then find a way to get rid of it. It'll be best for everyone in the long term.'

The team were starting to drift in now – their eyes inevitably flitting to the closed conference in Sanderson's office – so Gardam took his leave. He had delivered his message and departed quickly, sharing a word or two with people on his way out. Sanderson waited until he'd gone, then left the sanctuary of her office, aiming for Charlie's desk. As so often these days, Charlie was nowhere to be seen. DC Edwards was in, however, and Sanderson hurried over to him now.

'Any idea when DS Brooks is coming in?' she asked, keeping her tone light.

'She isn't,' Edwards responded, not looking up. He had clearly heard about their bust-up and was not keen to get involved.

'What do you mean?' Sanderson replied.

'She just called in sick. Texted me . . . ten minutes ago.'

Sanderson thanked Edwards and walked slowly back to her office. Charlie knew that she had to contact her superior officer if she wasn't coming in. The fact that she hadn't suggested she was up to no good. If she had ignored last night's warning and taken matters into her own hands, then she would be playing straight into Gardam's.

She liked Charlie, but was not prepared to sacrifice her career on the altar of their past friendship. If she *had* ignored her advice, then she would have no choice. She would have to call time on Charlie's career at Southampton Central.

41

Charlie sat in the dark room, her eyes glued to the vast screen. Cut off from the outside world, dwarfed by the images she was watching, she felt as if she was in another universe, as if she was watching someone else's life.

She was holed up in an edit suite at the BBC studios on Havelock Road. All of the local services were based here, including BBC Solent, the news channel which covered Hampshire and the Isle of Wight. Predictably they had gone to town on the Helen Grace story, dispatching reporters and crew to cover her arraignment at the Old Bailey and her incarceration at Holloway Prison. Charlie was glad of their interest now.

Something Steve had said last night had stayed with her. He'd suggested that Helen's nemesis would be long gone by now, having got what he wanted. In a way he was right – Charlie was certain that Stonehill had fled Southampton – but would he really leave the country? Would he absent himself from the climax of Helen's disgrace – her public trial in London? Having invested so much time and effort in engineering her downfall, wouldn't he stick around to enjoy the fruits of his labour? Only after she was convicted would he have got what he really wanted.

If he was holed up in an obscure part of the country, he would be virtually impossible to find, especially now that Sanderson had declared the investigation over. But Charlie had a theory as to where he might be. She knew she was chancing her arm approaching an old friend at the BBC, but it was a risk she had to take in order to test her theory. BBC Solent's news crews had been on hand to film Helen's journeys to and from the Old Bailey each day and had reported on her appearances in court. Was it possible that Stonehill had put in an appearance *there*? He would be taking a terrible risk, but having pulled off the crime of the century, wouldn't he want to be there in person to watch it play out?

Charlie chatted to the reporters who'd covered the case – who clearly thought she was mental – then asked to see the footage. There were numerous tapes – hours of footage of the Old Bailey on those hazy, autumn days – so Charlie was watching the reports on fast forward, her tired eyes straining to spot anything familiar in the staccato images.

Pausing briefly, she stole a look at her watch. Sanderson was bound to find out where she was eventually and would take a dim view of such an open act of defiance. Would it cost her her job? Quite possibly. Her only hope was to come up with something concrete, something to show for all her endeavours, but so far she had discovered nothing of note. She'd seen the gaggle of photographers running alongside the prison van, trying to snap shots of Helen through the blacked-out windows as she left Holloway. And she'd seen similar scenes at the rear entrance of the Old Bailey, as the G4S van had sped in.

She'd whizzed on now to Helen's departure from the courthouse. The defendant was once again hidden from view in the armoured van, but that didn't stop the phalanx of photographers pursuing her down the road. Why did they do this? Did they ever get any decent shots? Charlie rewound the tape – she realized she was getting tired now and wanted to double-check everything – and this time as she played it back she saw something that intrigued her. As the photographers ran off, they revealed a small knot of onlookers, members of the public who'd come to gawp. A couple of elderly women, a mum with a pram and, just behind them, a man. He was hard to spot at first, shielded by the other onlookers, but it was his hat that stood out. Charlie remembered that it had been a mild, autumnal day, neither rainy nor particularly sunny, yet this man was wearing a cap, pulled down low over his face.

It was no more than an instinct, but Charlie now called one of the technicians in and asked him to freeze and enlarge the image. Begrudgingly he did so and Charlie watched open-mouthed as most of Robert Stonehill's face came into view. You couldn't see his hair, but Charlie was certain it was him.

Hugging the surprised technician, Charlie hurried from the room. She ran out of the building and all the way back to her car. Her heart was still beating nineteen to the dozen when she climbed inside. Her persistence had finally paid off. As she'd hoped, Robert hadn't been able to resist watching Helen's disgrace. His mere presence there was intriguing enough – seeming to add weight to Helen and Charlie's versions of events – but it also provided a valuable lead as to his whereabouts. Two weeks ago, he had been alive and well in London.

Which was where Charlie was heading now.

42

Helen hadn't slept a wink and she could barely put one foot in front of the other. But she was aware that Cameron Campbell was watching her intently from the gantry above, so she shuffled her way across the canteen as fast as she could, keen to avoid any further confrontation.

Her ribs ached and she felt dehydrated, irritable and tense. She wasn't the only one suffering, however – everybody looked as though they had had a rough night. There was relief of course that they had made it to the morning unharmed, but the faces that turned towards Helen as she passed wore haunted expressions. Helen suspected they'd been up all night, watching their cell doors for signs of movement and she was not surprised to see suspicion and hostility mingling with their unease. Like Campbell, some of them clearly felt that Helen might be responsible for Leah's death. The question was what, if anything, they were prepared to do about it.

Heading towards the breakfast queue, Helen was dismayed to see Andrew Holmes approaching. The prison Chaplain had been very attentive since her arrival in Holloway – though whether this was because of her notoriety or because he thought she genuinely needed help she couldn't tell. What she did know was that she found him preachy and judgemental. She was a whisker away from telling him what she really thought of organized religion, so changing direction sharply she picked up a discarded tray and joined the back of the breakfast queue, successfully dodging his attempt to strike up a conversation.

As she waited patiently for her bowl of porridge and cup of tea, she suddenly realized how ravenous she was. It had been a long time since she'd eaten properly and though the stitches in her lip limited what she could consume, a large bowl of porridge would do the trick.

Having eventually been served, Helen made her way towards Noelle and Babs, who made an ostentatious display of making room for her on their table. Annie, who was eating two tables away, pointedly ignored the pantomime, but Helen felt sure Noelle's point had been made. The strongest signals in prison were those without words.

'You look like I feel,' Noelle said ruefully, as Helen eased herself gingerly down on to the bench.

'Thanks a lot. Talk about kicking a girl when she's down . . .'

'Could be worse. You could look like this one,' Noelle continued, gesturing to Babs. 'She's only twenty-five and look at her . . .'

'Fuck you very much,' the elderly prisoner shot back, suppressing a smile.

'You feeling any better after your boxing match?' Noelle went on.

'A little,' Helen lied. 'How are you?'

'My knuckles are a bit raw,' Noelle replied, holding them up for Helen to view. 'But hell, it was worth it.'

Noelle resumed eating, noisily gulping down her cornflakes. Helen did likewise, turning her attention to the bowl of porridge in front of her. The servers at the canteen had been friendlier than usual today, giving her an extra-large helping. Helen put this down to the solidarity engendered by collective fear, but as she took her first spoonful of porridge, she soon discovered how naïve she'd been. As she broke the thick skin, a fat cockroach wriggled to the surface, fighting for its life in the thick, milky brew. Helen jerked away from the bowl as if stung and looking up was furious to see the kitchen staff laughing at her.

She had endured many petty indignities during her time in Holloway, but Helen now found herself on her feet, struggling across the room towards them. Babs called after her, urging her to sit down, but Helen was wound too tight today. The red mist was descending, she could hear a strange buzzing sound in her ears, but as she approached the offending inmates, a hand reached out and grabbed her.

Spinning round, she saw Mark Robins holding her arm.

'Let it go, Helen.'

Helen tried to shrug him off, but he held firm.

'I said let it go. You're wanted elsewhere.'

Now, Helen relented. Her red mist was dissipating and she was relieved now that Robins's timely intervention had stopped her doing something stupid. But his next words sent her mood tumbling.

'We need a sample.'

Helen closed her eyes – could this day get any worse? The prison's random drug testing was one of the most humiliating aspects of prison life, as an officer, usually male, had to be present at all stages of the process. However, failure to provide a sample when asked to do so inevitably led to an official warning, loss of privileges and in some cases twenty-four-hour lock-up. Grim as it was, there was no dodging it. So, swallowing her pride, Helen let herself be led away, the sound of her fellow inmates' laughter accompanying her every step of the way.

43

From her viewpoint in the canteen, Alexis watched Helen depart. She was still seething following their fight and her mood had not been improved by the mockery she'd endured since starting work this morning. As soon as she'd arrived, one of the canteen workers had started up a chorus of 'All I want for Christmas is my two front teeth' and the rest of the kitchen staff had joined in. They loved it, laughing and shrieking, revelling in her misfortune.

Alexis had wanted to smack them all into the middle of next week. And she would have, if she hadn't already been under surveillance. Campbell had asked her about her missing teeth and had clearly not believed her weak explanation. As a result, he was keeping an eye on her, expecting trouble. So, as she was already on her last warning, she'd been forced to swallow her anger. The prospect of another stint in the Seg was too grim to contemplate.

Instead, Alexis had applied herself to her chores, thinking all the while about how to avenge herself on Helen Grace. The cockroach hadn't been her idea – it was something the canteen staff did most days to amuse themselves, but it bored her. That said, there was no question of letting her beating at the hands of Grace go unpunished. For weeks now she'd been bragging about sending Grace out of Holloway in a box and her missing front teeth were now an embarrassing testament to her failure. The indomitable police officer had ruined her life once before already – banging her up just for settling a few scores with the local Muslims – and now she was threatening to do so again.

She had to strike back. She had to be seen to break Grace, to come out on top in their continuing battle. If she could achieve this, then her missing teeth might eventually be viewed as a badge of honour. After all, there was no love for the disgraced former copper in here.

It would have to be something painful. It would have to be something that struck fear into the heart of all those other maggots out there. And as Alexis gazed across the kitchen, an idea started to take shape in her mind. It would be agonizing. It would be gruesome. But, best of all, it would be permanent.

44

It is amazing what hate can do.

Charlie was roaring up the M3 towards London, but her thoughts were not on the road in front of her. She was going to the capital in pursuit of Helen's nemesis, and while her mind was turning on the possibilities such a confrontation might throw up, she was also thinking about what had driven Robert Stonehill to wreak his terrible revenge.

He was Helen's only living relative. They were bound together by birth and history – she was his aunt and had felt duty-bound to protect him. She'd wanted to be his guardian angel and over time had hoped to forge a meaningful relationship with her nephew, but Emilia Garanita had put paid to that.

Charlie loathed the untrustworthy journalist, but she had never hated someone enough to want to harm them. The same could not be said of Robert Stonehill. Garanita had found out who he was and splashed his name across her newspaper. The national press had picked up on it and suddenly everybody knew that he was the son of Marianne Haynes, the infamous serial killer whose reign of terror had only come to an end when she was shot and killed by her own sister.

Charlie had been there on that awful day and she knew that Helen had done the right thing. If she hadn't pulled the trigger, Helen would have been killed herself and Marianne would have won. Robert didn't see it like that, however. He despised Helen for killing his mother, for destroying his ordered life by being the unwitting source of Garanita's scoop.

Clearly he would not rest now until Helen's disgrace was complete and this both cheered and concerned Charlie. It gave her an opportunity to apprehend him but also suggested he would fight to the death to see his plan come to fruition. Charlie was hunting him without official support, without any backup, and if she got into a scrape, she would have to deal with it alone. She had been in situations like that before and things hadn't always ended well for her.

She had no choice – she had to be brave and keep going – but she couldn't ignore the fear rising inside her. She was being driven by a sense of injustice and a desire to help Helen, but her adversary was being driven by something much more powerful – hate. Hatred of his own kith and kin. And it was this that made him dangerous. In situations like these, blood is much thicker than water.

45

Helen pulled down her knickers and placed the plastic cup between her legs. Robins stood in the corner, looking embarrassed but resolved, never taking his eyes off her for a second. There was a solid logic to this obviously, but it didn't make the task any easier. Over time, Helen had found that the only way to get through it was to close her eyes and try and kid herself that she was alone.

Helen could feel herself flushing, could sense Robins's presence in the room, but she forced herself to relax, slowing her breathing and finally the urine flowed. It was all over in under a minute and, relieved, Helen handed the cup to Robins. He took it from her, sealing it swiftly, before dropping it in the zipped sample bag.

Helen quickly pulled up her trousers, trying her best not to look embarrassed. She was waiting for Robins to dismiss her now, but he made no move to do so. Instead he handed her sample to Campbell, who lounged in the doorway, before returning his attention to Helen. As Campbell departed, Robins's eyes locked on to the heavy bruising on her face.

'You thought any more about what I said?' he asked.

'Sure thing,' Helen replied. 'But I'm doing ok, honestly.'

'Is that right?'

They both knew she was lying. The question was whether Robins was going to make an issue of it or not.

'If you point me in the right direction, I can make sure you're protected.'

'I don't think anyone can promise that in here.'

'I can talk to the Governor, see about getting you moved to another wing . . .'

'And why would you do that?' Helen was suddenly curious.

Robins looked at her, as if sizing her up, then explained:

'Because I think your life might be in danger.'

'You and me both. But I'm ok here. Thank you.'

Helen wasn't even sure she believed her brave words, but she couldn't leave the wing now, abandoning her friends and fellow inmates to an uncertain fate. And not when she had Bradshaw in play.

'Well, it's your decision. Now let's get you back to your cell.'

Robins ushered her from the testing room, but Helen wriggled out of his grasp.

'Actually I'm not going back to my cell straight away.'

'Are you serious?'

'It's association time, isn't it?'

'Are you sure that's a good idea?'

Helen was about to respond, but Robins cut in, before she could do so:

'Tell you what. Let me walk you back to your cell and maybe hold off seeing your friends until tomorrow?'

'You're very kind,' Helen said decisively in reply. 'But I'm going to have to decline.'

Robins looked surprised, eyeing her suspiciously, so Helen followed up quickly, keen to end this conversation:

'There's somewhere I need to be.'

46

Babs looked up from her novel, as Helen knocked and entered. Putting her book down, the septuagenarian curled up her legs to allow Helen space to sit on the end of the bed.

'How did you get on?' she asked.

'Well, Robins had a good look, but I still managed it, so . . .'

'I've been here nearly twenty years and I'm still not used to it.'

'Is anyone?'

'You'd be surprised,' Babs suggested, knowingly. 'Some of the girls actually enjoy trying to make the men blush. Others use it as an opportunity to challenge authority. Your sister was like that. Always used to stare directly at them. Showing them she wasn't embarrassed, making them look away first. She got away with quite a lot using that trick.'

It was said without judgement and in other circumstances Helen would have taken the opportunity to probe further – over the last few weeks Babs and other lifers had afforded Helen a privileged view of Marianne's time in Holloway. But she had come to see Babs for a reason, so resisted the temptation, getting straight to the point.

'I was wondering if I could have a look at your books? Your records, I mean . . .'

Babs looked at Helen carefully before replying:

'You want to look at my clippings?'

'If you're comfortable with that.'

'Can I ask why?'

'Because it's the best source of information in here. Because you know everybody . . .'

'I know what they've done, that's not quite the same thing.'

'True, but still, they could be invaluable.'

'Old habits die hard, eh?'

'Something like that.'

Babs paused for a moment to consider Helen's request, then said:

'Well, I'm willing to help you, but just be careful. People have been killed in prison for less than asking a question.'

'I'll keep my wits about me.'

Bending down, Babs reached underneath her bed and retrieved a battered cardboard box, which was full of scrapbooks. She was one of Holloway's 'cuttings merchants' and kept clippings on every inmate – past and present – who'd served time in Holloway. As an unofficial historian of the prison and its transient population, Babs was a font of knowledge.

Helen decided to tackle them in order, opening up book one first. She had time on her side and was determined to be thorough.

'What exactly are you looking for?'

'Someone with a taste for the exotic,' Helen told her, deciding to shield Babs from the worst details of Leah's death.

Babs seemed to understand and said nothing, sitting back to let Helen read without distraction. Helen flicked through the clippings fast – dismissing the drug dealers, prostitutes and thieves to concentrate on the murderers and those involved in sex crimes. Many of the faces were unfamiliar to her – dead or released now – but some of the lifers she recognized, people whose crimes were sufficiently serious for them still to be behind bars, with no prospect of parole or release. A gallery of downcast faces danced in front of her as she sped through the articles – women who'd killed their children, their parents, their siblings and even in one case a police officer.

She was moving fast towards the end of the book, then suddenly paused – her eye drawn to a small article with the headline 'Sarrington sentenced to life'.

Flipping the page quickly, she carried on her search.

'You can read it if you want.'

Helen looked up to find Babs smiling at her. She had clearly not missed Helen zipping past the article about her.

'I don't need to,' Helen replied.

'I don't mind. It's no secret.'

'Honestly, I'm fine . . .'

Helen finished the book and handed it back. It wasn't the done thing to ask what someone had got mixed up in to land them behind bars – if they wanted to tell you, they volunteered it, not the other way around.

'Aren't you a little bit curious?' Babs teased her.

'Maybe . . .' Helen shrugged. 'But it's not my place to ask.'

'Then I'll tell you to save you the bother. I'm here because I murdered my husband.'

Helen nodded, but said nothing.

'Does that shock you? Well, it should. I did it in cold blood and I meant it.'

Helen stared at Babs, unsure how to respond. Was that guilt she saw on Babs's face? Or something else?

'I married the wrong man. A violent, jealous, cruel man. He hit me nearly every day, even when I was pregnant. Smashed my head against the door, dragged me round by the hair, whenever he was in drink he took it out on me.'

Helen nodded once more – the echoes of her own father's behaviour were coming through loud and clear.

'Silly bitch that I am, I stayed with him. Had a kid. I thought that might make a difference, but it made things worse. One day I came home to find that he'd thrown our Jeannie down the stairs. She was only six, poor kid. She'd broken her arm, could have broken her neck – she was terrified. That night, I took a hammer to him while he slept. I made sure he would never hurt me or Jeannie again.'

'And they gave you life for that?' Helen said, angry that this seemed to be another instance of a woman being treated harshly by the criminal-justice system.

'Well, I was pretty thorough.'

Helen nodded, but the images Babs's words conjured up were not pleasant. Babs seemed to sense this.

'I'm sorry if that upsets you, but I'd prefer that you heard it from me, rather than one of the other girls.'

'I'm glad you told me.'

'People ask me if I regret it. Well, I regret being in here, that's for sure. I get lots of letters and cards from Jeannie' – she gestured to a neatly stacked pile of letters on her tidy shelf. 'But it's not the same as being with her, you know. Do I regret doing that to him? No, I'm not sure I do – despite what I might say to the prison therapist.'

Helen laughed and Babs resumed her reading, her confession over. Helen was glad of the respite, of the chance to gather her thoughts. She was pleased that Babs felt able to confide in her, but it also brought home to her the absurdity of her position. She was searching for a murderer in a sea of deeply damaged women. Moreover, in order to do so, she had just asked for the help of a convicted killer.

47

Celia looked at her watch nervously, as her officers trooped into the cramped meeting room. Benjamin Proud had insisted all prison staff attend the meeting, which meant the inmates were now in the care of auxiliary staff. This wasn't ideal at the best of times and the thought made Celia shudder now. The prisoners were on edge today. Did Proud really believe that part-timers could handle the situation if something kicked off? Maybe he just didn't care, knowing full well that the blame for any disturbance would land on *her* head.

'Now we're all here we can begin,' Proud declared, as the last of the officers shuffled into the room.

'Not before time,' Campbell said in a loud stage whisper, which was met with a dark look from Proud. Campbell predictably didn't seem to care – his contempt for the man in the expensive suit was evident.

'As you know, a very serious incident took place on Monday night. My team and I are now investigating and it is our job to make sure no stone is unturned, as we try to make sense of what happened.'

Celia clocked a few of the officers looking at each other. They could already tell where this was going.

'Anyone who was on site that night and who had access to B-Wing will be interviewed as part of this process.'

'You want to talk to *us*?' Mark Robins piped up, barely containing his anger.

'I want to talk to everyone who was here on Monday evening and I will be expecting your *full* cooperation.'

His gaze inspected the whole room, looking for – hoping for? – a challenge. Nobody confronted him directly; instead their eyes swivelled to Celia, appealing for her support. But Celia dropped her eyes to the floor, unable to meet their gaze.

'I'd like to make it clear that nobody is under suspicion,' Proud continued. 'This is a standard part of the process. But you *will* incur some disruption to your working day. We will be interviewing you all at various points over the next couple of days, but we are going to start with a search of the staff lockers and recreation areas.'

'You've got to be fucking kidding me?' Campbell suddenly exploded. '*We're* suspects now?'

Celia Bassett had known this was coming. She was just surprised it'd taken as long as it had.

'Nobody is a suspect, but the searches will be carried out. I have a warrant here –'

'Well, you know where you can stick that.'

Campbell was staring fiercely at Proud, challenging him to rise to the insult.

'Be that as it may,' Proud went on, ducking the confrontation, 'the search will go ahead and I'd be grateful if you could accompany my staff to your lockers and help them in any way they require. I don't need to remind you that failing to assist them constitutes a criminal offence.'

There was a long pause as the officers looked at each other, then at Campbell, unsure what to do next. Eventually, with a deep, weary sigh, Campbell rose from the table.

'Suit yourself. But it'll take you a day and a half to get through all the porn in Bradshaw's locker.'

He walked towards the door, winking at Sarah Bradshaw, who'd spent the entire meeting backed into the far corner of the room, watching carefully but saying nothing. She smiled awkwardly – like many in the room she looked uncomfortable and concerned.

Slowly the officers trailed past Celia out of the room. Many ignored her, others cast disapproving glances in her direction. Celia felt the colour rising to her face and stared hard at the floor. Although she didn't like it, she didn't blame her officers for their attitude. They were just letting her know what she had already acknowledged to herself – that the situation was spinning out of control and that she was now powerless to influence events. She had never felt so worthless and helpless as she did today.

48

He was looking at a soul in pain.

It had been a trying morning in the canteen and Andrew Holmes had soon retreated to his office in search of solitude. It was a small and not particularly prepossessing space at the far end of B-Wing but it was *his* space. Dusty, tranquil, calm – it was the perfect antidote to prison life. But not on this occasion. As soon as he opened the door, he saw the tall figure of Lucy, sitting on one of the battered chairs.

Feigning good humour and enthusiasm he didn't feel, Andrew had sat down with her to hear her latest woes. Lucy was a regular visitor – not because she liked him particularly or was especially religious, but because no one else would listen to her. In some ways, Andrew didn't blame the other inmates for steering clear. It wasn't that they were intolerant of transsexuals or even that they were particularly scared of this occasionally volatile character. It was more that she was often deeply depressing company for the very simple reason that she was . . . depressed.

Andrew had long made the case that she belonged in hospital rather than in Holloway, but nobody seemed to want to listen, so Lucy remained where she was. Sometimes she exhibited her deep misery through acts of wanton violence or repulsive 'dirty protests'. At other times, she seemed to lapse into an almost catatonic state of sadness which usually preceded an attempt on her own life.

At her best, Lucy was simply morose. This seemed to be the case now.

'My dad tries to put a brave face on it,' she was saying. 'But I can tell it's killing him, just like it's killing me. We've only got each other, see, and, despite everything I've put him through, he misses me, especially at Christmas.'

'You must try to be strong. I know it seems hopeless, but you've got each other and that's got to be worth something. Things *will* get better.'

'Perhaps,' Lucy replied blankly, dropping her eyes to the floor.

'You haven't had a falling out, have you?'

'Of course not, what the fuck are you saying that for?'

Having been placid seconds before, suddenly her eyes were blazing. This was classic Lucy – you could never predict from one moment to the next how she was going to react.

'No reason at all, just you seem doubtful about the future, about you and your dad –'

'Not because of him, never because of him. That man . . . that man is my rock. I'd die without him.'

It was true. Andrew knew that Lucy's father, Paul, had never judged or criticized his daughter – not even when she had stabbed a man to death with a broken pint glass. Lucy had been provoked with vile abuse, it was true, but still not many men would be so unfailingly supportive towards a child who'd caused so much grief over so many years.

'So what's the matter? Why are you so worried?'

'It's not him that's the problem. It's this place.'

'Lucy, I know you find it hard here –'

'You really don't get it, do you?' Lucy virtually snorted

in response. 'You of all people should be able to see it for what it is.'

'You're not making sense, Lucy, what do you mean?'

'I mean Leah.'

'What about her?'

'She was just the first.'

Andrew said nothing, regarding Lucy cautiously. It was often hard to tell whether she was talking rationally or retreating to a dark, fantastical place.

'She was a baby killer, the lowest of the low. And she was made to pay.'

'You don't know that.'

'Don't you feel it too? The reckoning is coming. And when it does, freaks like me won't stand a chance . . .'

Now Lucy suddenly looked terrified.

'That's when you need friends . . . and I haven't got a single one of those in here.'

She had pulled her legs up now, curling herself into a ball, as if to protect herself from the coming violence. There were tears in her eyes and her whole body was shaking, but Andrew remained calm, reaching forward to take Lucy's hands in his.

'You've got me.'

Lucy looked up sharply, surprised by this sudden show of affection, by the strength in his voice. She looked at him intently, as if wanting to feed off his confidence.

'I know you're scared, but I have someone very powerful on my side, who can be of help to you. So let's have no more talk of Leah or of vengeful justice. Let's concentrate instead on helping each other as good Christians should.'

Lucy nodded dumbly, moved by the Chaplain's words.

'Now I know I've not asked you this before, but would you like it if we prayed together?'

Lucy nodded again. She suddenly seemed as if you could lead her by the nose, such was her weakness. Andrew smiled warmly at her as he wrapped his hands around hers and continued:

'Good. Now would you like to begin or shall I?'

49

An hour had passed and Helen was no closer to identifying a suspect. Shutting the third book, she looked at the others spread out in front of her. Suddenly it seemed a hopeless task. She would persevere, but so far she hadn't found a single prisoner who fitted the bill. She had come across vile acts of murder and sexual brutality, but no mutilation on the scale Leah had endured. She had come across a lot of unnerving characters, but no one exhibiting the preternatural calm and expertise exhibited by Leah's killer.

'Want a hand?' Babs asked, putting down her novel once more. 'I'm not sure I can handle any more Marian Keyes.'

'If you want to,' Helen replied despondently. 'But to be honest I'm probably as well served going to the Craft department and asking if anyone's taken up sewing recently . . .'

'That's the spirit. I knew you'd get the Holloway sense of humour in the end,' Babs said, smiling.

Helen picked up book four and opened it. As she did so, Babs started to leaf casually through book five.

'You're the expert,' she continued. 'And I don't want to tell you your business, but have you considered the possibility that your killer might *not* be contained in the pages of these books?'

'Of course, but it seems a decent place to start.'

'Maybe. And I wouldn't fault you for thinking that. You're a copper and we're a bunch of killers, thieves and whores . . .'

'I never said that –'

'No, but it's what you think sometimes. You wouldn't be human if you didn't.'

Babs's tone was even. Helen didn't think she was being chided by the prison veteran but she wasn't sure.

'However, you shouldn't let your instincts, your history, blind you to the possibility that none of us are responsible.'

Helen knew where this was leading. The thought had certainly entered her head – only for her to dismiss it as outlandish. Babs, however, seemed deadly serious.

'You're looking for someone who had an axe to grind with Leah. Someone who had easy access to her cell, who could come and go as they pleased. Someone who feels they are *untouchable* in this place.'

Her words hung in the air for a moment, before Babs concluded:

'So doesn't it seem probable that Leah's killer was actually one of *them*?'

Helen stared at her. It was not a scenario she'd wanted to entertain, but Babs's logic was sound – and very disquieting. If she was right, if a prison officer *was* preying on his own charges, then no one was safe.

50

The officers stood silent as Proud's team went about their business. They had opened their lockers as requested, but protocol demanded they remain present while the search was conducted. It was humiliating for all of them, to differing degrees. Some lockers were total pigsties, others were scrupulously neat. Some contained embarrassing keepsakes – well-thumbed erotic novels or tatty pin-ups – others concealed more private, personal possessions: photos of ex-lovers or keepsakes of children who'd long since flown the nest. Everybody felt the tension – public humiliation was one thing, but there was the very real possibility that something more significant, something more sinister, might be uncovered by the search.

Sarah Bradshaw stood in silence. She just wanted this to be over. By the looks of things everybody else felt the same. Celia Bassett looked ill, Mark Robins was shifting uneasily from foot to foot and even Campbell seemed a little less cocksure now. It was excruciating to have to watch Proud's drones removing each item one at a time – discussing it, evaluating it. You could feel the silent judgement, from both searchers and colleagues alike.

The real question, and the one that was exercising Sarah this morning, was how *far* the search would go. Having your cache of empty chocolate wrappers and celebrity magazines paraded before your colleagues was embarrassing but was not a sackable offence. If, however, their investigation extended beyond the lockers to a full body or – God help her – a strip search, then things would be very different.

Sarah had Garanita's phone on her, but she could deal with that, as the mobile phone was unregistered and couldn't easily be traced back to its owner. She would have to explain why she had only one number in her contact list, but people knew she had no partner and assumed she had no mates, so perhaps she could convince them. More alarming was the paperwork she had on her, paperwork she'd lifted directly from the Governor's office not half an hour ago.

Using her reputation for clumsiness, Sarah had managed to get Bassett's PA out of the room by knocking a full cup of tea over her desk. The irate victim of this accident had fled down the corridor towards the cleaning station. It was a decent walk and negotiations would have to take place with the surly Head of Operations, allowing Sarah enough time to whip out the required papers and run off copies before the chuntering PA returned with a full kitchen roll and a serious case of the grumps.

Sarah had left soon afterwards and was on her way back to B-Wing when she'd been collared by a member of Proud's team. Her heart had been in her mouth, fearing her theft had already been discovered, but actually her apprehension was part of a general summons instigated by Proud. Sarah still had the papers in her hand and had had to think quickly as she made her way to the meeting room. Which was why she was sweating now.

She was standing perfectly still, trying to look open and honest, but her heart was thumping in her chest. A personal search would raise questions that it would be impossible to answer, questions that would inevitably result in her dismissal from the Service. Tucked down the back of her standard-issue charcoal grey trousers was a copy of the pathology report on Leah Smith. She had taken a terrible risk obtaining it and now Sarah Bradshaw feared she was about to pay the price.

51

'This is the guy I'm looking for.'

Detective Inspector Frank Percival looked at the picture, then at Charlie.

'He's wanted for a number of serious offences – assault and battery, aggravated burglary, identity fraud. He was spotted in North London roughly ten days ago,' she elaborated.

'Is he on the system?'

'Absolutely. We're not certain of his current alias, but all the details we *do* have have been inputted by our people. File Number HP1456.'

Percival nodded and started tapping the information into his laptop. Charlie smiled pleasantly at him and took the opportunity to take in her surroundings. The Met Police's Identity Theft Unit was well-staffed and significantly more high tech than their outfit. Initially, Charlie had been unsure where to start her search for Robert Stonehill, but as he had a history of credit card fraud and identity theft, the unit seemed as good a place as any.

Involving another police force was a risky play. Charlie knew that, but she reasoned that opting for serious but relatively routine offences would raise fewer eyebrows and might allow her to slip under the radar for a while. She had no idea how long her search would take – or even if it would be successful – and she knew she would have to manage the situation carefully if she wasn't to be exposed before she'd found her quarry.

'Up until three months ago, he was using the name Aaron West,' Charlie added.

Percival nodded and carried on typing. This was the trickiest part of their discussion as this could lead her Met counterpart straight back to the Helen Grace case and explode Charlie's fiction. But it was too important a detail to exclude and, as Stonehill had never been charged with anything, Charlie hoped it would only raise a hit on the system if he'd been using the same name while in the capital.

'Nothing coming up under that name,' Percival told her, shaking his head.

Charlie smiled – half relieved, half disappointed.

'And you say this guy is a priority?' he asked, looking up at her again.

'Absolutely. The attack on the shop owner was sustained and brutal.' Charlie winced at the 'memory' of this heinous crime.

'All right, well, I'd like to help, but I don't have the manpower to spare, so you'll have to do the digging yourself.'

He swivelled the laptop round towards her and pulled up a battered plastic chair.

'I can, however, stretch to a hot drink. I'd take the coffee, the tea tastes like dishwater.'

Thanking him, Charlie sat down and opened up their system. With each step she was getting herself into deeper and deeper water, but she didn't hesitate now. There were hundreds, possibly thousands of faces stored here and she would have to wade through them all in her hunt for Stonehill.

She clicked on the first one, then the second, then the third. A long and arduous day spread out ahead of her, but the first part of her mission had been successful, so there was nothing for it but to leaf patiently through this rogues' gallery of conmen and fraudsters, hunting all the while for a serial killer.

52

Her eyes swept the gantries, searching for her prey. Association time would soon be over and an attack would be much harder when the walkways were crowded with bodies. She had deliberately volunteered for extra kitchen duties so she could stay behind long after everyone else had headed for the yard, purely in the hope of getting a clean shot at Grace. But so far she was nowhere to be seen.

Alexis had seen her making off towards the far corner of the wing, where the Golden Girls' cells were grouped together. Since then there had been no sign of her. She must have been up there for nearly an hour. It was a strange place to linger if you were a marked woman. If it had been Alexis she would have been gathering people around her, calling in favours and bribing where necessary to get some muscle onside. In prison a show of strength is important, especially when you are expecting an attack.

But Grace was an unpredictable character, a loner with little interest in cosying up to the big dogs. Alexis hoped this would prove her undoing. Everyone had to strike a deal in here – whether you paid for it or not – otherwise you were always at risk of violence or worse. Alexis was planning the latter for Grace. Her first instinct had been to smash her face in, but on reflection she had decided for something more inventive and more painful.

She hit the button on the kettle for the fourth time and watched as the steam poured from the spout. She needed the water temperature to be just right, hence her constant boiling and re-boiling. And now as the noise of the kettle subsided she heard something she recognized. A voice. Grace's voice.

Grabbing the sugar from the shelf, Alexis emptied half the pack into the steaming kettle. Then carefully she lifted it off the base and started towards the stairs. This cocktail was hardly original, but it would be effective. The molten sugar would bind the boiling water to Grace's skin, making her burns all the more devastating. If she still had any face left by the end of this, she would be a lucky woman.

There was only ten minutes until the end of association. Alexis could see Grace two floors up, making her way back towards her cell. Padding quietly, Alexis slipped up one flight of stairs, then moved at double speed to the end of the corridor. Grace would have to descend a storey to return to B-Wing, so nipping in ahead of her, Alexis tucked herself into the darkened entrance to the library. Through the glass slit in the door, Alexis could see the bookworms browsing the shelves and prayed quietly that they wouldn't spot her and upset her plans.

Alexis could hear footsteps approaching now and slunk back towards the door. Grace passed by quickly, intent on getting back to the safety of her cell. Alexis counted to ten, then slipped out of her hiding place, hurrying along the corridor. Grace was only twenty yards ahead of her now, seemingly oblivious to the danger. Alexis picked up her pace.

Now there was only ten yards between them.

Now five.

Alexis flipped the lid of the kettle open and ran forward,

arm raised, but as she did so Helen spun round. Crouching low, she swung her right leg, connecting hard with Alexis's leading leg. Surprised and off balance, the burly thug crashed to the ground, boiling, sugary water splashing over her hands and arms.

Already Alexis was howling in agony, but Helen didn't hesitate, marching forward and putting her boot to her throat, pinning her down.

'Look at me.'

Helen's voice was calm and assured. Alexis squirmed beneath her, refusing to make eye contact.

'Look at me!' Helen shouted and this time Alexis did as she was told. She looked a pitiful figure, writhing on the floor, but Helen knew she could show her no mercy.

'This is your last warning. If you come for me a third time, I will kill you. Do you understand?'

Alexis nodded, riven with pain and terrified by the cold look in Helen's eyes.

'Tell your friends too. Playtime's over.'

Helen raised her foot suddenly and walked quickly away down the corridor. Alexis's cries were already attracting attention and it wouldn't do to be caught near the scene of the crime. Helen felt energized and alive – the adrenaline coursing through her – but also shaken, realizing how close she had just come to horrific injury. It was only the sound of the kettle lid opening that had alerted her to the danger and only instinct that had saved her from harm. It had been a close shave and one she didn't fancy repeating.

She hoped that her words had registered with Alexis. She didn't like what this place was doing to her, what she was becoming, but desperate times call for desperate measures. Bullies had to be dealt with, violence met head on, and if she didn't like the casual brutality of it all, one thing at least had been achieved.

She would live to fight another day.

53

'They're animals. What more do you want me to say?'

Cameron Campbell leant back in his chair, letting his words hang in the air. The locker search was over now and he'd been summoned to a private interview with Benjamin Proud in the Governor's office.

'I know we're supposed to think of them as our special charges,' he continued. 'But *you* spend a few weeks here, then see how you feel. This week I've already had to deal with a dirty protest from Juicy Lucy, three assaults, one ABH and some muppet who tried to choke herself to death by swallowing a sanitary towel. Guess who had to put their fingers down her filthy throat and pull it out. Not the man . . . or woman . . . in the suit.'

Campbell shot a look through the glass to Celia Bassett, who loitered outside, then returned his gaze to Benjamin Proud. Everything about this guy wound him up. The smart suit, the superior attitude, the refusal to smile – it all smacked of someone who had never been at the coalface, who'd never got his hands dirty.

'You know . . .' Proud finally retorted, 'I could have you up on a charge for those comments alone.'

'Be my guest.'

'Not to mention the contraband we found in your locker.'

'All for my personal consumption. You can't touch me on that –'

'Then you must like a drink.'

'If you worked here, so would you.'

Proud looked at Campbell, his face inscrutable. Campbell desperately wanted to provoke him, to make him lose his cool, but the guy refused to be baited.

'You're wasting your time here,' Campbell went on quickly. 'You should be talking to Grace. She's the one with form for this kin—'

'I'd rather talk about you, Campbell,' Proud interjected, sitting back in his chair. 'Can I ask why you work here, if you dislike it so much?'

'Who said anything about disliking it? I said they were animals and well . . . someone's got to work in the zoo, haven't they?'

'Why are they animals?'

'Search me. I'm not a psychiatrist or a priest. But I'm guessing the drink and the drugs and the fact that Daddy fiddled with them don't help.'

'You feel sorry for them, then?'

'They've had a rough start, but who hasn't? Doesn't mean you can't grow, that you can't change. But most of them just want to fight or fuck. So what does that make them?'

'Was Leah Smith like that?'

Campbell eyed Proud suspiciously. Now they were getting to the meat of the conversation.

'Smith . . . was an accident waiting to happen.'

'Meaning?'

'Meaning she had no friends. She stuck a six-inch kitchen knife into a pregnant woman's belly . . . and there's no coming back from that, is there? Certainly not for the baby . . .'

For the first time, Campbell saw a twitch of displeasure steal across Proud's face.

'The other girls were out for her. We did our best, but you can't watch them twenty-four/seven and I think that got to her. Which is why she caned the drink and drugs whenever she could.'

'How could she afford that? She doesn't have any savings, her mother is on benefits, how could she afford the inflated prices gangs charge in here?'

'Perhaps she begged. Perhaps she used what her mother gave her. There's no telling what these people will do.'

'Did you ever give her alcohol or drugs?'

'Fuck off.'

'Something from your little stash?'

Campbell shook his head slowly, as if he was dealing with a moron, but said nothing.

'She was a desperate woman,' Proud continued, 'in need of friendship, in need of release –'

'Do me a favour –'

'You said it yourself. She was all alone in the world. Who knows what she might do to curry favour, to get by. I'm going to be asking everyone this question, but I'm particularly interested in your answer, Cameron.'

Campbell flinched at the mention of his Christian name. He suddenly had the nasty feeling that the power balance between them had shifted.

'Tell me in your own words the precise nature of your relationship with Leah Smith.'

54

Jordi slipped her arm through Helen's and held it tight. This was not just a friendly gesture to her wing mate, it was a very public statement of support. Word had already got around of Alexis's abortive attack. Everybody knew Helen was responsible for the thug's unpleasant injuries and Jordi wanted Annie and everyone else in Holloway to know that if they came for her friend, they would have to deal with her too. Jordi didn't possess Helen's strength or agility but she was a street fighter, and, besides, statements were important in prison. Though perhaps in disarming and besting Annie's number one thug, it was Helen who'd made the most powerful statement of all.

'You're learning, kid,' Jordi said, squeezing Helen's arm. 'First rule of prison life – you've got to have eyes in the back of your head.'

'You could have told me that earlier,' Helen answered ruefully.

'Don't worry about it. They'll think twice before they come for you again now.'

Helen nodded, hoping she was right. She was glad to have Jordi's company today. Despite everything she'd been through – her life as a prostitute, the loss of her kids to the care system, a long life sentence stretching out in front of her – Jordi seemed incredibly normal. Helen knew there was no way they would have been friends on the outside, but in here Jordi's generosity of spirit kept Helen sane, reminding her that there was goodness everywhere if you looked for it.

'You sure you're going to be all right, now?' Jordi asked as they approached Helen's cell.

Helen was wheezing slightly, regretting now that she hadn't got her ribs X-rayed.

'I'm fine,' she reassured her. 'Just got a bit more exercise than I intended to this morning.'

'Well, you take it easy now . . . but don't let your guard down. Those bastards could come for you at any time.'

The meaning of Jordi's words was clear – a night-time attack – and Helen hesitated, before responding. Should she share her suspicions that a prison officer might be involved in Leah's murder or would that alarm her further?

'I'll keep my wits about me. You too. You're probably a marked woman now.'

'Just let them try.' Jordi winked at Helen, before sashaying theatrically away down the gantry.

Helen watched her go. She admired her defiance, but she could tell that beneath the exuberant display Jordi was as unnerved as the rest of Holloway's inmates. Night was falling now and the tension was beginning to rise.

Helen slipped into her cell and shut the door firmly behind her. Jordi was right, she should rest up, but she knew that she wouldn't. Somehow Helen felt she was already involved in a twisted game of hide and seek with a killer who appeared able to commit murder then vanish without trace. Any one of them could be next and she knew she could not rest until she'd discovered the truth behind Leah's bizarre and troubling murder.

Helen lay down on her bed to think, but as she did so,

her pillow shifted to reveal a small present tucked underneath. She had doubted Sarah Bradshaw – wasn't sure she had the nuts for the job – but the burly prison officer had delivered in style.

Nestling beneath her pillow in a plain manila envelope was the pathology report on Leah Smith.

55

Her phone buzzed insistently, demanding to be answered. But Charlie let it ring out, before turning it off completely. This was her fourth missed call of the day, all from an 'Unknown' number. That could mean only one thing – someone from Southampton Central was looking for her.

Charlie drained the last dregs of her coffee and threw the plastic cup in the bin. It was her third of the day and wasn't doing anything to calm her nerves. She knew by now that her absence had been noted, yet she still was no further forward in her hunt for Robert Stonehill. She would have to give up soon, if she didn't want to completely blow her chance of keeping her job. The thought of the long, lonely drive back to Southampton was depressing in the extreme.

She speeded up her sifting. There were still so many to check – she was barely a quarter of the way through – and by accelerating her search she knew she risked missing something important. But she wasn't sure when she would get another chance to do this, so flicked through them swiftly, looking for something, anything, familiar.

The faces flew by, while the hands on the office clock crept remorselessly round. She'd filtered by gender, by age, but still there were scores of faces to scrutinize, many of whom looked a bit like Robert: young men, with shaven heads and sullen expressions – she'd had several disheartening false starts already and by now the faces were beginning to blend into each other. She was slowly becoming face blind, fatigue finally overtaking her.

Then, just as she was tempted to turn the laptop off and call it a day, she saw something. She was going so fast, she almost shot straight past it, but scrolling back she realized now what had caught her eye. A cap. An old Portsmouth FC cap, which she was sure Robert Stonehill had been wearing when he entered the newsagent's in Southampton.

She scrolled downwards and there were a number of similar photos. From different days and times, but all in sub-post offices, located in newsagents' shops, cash and carries, and supermarkets. The file was still pending – an officer had not been assigned to it yet – but the implication of it was clear. The man in the photos had been claiming benefits that weren't his. Though the amounts were small, he was certainly prolific and over time had racked up a considerable sum. The man definitely looked like Robert, though as his face was seldom seen front on, it was impossible to be sure.

Charlie looked at the file for the names of those defrauded. None of the victims had been contacted by the police – the complaints had come from suspicious post office staff – which gave her an idea. She ran down the list of names – Arthur Reeves, Eric Pyke, Harry Wilmshaw – then googled the first.

She was not surprised to find he'd passed away. The same was true of Eric Pyke and Harry Wilmshaw too – according to an article in the local newspaper, which featured a report on the large amounts of flowers sent to the hospice where the respected charity fundraiser had recently died.

Now Charlie was whizzing back, searching the web for something – anything – on Arthur and Eric. They didn't appear to have made much of a mark in life, nor to have had much in the way of family to mourn them. But they did have one thing in common with Harry Wilmshaw.

Like him, they had recently passed away at Frances Hill Hospice in Holloway.

56

Alexis lay on the infirmary bed, her eyes clamped shut. She was raging inside and wanted to tear the place apart, destroying anything – or anyone – in her path. But it was agony to move, her arms and her legs having sustained significant second-degree burns, so she was forced to remain still, swearing violently at anyone who dared approach her.

Even though she'd been in shock, she'd insisted on walking to the infirmary herself. In the process, she'd aggravated her burns, with the result that the skin on her legs and arms was severely blistered by the time the doctors finally got hold of her. They had administered drugs straight away but still their every touch went right through her, as they tried to bind and salve her wounds. She had never felt pain like it, but this had now been replaced by something even worse. She was being tortured by a persistent, nagging agony – it felt as if someone was holding a naked flame to her limbs.

Some concerned friends had tried to gain access to the infirmary, but Alexis was in no fit state to receive them, unable to concentrate on anything except her own discomfort, so she'd refused their visits. Besides, she knew she looked ridiculous, with her arms and legs swathed in thick bandages and her front teeth missing. There was no way she would let them see her like this. She looked like a weakling, a broken woman. She looked beaten.

She would have to fight hard to convince the rest of the

prison that she wasn't. Her status, her position in the pecking order, even her life might depend upon it. But the truth was that she was defeated. She had taken on her nemesis twice and been bested both times. She had no doubts that this would have serious consequences for her life in Holloway and she cursed the Southampton police officer from the bottom of her heart.

She had never hated Helen Grace as much as she did tonight.

57

Helen feverishly drank in the report's details. The first surprise was contained in the opening paragraph. Cause of death: Unknown. Helen paused to take this in. She had been expecting a razor slit to the throat, a traumatic head injury or at the very least deep bruising around the throat. But if the report was to be believed, there was nothing remotely like this.

Furthermore, the livor mortis patterns suggested Leah had died as she was found – lying calmly on her bed. There was some evidence of enlarged vessels in the heart and in any other circumstances the pathologist would probably have marked Leah's death down as cardiac arrest or, if he wanted to cover himself, natural causes. But the mutilation of the corpse argued strongly against this.

Overdose was Helen's next thought. She sped to the appended blood analysis, but there was nothing particularly sinister here. Adrenaline levels were high, but you'd expect that given the situation Leah found herself in and the levels of paracetamol, ketamine and methadone were within normal parameters. Was she asphyxiated then? A plastic bag over the head would leave no marks on her body, but if that had been the cause of death, then you would expect a blueish discolouration to the face. Dr Khan made no mention of this and Helen suddenly realized how much she longed to see the body. It was a strange thing to wish for, but she was used to having all the evidence in front of her and she suddenly felt deeply frustrated. How could she possibly gain justice for Leah with one arm tied behind her back?

Helen flicked on through the report. Leah was slightly overweight, with plenty of body hair and evidence of sweat rash. Her arms exhibited track marks – both historic and more recent – as well as tattoos containing her sons' names and plenty of evidence of self-harm. In truth, her body was a bit of a mess, but Helen was intrigued to find no evidence of bruising or scratches on her hands or wrists. If she'd been physically attacked, you would expect some defensive wounds or evidence of restraint. But there was nothing.

Presuming that Leah wasn't a willing victim, then she had to have been restrained or disabled without a struggle. How was this possible? She didn't have any friends, was no favourite of the prison staff and so . . .

A thought now started to take shape in Helen's mind. There was one way to immobilize someone without laying a finger on them, but only prison officers would have access to the necessary equipment. A taser would disable a victim for long enough to kill them, though they would leave two tiny pricks on the victim's skin. Khan made no mention of this and Helen once more swore under her breath, craving more information. It was an intriguing possibility, but at this stage was no more than a theory and didn't explain how Leah had actually died.

Helen skipped on to Khan's internal examinations, hoping against hope for some clue that might unravel this bewildering murder. She was skimming the words now, expecting little, but as she reached the final paragraph, she suddenly came to a halt. Dr Khan had saved his most surprising and most important revelation until last.

Leah Smith was in the early stages of pregnancy.

58

Emilia Garanita punched in the final full stop and sat back to admire her handiwork. She had called the *Evening Standard* as soon as she'd taken her shots of the coffin leaving Holloway and predictably they had bitten her hand off.

She had been pleased to see that she was the only reporter at the back gates – clearly the other hacks hadn't heard about Smith's murder or had chalked it down as another suicide. Her bribe, slipped to one of the G4S guys on duty, had proved money well spent, as she'd not only been given the identity of the victim but also her estimated time of departure from the prison.

Further details were thin on the ground, as Sarah hadn't responded to her texts and the security guy hadn't been told much. But in some ways that didn't matter. Leah Smith had been murdered and, if the rumours doing the rounds were true, her corpse had been mutilated. That was more than enough for Emilia to go on – hinting at these horrors was often far more effective than spelling them out in great detail. Coupled with the grainy photos of the hearse leaving the prison after dark and a full rehash of Leah's crimes, this would be quite sufficient to intrigue and titillate the readers.

The link to Helen Grace was tenuous at best, but that didn't stop Emilia sketching it out. She wasn't going to come out and say that Helen Grace was responsible or even involved – she would leave the readers to draw their own conclusions from the coincidence of a grisly, unexplained death occurring just weeks – months really but who's counting? – after a serial killer was banged up in Holloway. Emilia already had a plan. She would hint at it in this initial article, and then in the ones that followed she would flesh out her suspicions, as more details came to light. She made a note to herself to track down the Home Office pathologist who had performed the post-mortem on Smith. If she could get hold of yesterday's register from the front gate, she should be able to find his name.

Emilia had that familiar feeling in the pit of her stomach – half excitement, half nausea – that always accompanied the birth of a new story. Something was brewing in Holloway – something big – and as usual Emilia's former nemesis was part of the picture. Emilia smiled to herself as she finished the last drops of her chai latte. This story just kept on getting better and better.

59

Charlie shut the car door and darted across the road. Frances Hill Hospice was in a quiet, residential part of Holloway and Charlie was keen not to draw attention to herself. She marched swiftly towards the back entrance of the building and was pleased to see that there were no CCTV cameras in evidence – clearly the fading hospice was not a target for burglars or thieves.

A mum with a buggy was making her way slowly down the road, chatting on her phone. Charlie smiled pleasantly at her and her child, letting them make their way past. As soon as they were out of view, Charlie looked up and down the street again then, wrapping her coat round her hand, grabbed the top of the wire fence and hauled herself up and over.

She landed safely on the other side and moved quickly towards the back of the building. This was the most 'risky' part of her approach, as a member of staff or even a patient might spot her and raise the alarm. But luck appeared to be on her side today and she made it to the back door undetected.

She had decided against a conventional approach. Normally she would have presented herself at reception and asked to see the suspect, but there was no way she could do that with Stonehill. As soon as he became aware that someone was asking for him, he would be off. Charlie knew that once he became aware that his cover had been blown he might vanish underground permanently and there was no way she could risk that.

So far Charlie's plan had worked fine, but now she hit her first stumbling block. The back door was security locked to prevent patients wandering off. It was a heavy-duty metal door with a smart-card system attached and there was no prospect of breaking it down. So Charlie did the only thing she could do. She knocked.

Silence. Charlie knocked again. She knew that what she was doing was unconventional and possibly illegal. Ideally she should have an arrest warrant, though at this stage she only wanted to ask Stonehill some 'questions', so maybe she could get away with it. She was, however, undoubtedly putting herself in danger and Helen – had she been here – would have counselled her against acting so rashly. But as far as Sanderson and Gardam were concerned this case was closed, so what choice did she have?

There was no movement or sound from the other side of the door, so Charlie knocked again, louder and longer this time. Silence once more, then finally signs of life. Charlie braced herself for what was to come. She had no idea if Stonehill even worked here. On the other hand, it was perfectly possible that he might open the door to her. She tensed as she heard the system ping and the door slide open.

'Who are you?'

The young woman in the cleaner's apron looked puzzled and suspicious.

'Police,' Charlie replied, flashing her warrant card. 'I'm looking for this man. Does he work here?'

She was clutching a photo of Robert Stonehill.

'Peter? Yes, he does. He's one of the porters.'

'Is he here now?'

'Yes,' the woman replied, clearly alarmed now by Charlie's urgent tone.

'Where is he?'

'In the storeroom, I think, shifting some furniture –'

'Where is it?'

The woman froze – caught in Charlie's fierce glare – so Charlie gripped her arm and whispered fiercely.

'Where?'

The woman pointed down the corridor. Charlie was already pushing past her. Having been anxious a moment before, now she was in the zone, determined to bring Stonehill in. He had caused so much misery, so much pain – she was damned if he was going to escape her now.

She pushed on down a narrow brick arched corridor. The house was Victorian and would once upon a time have had a number of subterranean rooms for coal and so on. The basement area was now being used as a storage facility for bedsteads, lamps, tables and other junk. There were a number of doors off the main corridor, but all were closed, apart from the very last one, from which a weak light spilled. But Charlie was not going to rush the job, now that she had Stonehill trapped and she worked her way quietly along the passage, teasing open each door and looking inside. The rooms seemed dusty and dead, so Charlie pressed on to the last door. Was this it then? Was she finally going to come face to face with Robert Stonehill?

She removed the baton from her hip holster and extended it to its full length. Then slowly she pushed the door open. Thankfully it made no sound and revealed a large, dusty room filled to the brim with the detritus of past lives. Old photographs and paintings, clothing and memorabilia littered the surfaces of sideboards, dressers and chests. These presumably were the possessions of those who had no one to claim them in death.

Charlie walked slowly into the room, her eyes flicking left and right. The light was still on – presumably somebody was still in here. But there were no signs of life and all was quiet. Gathering herself, Charlie pushed on, her baton raised. The shelving units were high and crammed with cardboard boxes, it was a maze in which it would be easy to hide.

Charlie kept one eye on the door, expecting Stonehill to make a break for it at any moment. In other circumstances, she would have called out to him, tried to flush him out. But Stonehill was an experienced killer and Charlie dared not give him any warning. She already felt exposed enough as it was.

She could see the far wall now. Pretty soon she would round the last shelving unit and be afforded a view of the far side of the room. But as she reached it she paused. A shadow crept out into the aisle from behind the unit – a shadow that looked very much like a foot. If it was, then it was a good place for an ambush, so Charlie suddenly ran forward, ducking low as she swung round the corner, lashing out with her baton as she did so.

But it met with fresh air. And looking up she realized that the shadow had been cast by a pile of old clothing – a shoe sticking out prominently from the bundle. Cursing quietly, Charlie straightened up – then immediately felt herself flying forward. For a moment, she was disoriented and confused, but then she felt a burning pain in the back of her skull and moments later a brutal second blow. This sent her crashing headlong into the shelving, her baton spilling from her hand. Charlie was now face down in old curtains and clothes, but she rolled quickly sideways, just as the chunky table leg came down once more.

Stonehill lifted his weapon again, but to Charlie's surprise he now launched it at her. Raising her arm, she deflected it away and scrambled to her feet. She was dizzy, she was hurting, but she was still standing and she could see Stonehill sprinting away down the corridor. Without hesitating, she raced after him.

The chase was on.

60

'Need to talk. Call me NOW.'

The text was short but not particularly sweet and it filled Sarah Bradshaw with dread. Since Grace had collared her last night, all sorts of shit had kicked off – the staff lockers had been searched, they had all been interviewed and the staff rotas were now being pored over. All this while Sarah had had Khan's path report on her. Thankfully Proud's team hadn't opted for personal searches and she'd managed to get it to Grace's cell without incident, but she'd aged five years in the process. And now Garanita was chasing her.

Sarah needed the money, but was it really worth the stress? She had never been in the top rank of officers, had few commendations on her record and knew that her services were likely to be dispensed with once Holloway shut down. She had limited savings and there was no way she could ask her mother for money, so she needed as much cash in the bank as possible. There was no saying how long it would take her to get a new job – people weren't exactly clamouring to hire a 48-year-old with no qualifications or specialist skills to recommend her. She could already see a dreary future as a low-paid security guard stretching out in front of her and anything which delayed that prospect was very welcome.

Garanita had given her £500 up front with the promise of much more to come. She had presumably heard about Smith's murder by now and clearly there were possibilities for financial gain, but could she continue to leak information to her? There would be so much scrutiny – both from within and from without – was it really worth risking her pension for? As ever, Sarah found herself caught on the horns of a dilemma.

She was so deep in thought that she didn't see Grace approaching until it was too late. She'd resolved to steer clear of the ex-copper now that she had the bead on her and turned on her heel, but Grace was too quick for her, grasping her arm and pulling her back towards her.

'I need to talk to you,' Grace whispered sharply.

'Campbell's on the wing,' Sarah spat back, gesturing over her shoulder.

Grace shot a look towards Campbell and released her arm quickly.

'Tonight then. Where can we meet?'

'I've done enough for you already.'

'Don't even think about welching on our deal.'

'My job's on the line here.'

'You should have thought about that before getting into bed with Garanita. You were seen in the infirmary last night. It won't take the Governor long to work out who took that photo of me – if someone gives her the appropriate information . . .'

'You'll get caught if you're out after lock-up . . .' Sarah countered, changing tack. She desperately wanted to find a reason to avoid playing ball.

'Let me worry about that,' Helen ordered her brusquely. 'Where can we meet?'

Sarah stared at her, but couldn't look her in the eye. The former police officer looked like a woman who would not be denied.

'The gymnasium. I can meet you there at nine o'clock. But I won't be able to stay long,' Sarah eventually muttered.

'It won't *take* long,' Grace replied, before going on her way.

Sarah watched her leave. As she did so, she felt her phone vibrate in her pocket. Another text from Garanita. Cursing her luck, Sarah too made tracks, smiling wanly at Campbell, who appeared to be watching her. Why was life never simple? Why did she never get the breaks? When she'd been approached by Garanita it had all seemed so straightforward, but things were getting more complicated by the hour. She was in too deep to pull out and if she was honest she wished now that she had never set eyes on Emilia Garanita.

61

Charlie hit the fence hard, heaving herself over it. Stonehill was only seconds ahead of her and the fence was still vibrating from his ascent. Dropping down on the other side, she turned and sprinted after him. The street was empty and Stonehill had a clear run, but Charlie was no slouch and knew she had a chance of taking him in a straight race. She had lost her baton, but still had her cuffs. If she could close the gap between them, she'd have a good chance of bringing him in.

Suddenly Stonehill lurched across the road and, casting a quick look over her shoulder, Charlie did likewise. He darted between two parked cars, stumbling slightly on the kerb as he did so. Charlie avoided making the same mistake and hit the pavement at speed. The gap between them was only twenty feet now. A year or so ago, when she was having difficulties shedding her post-baby fat, Charlie would have struggled to keep pace with the young man, but she was in good shape now and powered forward. All those sessions at the gym had been worth it after all.

Stonehill darted round the corner, cutting up towards the high street. Perhaps he hoped to lose her in the crowds, but his tactic was backfiring. He was running into traffic now – shoppers and other pedestrians – and it was slowing him down. Charlie was only ten feet behind. One more burst and she would be upon him.

He stepped off the pavement, running alongside the kerb

to speed his progress. The high street was just a short sprint away and though Charlie couldn't fathom his plan, she knew that was his goal. The noise of traffic was getting louder, the pavements busier and people seemed to be aware of them now, shuffling away from the edge of the pavement as they careered past. Whatever happened now, there would be no hiding it from her bosses back in Southampton – there would be dozens of witnesses to this chase.

They had reached the high street and Stonehill plunged headlong across the busy road without a second thought. Charlie did likewise, preparing to launch herself at him. It would be a dangerous manoeuvre, but she was so close now. She counted down in her head and prepared to dive. Three, two –

A piercing screech alerted her to the danger. The skidding car was braking hard, but not fast enough to avoid barrelling into Charlie, sending her spinning sideways. She rolled over three, four, five times, before coming to rest face down on the tarmac. Her lips were bleeding, she had cuts to her face, but she now found herself stumbling to her feet. The car hadn't gone over her and she seemed to be steady enough, so she cast around for Stonehill. Where the hell had he gone?

A scream made her turn and now she saw him, dragging a terrified teenager from his hatchback. Charlie was already on the move, scrambling round the stationary car next to her and running in Stonehill's direction. He was climbing into the car, but was boxed in by the traffic and there was nowhere for him to go. Charlie was close now and grabbed for the car door, but suddenly the vehicle drove up on to the pavement. Shoppers dived for cover, and as Charlie made a last desperate lunge at the car, Stonehill stabbed the accelerator, going hard for ten yards, before swinging back on to a side street.

Charlie watched him go. Her heart was in her boots, her body was aching all over, but she had already memorized the make, model and registration of the car as it sped away from her. So pulling her phone from her pocket, she flipped it open and dialled 999.

62

'I don't know what you're up to. But, whatever it is, be careful.'

Noelle's expression was stern, but not unfriendly. Shooting a quick glance at Mark Robins, who was patrolling the canteen, she extended her arm under the table, seeking out Helen's outstretched palm. She deposited two bags of cotton wool in it, before drawing her arm back again to continue eating.

'I will be,' Helen replied. 'I just need a bit of time out of my cell tonight.'

'Are you sure that's wise?'

Noelle was no coward, but even she looked uneasy tonight.

'Trust me. I know what I'm doing.'

'And what happens if you get caught by the screws? If you get banged up, you're going to need a clean record.'

'I'm not planning on getting banged up.'

'Well, I've got news for you, sister –'

'You know what I mean.'

'You really believe that you're going to beat the rap?'

'Yes, I do. I've got friends working for me on the outside and the truth will out.'

Noelle's expression changed and immediately Helen knew she had said the wrong thing. Noelle didn't have anyone working for her out there.

'So tell me how this works,' Helen continued quickly,

gesturing to the cotton wool she'd just concealed in her hoodie.

'It's pretty simple really. When the prison officers shut the cell doors at night, the locks trigger automatically. The bolts slide across, locking us in. The only way to stop them doing so –'

'Is to fill the holes that the bolts slide into,' Helen interrupted, getting it.

'Exactly. Pack the holes as tightly as you can, but not with anything hard that will make a noise. There should be enough cotton wool there, but if there isn't, tear open a few sanitary towels for the extra.'

'So young, but so knowledgeable.'

'It's an old Holloway trick,' Noelle explained, shrugging. 'But you've got to get it just right. If the bolts go in half an inch or more, then you're going nowhere. If they don't go in far enough, then you'll be found out.'

'What then?'

'Well, obviously, you wait until the guards have finished their rounds, then you slip your prison ID in the gap and card it like you would a normal door.'

Helen nodded, amused that Noelle assumed carding was common practice. Helen had done this, in fact, on more than one occasion in her career, and felt confident she could ease the bolt out of its mooring, as long as it wasn't lodged too far in.

'I get the picture.'

'I hope you do,' Noelle chided her. 'Because if you mess it up you're off to the Seg.'

Helen didn't need reminding. She knew full well the risks she was taking and what might happen to her if she was caught. She'd already decided not to give up Sarah

Bradshaw if she was caught – she would honour the agreement they'd made. The punishment would land squarely on her shoulders. The thought wasn't cheering, but Helen felt it was still worth taking the chance. The revelation that Leah Smith was pregnant had changed things completely. Thoughts of Wheelchair Annie were already receding, as new suspects pressed their way into her mind. But she needed more information if she was to make sense of this strange crime.

Thanking Noelle again, she took her tray to the slops bin, then made her way up to her cell. She was supposed to be on canteen clean-up tonight, but had reluctantly given her last book of stamps to Sandra Bellis as an inducement to make her take on the chore. Helen wanted time to prepare, and bounding up the stairs to Level Two, she then slipped into her cell.

Ripping open the plastic bags, she poured the cotton wool on to the floor. Checking that the prison guards were still occupied in the canteen, she now started shoving the small white balls into the lock grooves. One hole was soon filled, but she was only halfway through the lower one when her supplies ran out. Heeding Noelle's advice, she now turned to her stack of sanitary towels, but to her dismay these too ran out before the job was done.

She scrutinized the room. Scrunched-up paper would have sufficed but she'd given her writing pad away to another inmate. Her blanket was designed not to tear and for a moment Helen thought she might have to rip up her own clothes to plug the gap, but then her eyes fell on her mattress. She lifted it up quickly to reveal a canvas bag containing her treasure trove of goodies. There were tubes of sweets, a half-drunk bottle of Ribena, but more importantly four packets of Marlboro Gold. Helen hesitated – she had only smoked a couple and they were her only pleasure – but in reality she knew she had no choice. Pulling the cigarettes out, she snapped them in half and shoved them in the bolt hole.

A minute later the job was done. Now all she could do was sit and wait to see if her scheme would work. Helen felt excitement and anxiety swirling inside her. She was ready to go.

63

He looked around the room, surveying the damage. The prisoners had been hard at work today, creating displays for the forthcoming Christmas celebrations, but their industry in tidying up the mess they'd made in the process left something to be desired. They had been having a happy time of it, laughing and joking as they made Santas and Rudolphs, working right up until the dinner bell. But as soon as it had rung they were off, downing tools hurriedly and fighting each other to get to the canteen.

Andrew Holmes bent down and began to pick up the pens, rulers and blunt scissors that littered the tables. Picking up the discarded utensils was a big enough job, but the whole place seemed to be littered with scraps of paper and bits of tinsel. Funny how it always ended like this.

He had been cheered earlier. The inmates generally found Christmas extremely hard, as their separation from lovers, family and the real world hit home. Today, however, the group had seemed in good spirits and Andrew had patted himself on the back for his persistence in petitioning the Governor to allow decorations this year. In the past, they'd had to ban them, after a scoop by a national tabloid seemed to suggest it was a non-stop party for murderers and thieves in Holloway. He'd felt it was important to reinstate the tradition of inmates making their own displays and decorations with cannibalized bits of paper and tinsel. They wouldn't win any awards for craftsmanship but they cheered the place up and reminded people of the importance of Christmas.

It had been a good turnout today. Many of the usual faces – Magda, Jordi, Noelle – but a few new ones too. As a result, the mess was more extravagant than usual and he'd already spent twenty minutes on his hands and knees gathering together the abandoned material. And it was as he was doing so that he realized that his entire supply of cotton wool was missing. They were supposed to be using it for the beards on the Santa faces, but now it was all gone.

In his old life, he wouldn't have given this a moment's thought, but here it meant trouble. Cotton wool was used by inmates when injecting heroin – even now it was probably already being doled out to a crowd of needy junkies. Shoving the rest of the craft material back in the cupboard, Andrew Holmes felt the black cloud descending upon him once more. He had managed to moderate his moods of late – with various forms of 'spiritual' help – but small incidents like this set him back. He had worked so hard with these women, offered them the hand of friendship so many times and in return they lied and stole from him.

He had tried his best, but the simple truth was that you couldn't trust anyone in this place.

64

'What the hell were you thinking? I trusted you to do the right thing and you deliberately disobeyed me.'

DI Sanderson was apoplectic, but Charlie was not in the mood for a dressing down. She was battered, bruised and shaken by the day's events.

'You trusted me to do what *you* wanted me to do.'

'In case you've forgotten, I am your commanding officer –'

'For the time being –'

'So if I tell you the case is closed, then it's closed.'

Charlie just shook her head, staggered by Sanderson's intransigence. Perhaps she should have stayed in London – she should certainly have gone to a hospital – but instead she had come straight back to Southampton to make her case.

'What's he got on you?' Charlie replied witheringly. 'Or is it just ambition that's blinding you?'

'Don't you dare talk to me like that. There have been half a dozen opportunities when I could have moved you on, but I kept faith with you –'

'I'm touched.'

'But I'm fresh out of patience, Charlie. And if I'm not very much mistaken, so is Steve too.'

'What the fuck do you mean by that? Have you been talking to my boyfriend?'

'I hear things . . .'

'Well, hear this. I nearly got killed today, pursuing a suspect. A suspect who was living under aliases in Southampton, fraudulently using other people's credit card details to help him *frame* Helen Grace. And here he is today, living in London under an alias, using the identities of dead people to keep his head above water, as he waits for her trial.'

Sanderson tried to butt in, but Charlie wasn't finished, raising her voice so the whole of the team could hear.

'You can see him on the footage, waiting outside Holloway Prison, for God's sake. Why else would he be there?'

'You know all this for a fact, do you?'

'Well, I was going to ask him face to face, but guess what? He attacked me, fled the scene, then hijacked a vehicle to make his escape. Now you've been a police officer for a few years, Joanne. Does that not strike you as suspicious behaviour?'

Sanderson said nothing, glaring back at her. Charlie knew her words had struck home so carried on, determined to press her advantage.

'Now, I've tried my best to be nice. I've tried to work for you, despite the fact that you had a leading hand in a gross miscarriage of justice. But that ends now. I have given you evidence of Stonehill's wrongdoing. The Met have no knowledge of his actions, they think he's a benefit fraudster and a carjacker and won't mount a manhunt to catch him, unless you tell them to. So it's shit or get off the pot time.'

Charlie was expecting Sanderson to come back at her, but her boss seemed unsure how to respond. So Charlie decided to make things clear for her.

'Stonehill *is* responsible for three murders. We need to hunt him down now, before he has the chance to disappear for good. And I for one will not serve under an officer who can't or *won't* see that. Order the search or give me my P45, because I'm not playing this game any more.'

Charlie was already heading for the door. Sanderson made no move to stop her and Charlie didn't linger for the post-mortem. She had said her piece. She had made her stand.

There was no going back now.

65

His head hit the floorboards and he closed his eyes. The heroin was starting to kick in now, a pleasant numbness creeping up from his toes to his brain. His senses had been in riot all afternoon, but the opiate was finally working its magic and Robert Stonehill was once more at peace.

He had dumped the stolen car near King's Cross, then hurried back to the squat. There was no question of him returning to the hospice and, besides, he needed time to think. He'd no idea how she'd made the connection, but Brooks had blown his cover and he was now a man on the run. He hadn't seen anything on the local news, which was one small mercy, and his best hope was that Brooks was acting alone. If so, she would have trouble mobilizing the local police. The last thing he needed now was the Met bearing down on him, when his final victory was so close.

He had been so careful – leaving Southampton immediately after Helen's arrest and creating new identities for himself in London. He had even sought out this pitiful squat in Archway, full of dropouts, druggies and vagrants, as a way of remaining off the radar. He loathed the people he shared this crumbling space with – they were all just marking time until their deaths – but they did occasionally have their uses. The heroin he had just purchased was third rate, but it was having the required effect.

He kept his eyes clamped shut and tried to block out the aged beat box pumping out reggae – God, how he loathed reggae – as he desperately needed to sleep. But, try as he might, he couldn't switch off. This morning, everything had been fine, now everything was up in the air, the threat of capture a real possibility.

What should he do? Helen's trial was still a couple of months away. Should he just hunker down and sit it out? He dismissed this notion instantly – he would go crazy in this squat and, besides, he still had to live. Had Brooks worked out how he'd been supporting himself? It was a fair bet that she had, given her appearance at the hospice. He'd have to change tack, perhaps get a menial job somewhere that he could lift credit card details. It would have to be away from North London and it would have to pay – he refused to live like the animals around him and anyway his drug habit was becoming ever more expensive.

It was hard to know what to do for the best or what the next few weeks might hold, but one thing was not in doubt. He would never give up, nor would he relent in his bid to destroy Helen Grace. And if Brooks – or anyone else – smoked him out, he would fight them tooth and claw.

Whatever life might throw at him, he would see this through to the bitter end.

66

Every step was agony, but still she kept moving.

The nurses had wanted to keep Alexis in the infirmary, but the Governor had insisted that *all* prisoners were to be confined to their cells after dark, so they had relented, offering to ferry Alexis back to her cell in a wheelchair. She had refused of course and a fierce argument had ensued, her doctors accusing her of deliberately wanting to aggravate her injuries. The discussion quickly grew heated, but when it became clear that Alexis was happy to take their heads off to win the argument, they eventually gave in. Which was why Alexis now found herself shuffling along the empty gantries of B-Wing, two nurses following at a discreet distance behind.

The pain was insufferable and on several occasions Alexis thought she was going to faint, but she drove herself on. She had walked to the infirmary and she would walk back to her cell. She'd already made it through two wings and was so close to home but now, as she approached her cell, she suddenly sped past her own doorway, aiming for another three doors down.

'Alexis, we had a deal . . .'

The surprised nurses were already hurrying after her, but Alexis propelled herself forward. She was determined to see Wheelchair Annie before lock-up. Cameron Campbell, however, was halfway through his rounds and poised to lock Annie's cell, hence her sudden burst of speed.

'Please,' Alexis gasped at the prison officer, as she stumbled the last few yards, the searing pain robbing her of the ability to say more.

Campbell made no move to arrest her progress, seemingly more amused than angry. Ignoring the protests of her medical staff, Alexis put a steadying hand on the wall and craned her neck round the doorway to look into the cell beyond. Annie was lying on her bed, novel in hand, plucking chocolates from a well-stocked box next to her.

'All right, Annie?'

She'd tried her best to sound forceful, but her voice was reedy and thin. Annie didn't look up, seemingly engrossed in her book.

'Everything ok? You need anything?' Alexis persisted, hoping against hope for some sign of favour from her protector.

Now finally Annie did look up. Saying nothing, she ran her eyes over the pitiful figure in front of her, a frown slowly creasing her brow. Then, placing her book carefully on the table, she turned to Campbell, who stood in the doorway.

'You can lock up now, Mr Campbell.'

Turning away from the door, she continued reading. Alexis tried to protest, but she was too late. Campbell slammed the door shut and moved on to the next cell.

For a moment, Alexis wasn't sure what to do. Part of her felt like crying, the other half wanted to drag Campbell back and force him to open the cell. But in the event she did nothing, staring forlornly at the locked door.

'You're only making things worse,' she now heard one of the nurses saying. 'You'll only make them hurt *more*.'

They were right, but still she remained where she was. Her legs *were* numb and her arms felt like they were on fire, but the physical agony was nothing compared to the bitter pain of her rejection. Ever since her arrival in Holloway she had relied upon Annie to protect her, doing whatever vile deeds her mentor asked of her, but now she had been discarded.

Eventually she allowed herself to be led back to her cell. The nurses comforted her, but her despair tonight was total. There was no one to keep her safe now and when her cell door slammed shut behind her, it sounded to her like a death knell.

67

She was screaming at the moon, appealing to God to end her suffering. Lucy was in good voice tonight, cursing her birth, her mother, even the Almighty himself, as she railed at her fate. On nights like this she was difficult to ignore – already the catcalls were starting up in response – but Helen tried to block out the noise. She couldn't afford to be distracted. It was nearly a quarter to nine – the clock was ticking down to her meet with Bradshaw.

Lock-up had passed off smoothly. Campbell had slammed Helen's cell door shut, sending a few choice expletives her way as he did so. Then he was on his way – like most prison officers, he didn't linger while locking the inmates in for the night.

Helen had heard neither hide nor hair of him for over an hour now. She couldn't be totally sure he'd left the wing, but it was a chance she'd have to take, so, dropping to her knees, she pulled her ID card from her pocket. She wasn't sure that she had judged the distances correctly and took her time as she slid her card into the small gap between door and frame. She had to do this right – if she dropped her card, not only would her escape attempt be thwarted, but she risked giving herself away.

The edge of the card connected with the thick steel bolt. She pushed down on it, gently increasing the pressure. But it refused to move. She tried again, harder this time, but the card started to buckle and Helen withdrew it quickly, fearing it might snap. Cursing, she stood up and applied herself to the upper bolt. This bolt also refused to move and Helen was about to remove the card and admit defeat, when finally she felt a bit of movement. She reapplied herself, easing it along millimetre by millimetre and finally, with a satisfying sucking noise, the bolt withdrew from its mooring. Returning to the bottom bolt, she found the door was looser in its frame now and the steel bar yielded to her pressure. She had done it.

Teasing the heavy door open, Helen slipped outside. She lingered in the doorway, craning her neck to see if the coast was clear. To her relief, the wing was deserted and still. Even Lucy seemed to have calmed down now, so she pulled the door shut behind her, stopping just short of closing it completely. It wasn't perfect, but it would have to do. It was nearly nine now and Helen knew that Sarah Bradshaw would not wait. So double-checking that she was alone, she emerged from her hiding place and padded off quietly down the gantry.

68

From an elevated position, the figure watched Helen Grace steal along the walkway. It was no surprise that she was on the move. She had no faith in the internal investigation into Leah's death and had obviously decided to take matters into her own hands. Her methods had not been particularly subtle – she still had much to learn about prison politics – and she had provoked the ire of several interested parties in the process. Frustratingly, however, she seemed to be made of sterner stuff than anyone had anticipated – she had already survived two attempts to neutralize her. Would her luck continue to hold? Or would it be third time unlucky?

Grace had now left the wing and all was still once more. This was the best part of the day, when the sound and fury ebbed away, to be replaced by peaceful misery. The women were alone in their cells with only their consciences for company, reflecting on all they had done and all they had lost. It was a dark time, enjoyed only by the prison vermin.

How long would Grace be gone? Where was she going? It was risky making another move tonight, but there was no other way. Proud and his team were on the hunt, Grace too, so there was no telling what they might discover. Emerging from a shadowy doorway, the figure moved fast along the gantry, before descending quietly to Level Two. The cell numbers flicked by and before long the figure had reached

B33. The Judas slit slid quietly open to reveal a supine inmate inside. All was as it should be, so the figure now reached inside a pocket, fingers searching for the reassuring feel of needle and thread.

This was it then. There was no point delaying. It was time to go to work.

69

'It won't be pleasant, but you've got no choice. You have to kill this right now.'

Sanderson stared at Gardam, wondering whether his choice of words was deliberately graphic. Could it be that he was *enjoying* himself? Sanderson certainly wasn't – she had joined the police to catch the bad guys, not to sit in judgement on fellow officers.

Sanderson had not seen eye to eye with Charlie for some time, but there was no denying they had history. Charlie had joined Hampshire Police a little before her and had been kindness personified in showing her new colleague the ropes. As far as Charlie was concerned they were all in it together – she had never let her own hopes or ambitions colour her relationship with fellow officers. Sanderson couldn't say the same and now felt a twinge of shame, as she recalled how she had crawled over Charlie's back, then Helen's, to get to the top job. Put in the same position, Charlie would have behaved with more . . . grace.

'If you don't get rid of her, then the team will think there's something in what she's saying. More than that, they will think that you're weak.'

'They know me a little better than that, I think.'

'They all witnessed the confrontation. They probably heard her ultimatum. If you back down now, what does that say about you?'

'I understand that, but surely we need to take a moment to consider the evidence?'

'What evidence? DS Brooks can pursue her vendetta against Robert Stonehill all she likes, but it doesn't mean there's a grain of truth in what she's alleging.'

'He attacked her, fled the scene –'

'Because he's a crook. A benefit scammer and a thief who is being pursued remorselessly by an obsessive, unstable officer. There is no evidence at all to connect him with the murders and frankly I'm surprised that you're allowing a junior officer to lead you by the nose like this. What has Brooks actually proved so far? That Stonehill exists. We knew that already. He has a penchant for petty crime. Again this is not news –'

'But if we could talk to him, question him properly then we would at least have a chance to put this to bed once and for all –'

'You put this to bed twenty-four hours ago, in case you'd forgotten. "Case closed," you said. And that is the way I'd like it to remain. Let Brooks ruin her career if she wants to, but don't let her drag you down with her.'

Sanderson wasn't sure what to say in response, but Gardam hadn't finished yet.

'Her time is over. Yours is just beginning. So do the right thing, Joanne.'

70

The deserted gymnasium looked cavernous and cold in the moonlight. The discarded gym equipment cast long shadows and the heavy ropes that hung from the ceiling seemed strangely sinister, as if harking back to an earlier time when executions were carried out in Holloway.

Helen closed the door quietly behind her. The lifeless space made her shiver and she suddenly realized how vulnerable she was here. She had no weapon, no means to defend herself. If she was surprised here, there would be no one to come to her aid.

'Sarah?'

Her voice echoed round the empty hall, but there was no response. Had Sarah reneged on their agreement? Was it possible that Helen had somehow walked into a trap?

'Sarah, are you here?' she whispered, her strangulated voice sounding unfamiliar and unpleasant.

Now a figure emerged from the shadows. Helen squinted to see who it was, but it was impossible to tell in the half-light. Swallowing down her fear, Helen moved forward and was relieved to see Sarah Bradshaw's pinched face approaching.

'Say what you want, then go,' Bradshaw said.

She looked dreadful – pale, drawn and tense – so Helen asked her straight out:

'Did you know Leah Smith was pregnant?'

The look on Sarah's face suggested she did not.

'No . . . I . . .'

'Who are the likely candidates?'

'How should I know?'

'Because she doesn't have any male visitors. It has to be a member of staff. You've worked here long enough, you know your colleagues.'

'Are you sure . . . about the pregnancy, I mean?'

'It was in the pathology report. You didn't read it?'

'None of my business. I got it for you, like you asked, but that's it. I never wanted to be part of this.'

'Too late, so give me some names. Someone with a reputation, someone who's friendly with the girls. Someone who has access to the cells . . .'

Sarah paused, staring at Helen. Now she looked even less keen to be here.

'Don't hold out on me, Sarah. You have a lot more to lose than I have.'

'I've never seen anything . . .'

'But . . .'

'But you hear things.'

'About?'

Still Sarah paused – was that fear Helen now saw in her eyes?

'I'm not going to warn you again,' Helen threatened. 'A woman in your care was brutally murdered and violated –'

'Campbell.'

Sarah looked oddly relieved to have said it. She looked quickly at the door, then added:

'He's moved around a lot of prisons and, you know, rumours follow him. About how he used to treat the girls. I think he has an eye for the bad ones . . . but whether it's *that* kind of interest I don't know.'

'Meaning?'

'Well, I heard a story from Wakefield that he tasered one of the girls just for fun. I've never seen him up to no good, but that doesn't mean anything. The clever ones always hide in plain sight, don't they?'

An image of Jonathan Gardam trying to force himself upon her suddenly shot into Helen's mind, but she pushed it away quickly.

'What about the others? Robins, Kirkham, Malik . . . ?'

'Why not? They've all got dicks, haven't they? But, honestly, you're asking the wrong person. They don't talk to me, don't confide in me . . .'

'Who do they confide in?'

'Each other, I guess. It's a pretty closed club. Sorry, but that's all you're getting from me . . .'

Sarah didn't wait to be dismissed, hurrying past Helen towards the exit. Helen made no move to stop her – she had got the information she needed. She'd had her suspicions about Campbell – he was overly familiar with his charges and sadistic with it – and she now wondered whether his attempt to pin the blame for Leah's murder squarely on *her* had been a deliberate tactic to obscure his own guilt. Was he the one who had silenced Leah for good?

The door swung shut behind Sarah, making Helen jump and now she too headed for the exit. She had risked a lot to come here, but it had been worth it. Now the challenge was to get home safely.

71

The newspaper fell on to the desk as Celia Bassett collapsed into her chair. It had been a gruelling day – anxious inmates, mutinous staff and endless questions, questions, questions. The fact that Leah Smith had been in the early stages of pregnancy changed everything, putting her own officers squarely in the frame. She had to support the PPS investigation, while sticking up for her staff. It was a fine line to tread and Celia was unsure what to do for the best. Every which way she cut it, it was a no-win situation.

The *Evening Standard* led with the news of Leah's brutal murder. Celia wasn't surprised to see Emilia Garanita's name on the byline. She had already proved to be a thorn in Celia's side, trying on numerous occasions to breach the prison's security. The drone had been her most imaginative effort, though she had never admitted responsibility for it of course. Wasn't that journalists all over? Now she was all over the Leah Smith murder and had also found time to concoct an arresting centrefold spread focusing on Helen Grace, complete with an authentic photo of the badly beaten inmate resting in the prison infirmary. Put together, the stories painted a picture of Holloway as a lawless, dangerous place – which was no doubt the intention.

Celia had already fielded an anxious phone call from the Home Office and had promised a full internal enquiry into the leaking of the photo. Though what this would achieve she wasn't sure. It could have been an infirmary nurse, prison officer or even a fellow inmate. Whatever precautions they took, phones seemed to find their way into the prison and Celia knew that the culprit would be impossible to find. Still, she had to go through the motions.

She flicked through the newspaper, taking in Garanita's latest offering. The description of Leah's mutilation wasn't accurate, which would give the media liaison team something to work with, and the journalist didn't seem to know that the unfortunate inmate was pregnant when she died. But how long could they hold this information close? And what would happen when it did finally leak?

Her best hope was that the PPS now made a quick arrest, bringing the whole incident to a close before things could escalate, but how likely was that? The staff interviews seemed to have achieved little, apart from fostering mutual hostility, and Proud looked stressed and dissatisfied when he left her office tonight. How long would this nightmare go on for? More importantly, where would it end?

Celia had no husband to go home to. No partner to vent to. Which is why she was here, holed up in her office late at night, reading Garanita's ill-informed but devastating critique of *her* prison. Her one friend, if you could call it that, was nestling in the desk drawer in front of her.

It had been the hardest of days, so Celia now removed the bottle of Jameson's from her desk drawer and filled her glass to the brim. She'd promised herself that she would knock it on the head soon, but it was calling to her again and tonight she didn't have the strength to resist.

72

Sanderson removed a cigarette from the packet and lit it. She had bought a packet of twenty, rather than her usual ten, in expectation of a sleepless night.

She had never felt so boxed in. Gardam couldn't have been any clearer – he wanted Charlie out on her ear. Hours earlier, Sanderson had been ready to oblige. Charlie had lied to her repeatedly, challenged her authority and made her look a fool in front of her team. Sanderson had convinced herself that in order to maintain control of the unit, she'd have to get rid of her old friend.

Sanderson had sacrificed so much to get to this point. Arresting Helen was a massive gamble which could have backfired horribly. As it was she'd had to endure plenty of hostility and suspicion from other officers, who now wondered if they could trust her, given the alacrity with which she'd 'stitched up' her former boss. Yet in Sanderson's eyes she'd never had a choice. The evidence of Helen's guilt was there for all to see and somebody had to be arrested for those murders. After her apprehension, the murders had stopped and this more than anything had brought the team round. It had also allowed Sanderson to convince herself that she'd done the right thing.

Everything now demanded that she complete the process and rid Southampton of Helen's one remaining champion. And yet still she hesitated to pull the trigger.

Charlie's conviction was total. So much so that she had

risked her life today to prove that she was right. She was not crazy, nor was she stupid. Would she really do all that, given that she had a young kid at home, if she didn't *genuinely* believe that Robert Stonehill had framed Helen? He clearly had been outside the court building when Helen was arraigned, which invited a few questions. His disappearance from Southampton immediately after Helen's arrest was also suspicious. Was it possible that he had deliberately planted the evidence to destroy his only relative? Charlie clearly believed he had.

Was this enough? Was there sufficient doubt over Helen's conviction for her to jeopardize everything she'd been working for for so long? Was she prepared to take this gamble?

Sanderson stubbed out her cigarette and pulled out another. She had the feeling that she could smoke the whole pack and still be no nearer to making a decision. Whichever way she jumped, the path was fraught with danger.

73

Helen padded quickly along the gantry, keeping a wary eye out for prison officers. Her interview with Sarah had been brief, meaning there was a good chance she hadn't been missed yet. The night shift occasionally carried out cell checks in the dead of night, but such was the level of abuse they copped from those they awoke that mostly they didn't bother any more. Helen was only a minute or two from home and she hopped briskly up the stairs to Level Two, keen to get back to her cell.

As soon as she crested the staircase, however, she saw movement. A figure darting from a cell at the end of the gantry and disappearing fast around the corner. Such was the speed of its flight that Helen barely took in what she was seeing – it was just a dark blur in the corner of her field of vision. But instinct took over now and Helen chased after the fleeing figure. Had the killer struck again? If so, this would be Helen's best chance to catch him.

Helen paid no heed to her own safety or the stupidity of getting caught out of her cell at night, she just pounded along the gantry, devouring the yards to the end of the walkway. Her breath was short, her ribs were aching horribly, but still she pressed on. Spinning around the corner, she was just in time to see the swing doors ahead flap shut and she charged in their direction. Barrelling through them she was surprised to see that the corridor was empty. Then she heard footsteps on the walkway above. Immediately she was on the move again, taking the metal stairs three at a time. The muscles in her legs were burning now, her knees protesting, but she drove herself on. Reaching Level Three, the highest in the wing, she scanned to the left and right, before catching sight of a tall figure right at the end of the gantry, wrestling with the access door. If the door there was locked or inaccessible, the fugitive would be trapped – the only way to descend was via the staircase Helen had just mounted.

Helen upped her pace, pursuing the figure. She was getting closer, closer, closer – she could already picture herself crashing into him, smashing his tall form against the heavy door. But suddenly the figure moved, climbing up and over the gantry fence. Helen could scarcely credit what she was seeing and watched in disbelief as the figure leapt off the balcony into the void beyond.

Down, down, down he fell, before crashing heavily on to the suicide net below. The net was made of solid rope and Helen could hear the sound of the impact, as well as the strangled growl of pain that accompanied it. Reaching the fence, she leant over it. To her surprise, the figure was already on the move, scrabbling towards the Level One gantry.

Helen swung one leg over, then another. She was balanced on the edge now, ready to jump. The fugitive, however, had made it off the net by now and was limping away down the gantry.

And now Helen found herself climbing back over the fence. Whether this was cowardice or common sense she wasn't sure, but suddenly she didn't like the odds of such a long fall, especially with a busted rib cage. There was still a chance to catch the fleeing figure perhaps, as his movement appeared to be laboured now, so Helen tore down the staircase, leaping the last few steps, before racing down yet another set of stairs to Level One.

She was hoping to cut the killer off, racing to bring this troubling case to a conclusion, but as she reached the lowest level she was dismayed to discover that it was deserted. The cell doors were all closed, the gantries empty, there were no signs of life. Pushing the access doors open, she peered down the corridor. It too was empty and the doors at the far end were still. Helen slumped down to the ground, exhausted and despondent.

Her quarry had escaped.

74

Charlie stood on the landing, staring at the closed door in front of her. She desperately wanted to turn the handle and walk inside, to try and repair the damage that she'd done, but she didn't dare. The row she'd had with Steve, played out in fierce stage whispers so as not to wake Jessica, had been the worst they'd ever had. They were a loving but argumentative couple, used to solving their disagreements via a vigorous exchange of opinions. This, however, was on a whole different level and for once Charlie had no idea how to appease her partner of fifteen years.

She had returned home late, so Steve was already in a bad mood. When he saw the bruises on her and heard her explanation, his irritation had turned to anger and disbelief. He had always supported Charlie's desire to work and had altered his hours to allow her to do so. But there was one aspect of her job that he couldn't stomach – the danger it occasionally placed her in. Sometimes he blamed the nature of her work, at other times he blamed Charlie's impetuous nature. He had opted for the latter tonight.

'Forget about *me*,' he'd hissed. 'You have a *child*. A little girl who loves you and needs you. And yet you run into moving traffic, get knocked over . . .'

Charlie had tried to explain, but Steve was not to be silenced tonight.

'And then . . . then you don't think to go to a hospital?

Or to phone me? No, you go straight back to Sanderson to continue your stupid crusade.'

Charlie had objected to his description of her campaign to free Helen, but this was just deflection. Steve was right, she shouldn't have risked life and limb in the pursuit of Stonehill and she had been thoughtless in not letting him know what had happened. She was pretty sure there was no serious physical damage done, but she ached all over and it wouldn't have killed her to get herself checked over. She knew Steve only railed at her like this because he loved her, but that made it worse. His anger she could handle, it was the hurt that lay behind it that really struck home.

Moving along the landing, she settled down in the spare bedroom for the night. She hated being separated from him – she liked having his reassuring bulk next to her at night – and wondered how long she would be in exile for. As she pulled the blankets up around her, Charlie felt utterly miserable. She had let Steve down. She had let Jessica down.

And though she didn't want to admit it to herself, she had let Helen down too.

75

Helen stood in the doorway, sickened by the sight in front of her. Having failed in her pursuit, she'd retraced her steps to the cell which the fugitive had bolted from. To her horror, the cell door lay ajar and inside a prone form lay on the bed, covered from head to foot with a tatty blanket.

Trying to quell the roaring emotions inside her, Helen moved forward but as she reached out to grasp the blanket, she saw that her hand was shaking violently. She closed her eyes, breathing slowly in and out, trying desperately to regain her composure. But her heart was breaking and there was no way to quell her distress so taking the final steps, she gently tugged the blanket from the bed.

As it slipped to the floor, Helen reached out to steady herself against the wall. Jordi lay on the bed in front of her. Her eyes were sewn shut and a smile tugged at the corners of her mouth, where the stitching pulled upwards. Instinctively Helen wanted to run from this terrible scene, to hide from the gut-wrenching sight of the dead mum of two. But she now found herself kneeling down by the body. Pulling her sleeve up to cover her hand, she stroked Jordi's cheek, uttering a silent prayer for her. Helen wasn't religious in the slightest, but Jordi was and Helen felt it was important that she should leave this world bathed in love and tenderness, rather than tainted by a killer's cruel touch.

Tears filled Helen's eyes now, but she wiped them roughly away. Jordi's body was still warm but Helen could see that rigor mortis was starting to set in. This spurred her on – as broken as she was by the sight of her brutalized friend, Jordi's body would become increasingly hard to manipulate. She had to examine her now.

As she'd expected, Jordi's ears were full of a thick, clear jelly. Helen didn't dare touch the body, so instead leant in close to smell the substance. It had a strong odour of petroleum so was presumably Vaseline. Moving her gaze further down, she was distressed to see that Jordi's vagina had been sewn shut. She thought about rolling Jordi over to check her rear, but every second counted now, so she would take it as read that her killer had been thorough in their work.

She moved upwards to examine Jordi's face and neck. No scratches, no bruising. Likewise, her hands exhibited no defensive wounds and her long, glamorous nails were all intact. Was it possible the killer drugged her? Creeping up on her while she slept and applying chloroform or similar? Helen leant down until her nose was nearly touching Jordi's – she couldn't smell anything, but that didn't prove a thing. There were odourless equivalents.

A sudden noise made Helen look up and she glanced nervously at the door, but it was just another inmate crying out in her sleep. Helen returned her attention to the body, running her eyes over the surface of her skin, looking for the puncture marks of a taser's pins. There were plenty of tattoos, old scabs and scars, even the legacy of childhood burns, applied by her sadistic mother. But no sign of the skin on her face, neck or arms having been broken in the last few hours. In fact, her skin looked largely unblemished, her upper torso as toned and alluring as always, her silver crucifix resting gently on her generous bosom.

Pulling her hand deeper into her sleeve, Helen now moved Jordi's left arm up so she could examine that side of her torso. Nothing suspicious – so Helen did the same with her right arm and, this time, as she bent closer to examine the skin underneath she noticed something. In Jordi's right armpit was a small pink mark. It would have been easy to miss, buried as it was in the dark stubble of her intermittently shaved armpit, but it stood out to Helen like a sore thumb. It was a needle mark, raw and fresh. Jordi had been making great efforts to wean herself off heroin, so what did this signify? Was it self-administered in a moment of weakness? Or had someone injected *her*?

Helen continued her examination, but her mind was now turning on the needle mark and seconds later she stood bolt upright, cursing herself for her stupidity. Now she didn't hesitate, turning on her heel and heading for the door. As she did so, she rammed the suicide alarm with her elbow.

A second later, the shrieking alarm rang out, but Helen was already gone.

76

Helen ripped the broken cigarettes from the long holes, then set to work on the cotton wool. Prison officers would be passing her cell any moment now, as they responded to the alarm, so there was no time to waste. Seconds later, the grooves were clear of obstruction and grabbing hold of the Judas slit, Helen heaved the door towards her. It slammed shut, the bolts sliding back into place with a satisfying click.

Breathing a sigh of relief, Helen hurried back to her bed, pulling Leah's pathology report from its hiding place under her mattress. Then, climbing on to the bed, she pulled the blanket up and over her. If anyone looked through the Judas slit, they would assume she was just another callous inmate, trying to block out the wail of the suicide alarm in order to get some sleep.

Already she could hear prison officers pounding the gantry, swearing and shouting as they did so. But Helen tried to block out all thoughts of the outside world – she *had* to concentrate. Leafing through the report, she sought out Khan's external examination of Leah's torso. And there it was, buried amid the detail of the historic injuries and tattoos – a small puncture mark in her right armpit. There was nothing particularly remarkable about that, though Leah too had been detoxing recently. Leah was left-handed, which made sense of the location of the puncture mark. But Jordi was not. How likely was it that a right-handed person would inject themselves in their *right* armpit? She would be unlikely to use her weaker left hand for the job and injecting herself with her right hand would be awkward.

No, Helen was sure that the presence of the fresh needle marks on the bodies of both women was significant. Had they both been injected with contaminated drugs? Campbell would certainly have known about their drugs history and could have used this to dispatch them. Then again, so did every other member of the prison staff.

The culprit had to be someone who had easy access to cells, who could pick them off at will, so Helen cast her mind back to the fleeing killer. It certainly looked like a 'he' – the figure was tall, muscular and athletic and was wearing dark clothing, suggestive of the prison officer's dark blue uniforms. Helen cursed herself for not getting a better look. She had strong suspicions, but at the moment that's all they were. She needed certainty, she needed facts.

There was shouting in the corridor outside now, as one of the prison officers was dispatched to fetch the Governor. The rest of the prison was waking up to the situation now, realizing that this was not another code black. The inmates were calling to each other, seeking more information, even as the prison officers bellowed at them to be quiet.

Helen could hear the fear in the prisoners' questions, could sense the growing panic within the prison, but she knew she had to keep her head. It had been a horrific night, which would have terrible repercussions for all concerned, but she had just made the first major breakthrough in this worrying case and it was up to her to act on it.

She owed that to Jordi.

77

'Are you completely insane?'

It was early in the morning, but Gardam was not holding back, reacting with fury to Sanderson's announcement that she wanted to reopen the Helen Grace case.

'With respect, sir,' Sanderson responded coolly. 'I'd prefer it if you didn't talk to me like that.'

'Well, how would you like me to talk to you, when you've obviously lost your mind? I was very clear last night –'

'I know you were and I've reflected long and hard on that, but in the end it's my decision. I was . . . I *am* the SIO on the Helen Grace case and I think we need to look deeper into Stonehill's involvement in the murders of Jake Elder, Maxwell Car—'

'I can remember their names, Inspector,' Gardam interrupted. 'I also remember the body of evidence implicating DI Grace. This case is clos—'

'It's closed when I say it's closed, sir.'

Sanderson's challenge didn't need to be spelt out any further – if he overruled her and shut it down, she would be forced to take it up with *his* superiors.

'And DS Brooks?'

'She has unearthed a potentially significant line of enquiry, so she will be assisting me with –'

'You really think she's worth burning your career for?' Gardam interrupted brutally.

'That's not what this is about.'

'Believe you me, it is. I promoted you to the rank of Inspector and I can see to it that you slide back down the pole again.'

'I don't like being threatened –'

'It's a statement of fact. You are dependent on me for your future prospects – no one else – so be under no illusions what your decision will mean. I have backed you in the past and I'll back you again if you show sound judgement and a desire to swim with the tide now. So you have to decide if you want to be a career police officer, with commendations, generous pay and a comfortable retirement. Or whether you want to be a fuck-up, an also-ran.'

Gardam moved in closer, invading her space.

'Which is it to be, Joanne? What do you *want* out of life?'

Sanderson stared at her shoes, avoiding the fierceness of his gaze. Then finally, she raised her eyes to meet his.

'I want to be right.'

78

Celia sat with her head in hands, exhausted and dismayed. It had been a horrific night and the morning wasn't proving to be much better. She wanted to close her eyes and blot it all out, but when she looked up Benjamin Proud was still there, looking frustrated and angry.

'I will have a riot on my hands,' she eventually muttered.

'An unfortunate choice of words.'

'You know what I mean,' she continued irritably. 'My officers will down tools, call the union in. I know why you feel you need to do this –'

'So why are you fighting me?'

'Because I don't believe one of my officers is responsible for these murders and I can't risk alienating my workforce. We are running a skeleton crew as it is, they are exhausted, running on fumes –'

'They are legitimate suspects in a double murder and will be treated as such until every single one of them is exonerated –'

'We don't know enough about Jordi Baines's death to –'

'I know more than enough about Leah Smith's death to recommend this course of action and I expect you to comply.'

'Can we at least exclude the female officers?'

'Yourself included?'

'Well, I'm not likely to have got Leah up the stick, am I?' Celia sneered. 'And in case you hadn't noticed, my officers are currently searching every cell in B-Wing, looking for the evidence that your team have so far failed to find. I need as many officers on the ground as possible –'

'Be that as it may,' Proud interrupted. 'I would like *all* the officers tested. I would have thought that would make your life easier, as it avoids any suggestion of special treatment –'

'You're going to have to give me time to think about it. The staff are all very upset after last night's incident –'

'Can you even hear yourself?'

Proud's contempt for her was all too evident now.

'Two murders . . . two brutal murders have taken place in the last forty-eight hours and you want time to think? The time for reflection is long over, Governor.'

His tone was brutal, stinging Celia into a reaction, but as she opened her mouth to speak, Proud kept up his barrage:

'Believe me, you are *this* close to getting put into Special Measures. So I would think very carefully about your next move. Do as I say or get out the way, because this thing is happening.'

Proud walked out of her office, slamming the door shut behind him. Celia's head drooped once more. She was hungover, sleep-deprived and painfully aware that things were going to get a lot worse now before they got better. She was no longer worried about her career or her future – she could see both of those going up in smoke right in front of her – it was her conscience that worried her. How could she live with herself if Proud was right? What could she say to Baines's daughters? To Leah Smith's boys?

Had she really been harbouring a serial killer in Holloway all this time?

79

They were crammed in like cattle. The worried inmates had been marched down to the canteen first thing, so that their cells could be searched. Normally this would have worried the prisoners – all sorts of contraband items were concealed within their small cells – but today nobody seemed to care. All eyes were on cell B33 – Jordi's cell.

From their viewpoint below, the inmates could see the PPS officers at work, in their white, sterile suits. Some passed in and out of Jordi's cell, carrying evidence bags. Others crawled along the gantry, conducting a fingertip search for clues. They made a very odd sight in the old prison, raising the inmates' anxiety levels still further.

Helen sat at the breakfast table, flanked by Noelle and Babs. There was a gaping hole where Jordi should be – she never missed breakfast and was always a lively presence – and no one seemed to know what to say. What *was* there to say? The world seemed a poorer, darker place this morning.

Casting her eye around the room, Helen saw the familiar groupings drawing together. Those who could afford to pay for protection cosied up to the gangs, while those who couldn't tried desperately to find a clique to belong to. To Helen's surprise, the only person in the room who seemed isolated was Alexis, who sat on her own in the corner of the room. Had something happened between her and Annie? Was it possible she had been discarded by her boss? If so, then she faced an uncertain future.

'What are you going to do?' Babs said suddenly, intruding on Helen's thoughts.

Helen turned to find both Babs and Noelle looking at her.

'Are you going to tell them what you saw?'

Helen said nothing, staring at the untouched food in front of her. She had been wrestling with this dilemma all night. She *should* say something to the authorities – she had seen Jordi's attacker – but to do so would reveal her own wrongdoing. And could she trust them to take her seriously? How much stock would they put in the word of a 'serial killer' awaiting trial? Once she had made her statement, she would have exposed her hand, and if the killer *was* a prison officer, as Helen increasingly felt sure he was, then she would be putting herself in danger.

'I don't know,' she eventually muttered. 'I need time to think.'

'You didn't recognize him? Didn't see his face or nothing?' Noelle finally said, staring at her cracked nails.

'He was too quick. I saw him from behind, but it was dark –'

'Have you thought about where he could have disappeared *to*?' Babs interjected. 'When you lost him?'

Helen had been thinking of little else. The attacker could have disappeared into one of the cells at that end of the gantry, but to do so would have risked alerting the inmate sleeping inside. Far more likely then that they would have vanished through the access door to the next wing. But to do that, they would have needed an electronic swipe card – and only prison officers had those.

'I think he escaped to C-Wing.'

'In which case, say nothing,' Babs said quickly, nodding urgently at something over Helen's shoulder.

Puzzled, Helen turned to see Cameron Campbell walking towards her.

'On your feet, Grace,' he said brusquely.

'I think it's best if we skip the fun and games today, Mr Campbell. Nobody's really in the mood.'

Babs was already struggling to her feet. But Campbell dismissed her out of hand.

'No need to get excited, Grandma. I'm not here for *fun*.'

Babs glared at him and for a moment Helen feared she might do something stupid.

'I'm here on official business,' he continued, turning his attention to Helen. 'I have bad news for you, Grace. You failed your drugs test.'

For a moment, Helen said nothing – she was too stunned to react.

'That's impossible . . .'

'On the contrary. You tested positive and you know what that means . . .' he continued.

Helen stared at him in horror, knowing full well what was coming next.

'You're off to the Seg.'

80

Suzanne and Chloe sat on the creaking chairs, their fingers entwined in a hard, loving clasp. The teenage girls had had a chaotic life – years spent with foster families and in care homes, in between brief periods with their mother – but the one thing they had always had was each other. They were two halves of a whole and glad of it now.

Suzanne stared at Verity Young, the care home's youthful manager, barely taking in what she was saying. You only got called to her office if you were being transferred or in trouble. Neither was the case for them and Suzanne had smelt a rat straight away. Verity was usually brisk and business-like with the kids but today she was warm and welcoming. She'd even let them take a couple of biscuits from her secret stash – a sure sign that something bad had happened.

Suzanne had felt the fear rising inside her and had sought out her younger sister's hand. This was partly to reassure Chloe, who was always prone to histrionics, but also to reassure herself. Something in Verity's expression suggested that their world was about to be turned on its head.

This had been the calmest, least eventful year of their lives. The care home in Colindale wasn't glamorous, but it was comfortable and safe. Suzanne was sixteen and Chloe fourteen – they were at the upper age of kids in the home and were able to take care of themselves. The daily routine of studies and chores was dull and the food dire, but they got by. The girls had experienced many things in their lives – they had been beaten by their father, manhandled by their mum's clients and on one occasion even slung out on the streets. At least the dullness of their current lives was predictable and reassuring.

And yet for all the apparent cosiness of their existence, Suzanne still dreamt of escaping. She knew that their mother loved them – she had screamed like a banshee when she was dragged away from them – and Suzanne never stopped hoping that one day she would turn up and whisk them away. Their mum wasn't much of a letter writer, but she sent notes when she could and occasionally managed a phone call. Prison visits were harder to organize, but when they did happen, she was always very loving – crying with pride and happiness at how her two little girls had turned out. They were fighters like her, she always said.

Suzanne had never resented her mother or bemoaned their fate. It was her dad's fault that that bloke had died – their mum just happened to be there – and she knew . . . she absolutely *knew* that her mum would come for them, that they would be together again. At least she did until today.

'How did she die?'

The words came from her mouth, but she hadn't meant to say them. It was just that Verity was waiting for some kind of response and Chloe was looking at her older sister in dull shock. A cloud passed over Verity's face, like this was the one question she didn't want to be asked, then lowering her eyes she said:

'We believe she was murdered. I'm very sorry.'

The symmetry of it was horrifying. She was doing time for murder and now she too had been murdered. Was this how the world worked? Was this *justice*?

Suzanne felt she ought to ask some more questions, to take command of the situation, but what else was there to say? Chloe was already starting to cry, the enormity of this tragedy overwhelming her, and Suzanne suddenly felt consumed with misery too. She had pinned all her hopes on their mum, all her plans for the future were based on them being together. Being a family. But that would never happen.

Their life was their prison now and there was no one coming to rescue them.

81

'It's extremely important that I talk to her. So please put her on the phone.'

Charlie was trying to be polite, but was growing increasingly exasperated with the operator. She was pacing the car park at Southampton Central, her mobile phone clamped to her ear, and must have cut a pretty comical figure, gesticulating and remonstrating as she tried to get the receptionist at Holloway to play ball.

'I'm afraid I can't do that. She is not on my list of inmates who can receive prearranged phone calls –'

'Check again. Her name is Helen Grace. I speak to her every week around this time –'

'I've already checked twice –'

'She is *on remand*. I shouldn't have to remind you that all remand prisoners have certain rights and privileges –'

'Hold on a minute.'

Charlie cursed under her breath, unimpressed by the rude way in which she'd been interrupted. But she said nothing – she could hear the operator conferring with a colleague and hoped that things would be swiftly resolved.

'All her privileges have been revoked.'

Charlie was struck dumb for a moment, before finally finding her voice:

'That's impossible.'

'It's what the system says.'

'When were they revoked?' Charlie persisted, her uneasiness growing.

There was another short pause, then:

'This morning. Nine fifty-three a.m.'

Charlie's head was spinning, filled with unpleasant scenarios.

'Look it's really important that I get a message to her. I have important news regarding her trial defence –'

'Then I'll have to transfer you to the Governor – normally no messages are allowed when a prisoner is in the Segregation unit.'

Without waiting for a response, she ended the discussion and Charlie now found herself on hold, waiting to be connected to the Governor's office. What on earth was Helen doing in the Segregation unit? None of it made any sense.

Charlie paced up and down for another ten minutes, then rang off. It was clear that the Governor's secretary was not answering calls this morning. Another thing that made Charlie nervous. She knew there had been a problem at Holloway earlier this week – a death in custody had been reported in the papers two days ago. Was it possible these events could be connected?

Looking up she was pleased to see Sanderson coming towards her, car keys in hand. Charlie was already fired up about their mission to London, but she was doubly determined now. She had no idea what was going on in Holloway, but the sooner she could get Helen out of there the better. Suddenly something told Charlie that her old friend was in danger.

82

Helen paced the floor of her tiny cell, her hand clamped to her nose in a vain attempt to block out the overpowering stench of urine. She would be locked in here for twenty-four hours with nothing but the odours – piss, vomit, decay – and the catcalls of her angry neighbours for company. She was in with the sex offenders, the psychos and the determinedly suicidal. She had thought she was in Hell previously. Now she realized how wrong she'd been.

Everything about the tiny box she now found herself in was crushing. It wasn't just the dirt and the squalor, it was the misery that surrounded you. The segregated prisoners had found ways to mark their time, using stolen pens, coins, even their fingernails to carve their despair on to the walls. There were obscene drawings, screeds of abuse and in one case a long line of crosses, marking the number of days that prisoner had spent in this glorified coffin. Helen counted them – twenty-one days in all – and shuddered. If the poor woman wasn't mad when she'd arrived, she would have been by the end of her stay.

Helen knew she should sit down and rest – try to preserve her strength for the trials ahead – but she was too wound up. So she walked up and down, trying to make sense of her sudden segregation. It was inconceivable that she had failed the drugs test – she hadn't touched drugs since she was a teenager – so her sample must have been tampered with. It would have passed through many hands at the laboratory and Mark Robins had been present when she provided the sample, but so was Campbell and Helen's suspicions were now aimed very much in his direction. Why had he felt the need to do this? Helen had the nasty feeling she was in the Seg for a reason, though what this was exactly she couldn't say. Whatever the motivation behind her unjust punishment, she would need to be on her guard from now on.

The Judas slit snapped open and Helen looked up sharply. To her relief it was just the meal tray, albeit a rather meagre one, given that she was here to be punished, rather than protected. Somewhat reluctantly, she took hold of it and was surprised to find an envelope underneath. Peering through the slit, she saw Bradshaw's weak green eyes staring back at her.

'Preliminary findings from your mate's post-mortem,' she whispered hoarsely. 'Read it, then eat it, unless you want to spend a month in here.'

Helen nodded and pulled the tray towards her, but Sarah Bradshaw held on to it grimly.

'You know the drill,' she continued quietly.

Helen eyeballed her – suddenly furious and ashamed at the indignity of her position – but there was nothing for it, so acceding to her demand she placed the tray down on the bed and turned to face the slit. Sarah looked back briefly over her shoulder, then raised her smartphone to the opening. Helen tried her best to look surly, but she knew she probably just looked pitiful, framed by the squalor of the minuscule cell. A quick flash, then Sarah Bradshaw was on her way, not daring to check the image before making her escape. Helen wondered whether it would appear in tonight's *Standard*. Knowing Emilia Garanita, it probably would. She wasn't one to let the grass grow under her feet and wouldn't be able to resist offering her readers the latest images of Helen's disgrace.

Helen was happy to let her and the prison authorities believe she was beaten. It might buy her some time – time she dearly needed to make sense of these dreadful crimes. So sitting down on the hard bed, she opened the envelope, removed the two sheets of A4 paper, and began to read.

83

'I'm saying I made a mistake. I can't put it any other way.'

Jonathan Gardam tucked his hands behind his back and stared at his superior. Chief Constable Alan Peters was a canny operator, so Gardam kept his expression neutral. Excessive contrition on his part would arouse his suspicion, so he'd decided to go for a bald statement of fact instead.

'I thought DI Sanderson had the experience and where-withal to handle her promotion, but it appears I was wrong. Put simply, she is too close to the foot soldiers and seems unable to manage or guide her team.'

'Where are they now? Sanderson and Brooks?'

'To be honest, I have no idea. Which reflects badly on them and me. The team are in the dark too . . .'

'Have they gone to London?' Peters pressed further, irritation now seeping into his tone for the first time.

'I'd say that's very likely. As soon as we are finished here I will be contacting my colleagues in the Met.'

'Be sure that you do.'

'Of cour—'

'I'll be interested to see what progress they make.'

Gardam was so surprised that for a moment he couldn't find the words to respond.

'I'm not sure I follow, sir. The investigation into those murders is closed. We all know the damage Helen Grace did to this Force, the shit storm that you and I had to weather as a result —'

'You don't need to remind me, Jonathan. I was there too.'

Gardam nodded, but said nothing, unnerved by the gentle sarcasm in his superior's tone.

'And I'd like to know for sure that the pasting we received at the hands of the press, in Helen's name, was fully justified.'

'It was, we know it was –'

'Yet there do seem to be some questions that need answering. Whatever we may think about the manner of DS Brooks's police work, you can't deny that she has unearthed some interesting possibilities.'

'Look, I'm probably being obtuse, but –'

'I know your feelings on this, but I'd like to run Stonehill to ground. His recent actions suggest that Brooks's version of events is not entirely implausible. Let's double-check before putting this thing to bed, shall we?'

Gardam agreed with as much grace as he could muster, before making his excuses. He'd had no choice but to play ball, but Peters' attitude made him nervous. Had he misjudged the mood of the station? And people's attitude towards Brooks? He'd assumed she was a sacking waiting to happen, but perhaps he was wrong.

Gardam went back to his office and shut the door firmly behind him. He needed time to think. The ground was shifting beneath his feet for sure, but so far he'd only lost one battle. He hadn't yet lost the war.

84

They sat in silence, focusing on the road in front of them. Charlie hadn't felt much like talking, following her disquieting phone call to Holloway, but fortunately neither had Sanderson. There was a lot to do today – Sanderson had already contacted her Met colleagues to discuss putting out a general alert for Stonehill – but Charlie suspected her colleague's thoughts were focused rather closer to home. There was no question that she was risking a lot by backing Charlie. Disobeying Gardam could cost her her job, especially if they failed to find Stonehill or secure the evidence they needed.

'I'm sorry, Charlie.'

Charlie was so wrapped up in her thoughts that she jumped slightly when Sanderson spoke. Her new boss was concentrating intently on driving, though whether this was for safety reasons or to avoid looking at her colleague was unclear.

'I should have listened to you. You're a good copper and I should have taken your concerns more seriously.'

Charlie wasn't sure how to respond at first. She had been trying to make herself hate Sanderson for weeks now.

'You were following the evidence. I don't blame you for that,' Charlie eventually replied.

'I was following the evidence as I wanted to see it. Because it fitted so neatly, because it served my purpose . . .'

'Helen lied to us,' Charlie conceded, softening. 'I understand why she did it, but it was always going to cause problems once her duplicity was revealed. You'd be a strange person and a pretty poor copper not to be suspicious of someone who'd lied to you so blatantly.'

'I think I was so blinded by . . . the drama of it that I didn't hesitate. It was the most shocking, most newsworthy case I've ever been involved in and I had the chance to bring it in. I guess I couldn't resist that, though I'm embarrassed to admit it now.'

'Listen, I don't blame you for it. And in spite of everything, I'm sure Helen feels the same way.'

Sanderson glanced sheepishly at Charlie, clearly not entirely convinced that Helen would be so forgiving.

'I just worry . . .' Sanderson continued, after another long pause. 'I worry that maybe I did *exactly* what Stonehill wanted me to do.'

Charlie didn't contradict her colleague. She'd felt the same way for a while now and had previously cursed Sanderson for it. But now she felt nothing but sympathy for her old friend.

'Then let's take the fight back to him,' she answered calmly.

Another fleeting smile from Sanderson, then she pressed down hard on the accelerator, bringing their speed up to the 90 mph mark. They were gambling a lot on their mission to London and suddenly it felt as if every second counted.

85

Emilia punched the delete key and a morning's work disappeared. Normally this would have been the cue for a volley of profanities, but not today. This morning, Emilia had been more than happy to junk her carefully crafted copy, because something much juicier had fallen into her lap.

Another picture from Sarah Bradshaw. But this easily trumped her previous offerings. In this one, a pale, battered Helen Grace was standing in a tiny cell in Holloway's legendary Segregation unit. Emilia had actually squealed out loud with excitement when she saw the image, arousing the interest of other coffee drinkers nearby. But any embarrassment she felt was soon replaced by excitement about what this image could mean.

The accompanying text from Sarah had been brief, but confirmed that a second murder had taken place and that Grace was now in the Segregation unit. The two incidents weren't necessarily connected, but that didn't really matter – the coincidence was a gift. Experienced hands would point out that a stint in the Segregation unit was not uncommon and that Helen might have been put there for her own protection, but the uninitiated would instinctively make a different connection.

The psycho cop was preying on her fellow prisoners. It was a simple conclusion to draw from the morning's events and an exciting one. Could there be a more delicious form of justice than Helen Grace unleashing herself on the bad girls of Holloway? An article was already forming in Emilia's mind and she had high hopes that some of the classier national tabloids would take this one. She would have to be careful of course – she had few facts to go on at this stage and she couldn't come right out and accuse Helen of the murders. But a few salient facts, coupled with the ghostly photo of an inhuman-looking Helen Grace, would do the job. This was the power of innuendo.

The wider public had already made up their minds about Helen, even though she hadn't had her day in court. What Emilia would write today would further cement their image of a renegade cop gone bad. Mud sticks and Emilia would enjoy throwing as much of it as she could, whether it would prejudice court proceedings or not. This after all was modern justice.

This was trial by media.

86

Helen sat on the hard bed, fighting tears as she read Dr Khan's preliminary findings for a second time. The cause of Jordi's death was clear – cerebral haemorrhage brought on by cardiac arrhythmia. The state of the body after death had suggested a heart attack – the waxy complexion, the profuse sweating – as had the initial bloods, which were high in adrenaline and low in glucose. The internal examination all but confirmed it. Jordi's heart was grossly enlarged and utterly spent.

Helen shoved the image of a convulsing Jordi to the back of her mind and tried to focus on the details. As Helen had noted previously, there were no defensive wounds on Jordi's hands and her long nails remained intact. Khan had garnered scrapings from underneath these elegantly decorated talons, but he wasn't convinced they were significant. Lab testing would provide more information but his instinct was that they were dirt particles, rather than skin cells or hair. More instructive, however, were the samples lifted from Jordi's teeth. Analysis was pending, but Khan was convinced that he'd found semen residue.

Helen should have been cheered by this discovery. DNA is easy to harvest from semen and would certainly guide the authorities towards the culprit. But actually Khan's discovery made her sad. Jordi had been trying so hard to clean up her act and had sworn blind she would never prostitute herself again. What had gone wrong? Helen quickly went through the toxicology report. Jordi's blood samples showed traces of paracetamol and ritalin, but no evidence of heroin or cocaine, which puzzled her. If Jordi *had* resorted to using sex as currency again, then Helen would have expected hard drugs to be the payoff – she had been struggling for years to kick her habit. There was no evidence of sexual assault, however, according to Khan, so had Jordi succumbed to someone's advances *willingly*? If so, who? And why?

There were lots of questions that remained unanswered, but Helen felt sure that the recovered DNA would prove crucial. If the killer *was* a prison employee, as she was convinced he was, then testing would smoke him out. So far he had proved a devious and elusive adversary, but if Helen's instincts were right, this cruel phantom was about to be revealed.

87

'Are you completely spineless? When are you going to grow a pair and tell them where to go?'

Cameron Campbell fired the words at Celia Bassett, flecks of spittle flying in her direction. Celia knew she should reprimand him on the spot, suspend him for this abusive tirade, but somehow she didn't have the strength this morning. He had burst into her office without warning, despite the fierce resistance of her loyal PA, and seemed determined to have his say. So Celia had relented, ushering her assistant out and pushing the door to, in an attempt to shield the rest of her team from Campbell's fury. But allowing him an audience didn't seem to be working – he was more enraged now than when he started.

'From the beginning, you've rolled over, allowing them to do whatever they want –'

'That is their prerogative. I can't stop them –'

'It's not a question of stopping them. You have to *handle* them.'

'Two murders have been committed. I have to let them invest—'

'You let these suits think you're weak and they will walk all over you. You have to make a stand.'

'And what would be my rationale for refusing their request? Leah Smith was pregnant. We know that Jordi Baines had semen on her teeth. Surely you can see that DNA testing is a sensible move?'

'What is *sensible* about alienating your entire staff in one fell swoop? The only reason this place isn't in Special Measures already is because of the work that I and others like me do to keep these women in line. We do it every day for terrible pay, no thanks and fuck-all pension. The very least we deserve is the respect and support of those who claim to lead us.'

Campbell was staring directly at her now.

'Well?'

'Look, Cameron, I appreciate everything you do, but I can't impede their investigation. Putting aside the fact that it would be wrong, what would happen if this got out? That we'd been deliberately obstructing justice?'

'So it's the headlines you're worried about is it? Think they might affect your next move?'

'Frankly, yes and so should y—'

'Jesus Christ, you're even more of a brainless bitch than I gave you credit for.'

'For God's sake, Cameron, I'm trying to be civil here –'

'Oh, I think we're past that. Fuck it, do what you have to do, but be aware that there will be consequences.'

'What does that mean?'

'You'll find out.'

Glaring at Celia, Campbell turned and stormed out of her office, slamming the door on the way. Celia watched him go, embarrassed, but also a little relieved. Pulling open her desk drawer, she removed the bottle of Jameson's and filled her empty glass. Her nerves were jangling and as she raised the glass to her lips, she was surprised to see that her hands were shaking. She would never admit it to others and often tried to deny it to herself, but the truth was that she was more than a little scared of Cameron Campbell.

88

Benjamin Proud stood alone in the cell, taking in his surroundings. He had sent the rest of the PPS team for a break and wanted to take advantage of their absence to gather his thoughts. This case was proving to be particularly complex. Bassett was turning into a liability, her staff were openly hostile and there was unrest among the inmates too. Proud had been involved in a prison riot once before and had no desire to experience another. It was vital that he solved these confusing murders as swiftly as possible, but still so many pieces of the puzzle eluded him.

Crouching down, he looked again at Jordi Baines's bed. She had gone to sleep last night, little suspecting that she wouldn't see another sunrise. What had happened in the interim? And why had she gone so willingly to her death? Did she have a lover? A lover she shared with Leah Smith? It was possible, but didn't get them much further on. They had no confirmed cause of death for Smith, though they would look again at cardiac arrest now, nor any clear sense of how the women had died. It was as if the women had simply gone to sleep, never to wake again.

The fun didn't stop there, the killer taking his time to mutilate and stuff the victims. Was this the enjoyable part of the experience? Was this his signature? Proud had spent most of last night poring over past cases on the police databases, looking for similar MOs, but had found nothing. Their killer was one of a kind.

There was nothing around the bed of any interest so Proud now paced the room. Jordi Baines had been in this prison, and in this particular cell, for over four years now, but you'd never have known it. Her neat, ordered cell had very little in the way of decoration or personal possessions. There was a handful of photos of two very cute-looking girls Blu-Tacked to the wall. They reminded him of his own baby girl and once again Proud felt a stab of sympathy for Jordi Baines. Like Smith, she seemed to have something – or someone – to live for, but had ended her days here, the plaything of a twisted and devious killer. It was a terrible waste and made him very glad that his own wife and baby would never experience what these women had been through.

Beyond the photos, there were a couple of newspaper clippings, a few celebrity magazines and a necklace, which hung from a nail next to the bed. And that was it – the sum total of Baines's possessions. It was precious little to show for nearly thirty years of life. She hadn't made a mark on this world, Proud thought as he walked to the door, except of course on the lives of those she'd left behind. Those smiling girls had no mother now. And Proud knew from his own bitter experience how hard it was to recover from that.

89

The tight pellets of paper stuck in her throat, but Helen swallowed hard, forcing them down. She had committed Khan's findings to memory and was now destroying his report. As she swallowed, her mind turned on what he had found. Helen had initially thought Leah's death was a grim example of prison justice, but that seemed unlikely now. It was true that Jordi *had* argued with Wheelchair Annie and it was possible her card had been marked too, but the sexual aspect of these crimes and the precise, intimate nature of the mutilations argued against this theory. The murders exhibited too much imagination, too much control to be the work of prison thugs.

Taking in the latest developments, Helen's first thought had been blackmail. If Campbell *was* sleeping with his inmates, then it would be an obvious angle to exploit and prisoners seldom missed an opportunity to improve their situation. If Leah had known about her pregnancy, then she would have possessed a pretty powerful bargaining chip. And Jordi? Was she sleeping with Campbell? Had she kept that knowledge close after Leah's death, intending to use it against him? Was that why he'd gone to her cell that night? To silence her?

It was a credible theory and she could see Campbell acting decisively to protect his position. And yet surely the evidence in front of Helen implied something more complicated than simple blackmail gone wrong? The signs of sexual activity discovered by Khan revealed that the killer had feelings for these women, however depraved or base these might be. But the sewing up of their mouths, eyes, vaginas and the stuffing of their other orifices revealed there was a flip side to this desire.

Pacing her reeking cell, Helen wondered now if the killer desired his victims, but also hated them. It was possible that having had his way with them, Campbell felt the need to destroy them, rendering them unusable by other men. He had already left his mark on these women – internally as well as externally in Leah's case – so was the extensive mutilation an attempt to claim them wholly for himself?

This might explain why the bodies had been covered. There was no way that hiding them beneath a blanket would conceal their deaths, so was it possible that there was something simpler driving this? A desire to hide them away from other men? Or perhaps even a desire to hide the women from the killer himself?

If Campbell did harbour strong feelings for the women he had killed in spite of everything he'd done to them, then this would make sense. Helen had seen this hate/guilt equation before, killers rolling the corpses on to their front and even turning down family photos, so as not to have to look at the deceased's loved ones.

Crossing the cell, Helen sat down and let her mind turn on the possibilities this threw up. The mutilations had led her to believe that this was some kind of ritual killing. But maybe it was more complex than that. Was it possible that their murder was a twisted act of love? This could explain why there were no defence wounds on either victim. If the killer was someone the women had cared for, someone in authority whom they had grown to trust, then perhaps they had *allowed* themselves to be injected?

Helen closed her eyes, picturing Campbell in this scenario. If she was on the right track, what was driving this sudden explosion of violence? Why was Campbell turning on his girls? And how was he doing it? If he had induced a cardiac arrest in these women, as now seemed likely, why not use spiked drugs? The women would presumably be happy to accept free narcotics and the post-mortem wouldn't reveal anything suspicious, given the girls' drug history. But the blood analysis revealed nothing remotely like that. So what was he using? And where was he getting it from?

Helen sat stock still, mentally poring over the details of Khan's report, searching for clues. But the answers eluded her. She had the nasty feeling she was still missing a large piece of the jigsaw and until she found it many lives – not least her own – would continue to hang in the balance.

90

The needle drove into his finger and immediately a large bead of blood sprung to the surface. Andrew Holmes flinched, but continued to smile. He didn't like needles, didn't want to be here, but knew it was best to play ball and say nothing. The sooner it was done, the sooner he would be out of here.

His finger was now pressed down hard on the sterile swab, the blood soaking into the cotton wool. The attending officer, wearing latex gloves and working in diligent silence, now bagged the swab, sealing it in a ziplock bag. Pulling off his gloves, he now picked up a battered biro and prepared to fill out the accompanying forms.

'Full name?'

It was brusque to the point of rudeness, but Andrew let it go.

'Andrew James Holmes.'

'Position?'

'Prison Chaplain.'

It felt funny saying it out loud. Normally when people asked him what he did, he just said he was a vicar and left it at that. He was aware that people saw his dog collar and expected him to be a trendy inner-city vicar or better still the shepherd of a bucolic rural parish. He always sensed their disappointment when he admitted to being a prison chaplain. If he was honest he felt it too. This was not where he had imagined himself ending up.

'Do you need anything else?' he asked, as the officer continued his paperwork.

'Not for the time being. Send the next one in, will you?'

He didn't even look up and for a moment Andrew felt a flash of anger. It was all so impersonal, so mechanical, taking no account of the fact that they were dealing with human beings. People who had feelings, thoughts, desires. It was a cattle drive, the officers carrying it out mere cogs in the system. Maybe they did this kind of thing every day and were bored of it. But how could they be bored of *this*?

Turning on his heel, Andrew left without a word, pushing the door gently to behind him. As he stepped outside in the waiting room, he was surprised to find that it was now busy, a long line of prison officers awaiting their turn for testing. And at the very front of the queue was Cameron Campbell.

Andrew was aware of the ructions the testing had caused among the staff and was surprised to see Campbell here. He was even more surprised by the broad grin on the officer's face.

'Didn't realize you were in the frame, Chaplain?'

'I'm not,' Andrew responded acidly.

'Wouldn't be here if you weren't. Still, I suppose it proves you're still in *full* working order . . .' Campbell insinuated, dropping his eyes to Holmes's groin.

'I'm just doing as I'm told,' Andrew retorted, brushing past Campbell and walking to the door.

'Course you are. Don't worry, we're not judging you.'

Andrew had reached the door, but something in Campbell's tone made him turn – the burly prison officer clearly wasn't finished.

'After all,' Campbell concluded grimly. 'We're all in the same boat now.'

91

'We've got to get organized.'

Babs's voice was calm and authoritative, silencing the unruly crowd that had gathered in the canteen. The tension in the prison had been building all day, gradually morphing into fear and now naked panic. Jordi had been a popular member of the prison and her brutal murder had tipped the inmates over the edge. Not a single one of them felt safe in Holloway any more and many of the sixty-strong crowd were all for storming the perimeter fences in order to escape the death sentence that now seemed to hang over all their heads.

'Smashing the place up or climbing the walls isn't going to get you anywhere. Except perhaps the Seg. There is no way they're going to let the likes of us out, but there *are* steps we can take to protect ourselves.'

'Yeah, try not sleeping for a start.'

'And keeping a shiv by your side.'

'Thank you, ladies,' Babs resumed. 'Very helpful suggestions, but we need to be smart here. And we need to stick together. If we present a united front then the Governor will have to listen.'

There were grumblings from among the crowd, but no one shouted her down, so Babs pressed on.

'I'd like three volunteers to come with me to the Governor's office to make our case. Security has been dire in this place for months and we can't rely on them to protect us any more. So come on, who wants to help?'

Babs wasn't surprised to see Noelle step forward – she liked nothing better than a good scrap. The others hesitated – turning to each other – and for a moment Babs feared her words had fallen on deaf ears. But then Isobel, the Lithuanian fraudster, and Maxine, Islington's infamous madam, stepped forward. Babs thanked them and together they turned and advanced on the wing doors.

It was time to do battle.

92

Charlie yanked open the shop door and marched inside. She was exhausted after their morning's work, but was determined to remain optimistic, despite their total lack of progress. She could tell that Sanderson was disappointed too – like Charlie she had been hoping for swift results – but was resolved not to let her partner down, nor slacken off the pace.

On arrival in London, they'd gone straight to Scotland Yard. The Force coordinator was expecting them and they'd been ushered into an internal briefing involving CID, press liaison and representatives from the Chief Constable's office. Sanderson outlined the details of the case and shared Stonehill's new arrest warrant, before circulating the latest e-fit, which Charlie had created following their recent encounter. It was agreed that this would be put out via local media and given to officers on the ground. Charlie and Sanderson had immediately offered to help coordinate the search for Stonehill, as neither fancied hanging around in an unfamiliar control room waiting for news.

Stonehill had defrauded nearly two dozen sub-post offices, using the identities of recently deceased people to claim their benefits. Was he likely to return to old haunts, given his recent brush with the law? It was hard to say, but they had no other known addresses for him – none of his aliases featured on electoral rolls or rental lists – so these convenience stores and mini-marts were their best bet.

The Polish owner accepted the e-fit from Charlie and took a good look at it. There was a £10,000 reward for information leading to Stonehill's arrest and Charlie hoped this would have the desired effect – but after a few moments' consideration the shopkeeper shook his head.

'He's not been round here.'

It had been the same at every outlet they'd visited and for the first time Charlie felt her optimism waver. The shopkeeper promised to stick the poster up, but Charlie sensed that he was just paying them lip service and that it would end up in the bin the moment they were gone. She suddenly felt furious with him – with everyone they'd spoken to today. It was as if nobody grasped the importance of what they were doing and, worse, nobody cared. Was it possible that all this had been for nothing? Was it possible that the man she had been hunting for weeks now would silently slip through their net?

93

He stared at the TV screen. The picture on the cannibalized set was fuzzy, the sound patchy, but he could still make out the report on LDN, could still see the black-and-white e-fit staring back at him. It was not inaccurate and he was pleased by his thin, streamlined face, but they had got his eyes all wrong. They made him look peevish and nasty, whereas in reality his eyes were one of his best features. When people looked into his large, emerald eyes they seemed to trust him, to like him even, which had come in handy during the last few months.

Casting a look around the squat, he was pleased to see that nobody else had noticed the bulletin. The retards who shared this dirty space with him were too busy smoking pot and playing songs to see the drama playing out beneath their noses.

Switching the TV off, Robert walked round to the back of the set. The power cable was connected to a dodgy socket nearby and removing it from the wall, he tugged the plug clean off, leaving only the exposed wires behind. There would be accusations and recriminations once this casual act of vandalism was discovered, but it was better to be safe than sorry.

The manhunt was a worrying development. Brooks had raised the stakes considerably and there was no question that a full-on search was now in operation. Helen's trial was still a while away, but he now knew that it would be madness to stick around, so crossing the squat quickly, he made his way into the bathroom, locking the door behind him. He turned the tap on and it coughed and spluttered before reluctantly offering up a steady stream of cold water. He scooped it up gratefully, pouring it over his head, over and over again, until his hair was saturated. It wasn't long, but it was a distinctive colour, so it had to go. Squeezing some shaving foam into his hands, he slathered it over his skull, then picked up the nearest razor.

He made short work of it – great clumps of hair falling into the grotty basin – and in under five minutes his head was completely clean-shaven. He stared back at his un-familiar self, disconcerted but also pleased. He was damned if he was going to let Brooks take him down and this was the first small step towards ensuring his liberty. He hadn't planned it this way, but he felt pleased to be finally taking control of the situation. It was time to give up this hand-to-mouth existence in the capital.

It was time to disappear.

94

Helen looked up as the footsteps approached. She had been left alone with her thoughts for the whole day and craved some kind – any kind – of human contact. Her fellow inmates in the Seg had fallen silent, which was almost worse than their customary screaming. Sometimes the silence in this place was so total, so deafening, that you could believe you were the last person left alive on earth.

The Judas slit eased open and a voice barked out:

'Tray.'

Helen roused herself, rolling off the bed and carrying her tray over to the opening. Mark Robins was on the other side, her meagre dinner offering in his hands. He took her empty tray, before handing her the new one, but Helen stepped back, refusing to take it.

'Just take it, Grace, I haven't got all day.'

'I need you to do something for me first.'

'I'm not here to bargain. If you don't want it, someone else will.'

Helen didn't doubt it, but had already decided to risk an empty stomach in order to get someone to listen to her. She hated this place and had no desire to be here after nightfall, so had resolved to beg for help. She was pleased that it was Robins who'd turned up, given his recent concern for her.

'I just want you to talk to the Governor,' Helen persisted. 'You know I'm not a junkie, I don't do drugs. Something must have gone wrong with the tes—'

'You think she hasn't heard that a thousand times before.'

'I know, but you can talk to her on my behalf.'

'You and everybody else in here –'

'For God's sake, just listen to me, will you?'

Helen hadn't meant to speak harshly, but Robins was being oddly uncooperative. He eyeballed her, looking unimpressed, so she continued quickly:

'I'll happily submit to another test, accept twenty-three-hour lock-up, whatever, but I can't stay in here.'

'Why?'

'Do you really have to ask? I mean just look at this place.'

'Too good for the likes of you, is it?'

'I'm sorry?'

'The famous copper forced to live with the dregs and now she doesn't like it? Well, my heart fucking bleeds.'

Helen stared at Robins, unsure how to respond. There was a coldness in his eyes that she'd never seen before.

'I'd say you'd better get used to it,' he went on. 'Because from what I hear, you're not going anywhere fast.'

He pushed the dinner tray roughly into Helen's hands and walked off, cursing under his breath. Helen watched him go, confused and alarmed by this encounter, and it was only as Robins wrenched open the access doors to depart that Helen saw what was worrying her. Robins was limping. He had clearly injured his right foot and was hobbling away from her fast.

Now Helen realized how blind she had been. She had marked Cameron Campbell down as a vicious killer, but in fact it was gentle, kind Mark Robins that she'd chased from Jordi's cell last night.

95

'Absolutely not. There is no way I can agree to that.'

Celia Bassett's outraged response was utterly predictable, but Babs persevered nevertheless.

'It's just a temporary measure. Three people per cell per night until you've caught whoever is responsible.'

'You don't know what it's like being in those cells at night,' Noelle said, overlapping. 'Sitting there, wondering if you'll be next . . .'

'I completely understand your anxiety but I'm simply not allowed to do it. Inmates are housed in individual cells for security reasons.'

Which got the snort it deserved, but Celia carried on regardless.

'And I would be breaking Home Office rules if I allowed you to group together in that way.'

'I'm not sure the normal rules apply any more,' Noelle snapped, glaring at the Governor.

'We're happy to consider alternatives,' Babs offered, in more emollient tones. 'But we need something that's practical, something that will *work*.'

'I've already asked the officers to cancel their leave,' Celia informed them. 'We will be doubling the number of night patrols –'

'But it's one of them that's doing it!' It was Maxine's turn to get involved now.

'We don't know that –'

'You might not, but we do.' Maxine shook her head in disbelief. 'So, what? You're happy to just abandon us to them?'

'Of course not –'

'Then *do* something.'

'I will do everything in my power,' Celia reassured them weakly, more out of duty than conviction. 'But I cannot change the way in which you are housed. I'm sorry but that's the way it is.'

She had meant it to sound decisive and final, but nobody looked convinced. Babs in particular looked unimpressed.

'Have you been drinking?'

'No.'

It came out too quickly, merely confirming what everyone was already thinking. Noelle now moved in closer, sniffing her like she was some kind of animal.

'You bloody have, I can smell it on you.'

'I'd like you to leave now,' Celia said, returning to her desk.

But when she looked up they were all still there, staring at her accusingly. Babs crossed the floor towards her and for a moment Celia thought she was going to strike her. But instead she leant in close.

'You're a bloody disgrace,' she hissed, before turning to leave, the others following behind.

Celia watched them go, feeling wretched. She was trying to be strong, trying to do the right thing, but nothing seemed to be working. Inmates now suspected one of her staff was responsible, as in truth did she. Any trust they'd ever had in authority had now evaporated.

It was a toxic situation – one which could ignite at any moment.

96

Helen thumped her head against the wall, gently but repeatedly. She realized now that her hatred of Campbell had blinded her to what should have been obvious. Campbell's sadism, his desire to dominate, his bad reputation had skewed Helen's judgement, allowing her to walk straight into Mark Robins's trap.

It was Robins who'd pulled her out of the canteen for her urine test, insisting that she complete it without delay. Furthermore, he had attempted to ingratiate himself with her afterwards, chivalrously offering to walk the injured Helen back to her cell. Was this how he operated? She knew a few of the girls were soft on him because of his boyish good looks, tousled hair and deep, chocolate eyes, but Helen was largely immune to his charms. Was he setting his cap at her that day? Lining her up as his next conquest? The thought made her shudder.

Leah didn't have a friend in the place and Jordi, though popular, was prone to bouts of despair. She missed her old life, she missed her family and, in truth, she missed men. Robins would happily have taken advantage of that. He wasn't married, had no girlfriend, in fact he was a bit of a mystery man, which only seemed to increase his appeal for some girls. How gullible, how trusting they had been. And how naïve *she* had been. She had been searching, searching, searching for Jordi's killer, but Robins had flown under the radar the whole time.

He could have doctored her urine sample at any point, ensuring her segregation and thus taking her out of the equation for twenty-four hours. Was this simply so he could frustrate her investigations or was there a more sinister purpose for her isolation? Was he planning to strike again *tonight*? Was it even possible that he was coming for her? If so, this would be a great place to do it. There would be no chance of being disturbed and if any of the crazies happened to see or hear anything, who on earth would believe them?

Rising, Helen marched across the cell and slammed her fist into the suicide alarm. To her horror, nothing happened. No bells, no piercing alarm, just a horrible, empty silence. She punched it again. And again. But still nothing.

Now Helen was filled with a violent anger, furious at how this quiet, unassuming man had deceived her so completely. She was the only one who knew what he was doing but whom could she tell? There wouldn't be an officer on duty until morning, which meant that she would spend the night here alone, miserable in her knowledge and utterly cut off from the world.

97

Emilia stuffed her phone into her bag and rummaged in her coat pocket for some cigarettes. Lighting one quickly, she inhaled deeply, hoping the nicotine would calm her jangling nerves. But the cigarette had little effect – her head was spinning and she was still trying to make sense of what she'd just been told.

She was tempted to call Alan Stark back, but what would be the point? Her tame PC at Southampton Central was seldom wrong and his information had come from good sources. Emilia didn't want it to be true – she *really* didn't want it to be true – but it was.

Hampshire Police had issued an arrest warrant for Robert Stonehill. Stark had confirmed that officers from Southampton Central were involved in a joint operation with the Met and were currently combing the streets of London in search of Grace's nephew.

Emilia finished her cigarette and lit another, scarcely registering what she was doing. She had been dining out on Helen's disgrace for months, staking her whole reputation on having broken her sensational story. She had given up a good job in Southampton, pissed off her family, burnt some serious bridges and gambled all on making it in London. Was it possible that she had been . . . wrong?

She had gambled a lot on Helen's guilt. Gardam had too. If they had sent an innocent woman to jail and allowed a serial killer to walk free, then they would be finished.

Laughing stocks in the eyes of their colleagues and the world.

Emilia had been so sure and yet . . . Brooks had always believed in Grace's innocence and now seemed primed to land a sensational coup. Emilia's slim hopes now rested on Stonehill evading capture. This gave her some comfort. He was adept at disappearing from view when he needed to. But it was still a desperate state of affairs. She had hoped Helen Grace would be her meal ticket, but she might yet be her undoing – unless a multiple murderer could vanish for good. In spite of herself, Emilia knew she would be cheering him on all the way.

98

She was screaming and shouting for all she was worth, hammering on the door with her fists. It was probably futile – she had already been at it for half an hour – but she had to try. Somehow she had to raise the alarm.

Her hands were stinging, her wrists were sore and, pausing momentarily in her assault on the metal door, Helen was depressed to see bruises forming on her knuckles and palms. It was early evening – she still had another twelve hours in this hellhole and risked doing herself some serious damage if she kept this up. But what was the alternative?

Suddenly she found herself marching over to the wall. It was made of thick concrete but she banged on it nevertheless.

'Groves? Groves, can you hear me?'

Her voice was loud but controlled. It seemed to echo around her cell, but there was no response from Groves, a petty thief who spent most of the time in the Seg thanks to her penchant for starting cell fires.

'Groves, it's me, Grace.'

'What is it?' Groves finally replied, her voice low and sombre.

'I need your help.'

'You and everybody else in this shithole.'

It was one of Groves's more endearing features that she

assumed everybody in the prison relied upon her good counsel. She was Holloway's answer to Buddha, with a girth equal to the original.

'This is serious, Groves. I need you to punch your suicide alarm.'

'Are you kidding? I'm eating my bloody dinner.'

'That can wait. Just punch the alarm and I'll give you whatever you want when we're out of here. Stamps, phone cards . . .'

'But I'm feeling pretty happy today –'

'That's not the point. Mine isn't working –'

'So are *you* topping yourself?'

'No, of course no—'

'Then why do you want me to hit it?'

Helen swallowed an expletive.

'I need to get out of here, ok? My alarm's not working, so I need you to hit yours.'

There was a long pause, then Groves said:

'I ain't falling for that.'

'What do you mean?'

'I hit the alarm, they pile in, find nothing wrong. And then when they ask you what's up, you say, "It's nothing to do with me, boss –"'

'It's not like that.'

'I get another two days in here and for what?'

'Look it's a matter of life and death, so please will you just do it?'

'Fuck you, pig. I ain't doing shit.'

Helen's blood was boiling now and, crossing the cell, she hammered on the door once more. She was screaming for all she was worth and now her fellow Seg inmates started to join in – shrieking, crying, howling like wolves. It was deafening, insane, obscene, and Helen eventually slid to the floor in defeat. There was no way out of here, she was trapped. Trapped in the madhouse.

She sat in silence, her head resting on her knees, as all around her the hideous cacophony grew.

99

The pain from his viciously swollen ankle arrowed up through his leg, but still he kept going. His shift was finished and, if he was quick, he could make it out of the building without meeting a soul. He had been working here long enough to know Holloway's shortcuts.

Robins knew he was on borrowed time, but he had to get away. They had been called in one by one this morning to give their DNA samples, which were then whisked off to the Forensic Service labs in Hammersmith. As he'd given his sample, his eyes had strayed to the red flag on the corner of the zip bag and the single word written on it: 'Urgent'. He didn't know how these things worked – did it take them hours or days to process them? – but he didn't want to find out. He had to escape this place, to gather his thoughts and form a plan.

Initially he had been elated to escape Grace. His plunge on to the suicide net was a desperate act, but it had worked. Grace had hesitated to follow and, though he had hurt himself in the fall, he'd got away, limping to the safety of C-Block. He didn't think Grace had clocked that it was him – she still seemed to regard him as a friend during their recent conversation in the Seg – and in normal circumstances he would have breathed a sigh of relief. But nothing was normal about this current situation. Proud in particular seemed determined to run this one to ground and there was no telling what Grace might do, once her brief spell in the Segregation unit was over.

As Robins neared the back exit, he suddenly wondered if he would ever come back. It would be incriminating for sure, but perhaps it would be best to flee? He had savings, a car . . . He could go to Holyhead? Or Dover? There were plenty of places to hide out. He could start again. Reinvent himself.

The staff exit was only fifty feet away now and, buoyed by these thoughts, he picked up the pace. But as he neared the door, he suddenly became aware of movement close by. This exit was always deserted, but suddenly there were bodies in front of him. Men in suits, cutting off his escape route. Instinctively, Mark turned around, but here his way was blocked too. Benjamin Proud was hurrying towards him, a grim smile on his face.

'Now where are you going in such a hurry?' Proud said coolly.

Robins didn't know what to say, flustered by Proud's sudden appearance.

'Can't remember? Perhaps it'll come back to you once we're inside. I'd like a word with you, if I may.'

Proud gestured towards the staff quarters, a look of triumph writ large on his face. And in that moment, Mark Robins knew that all was lost.

100

'Shut up, will you? I'm trying to listen.'

'You shouldn't be up there. If Bassett finds you –'

'She's going to do what? She's finished here in case you hadn't noticed. Now pipe the fuck down . . .'

Campbell turned away from Sarah Bradshaw and put his ear to the wall. He was standing on a rickety wooden table, hanging on to the heavy-duty water pipes above his head. The entire storeroom was full of junk and normally Cameron would have avoided it like the plague – he was old school and liked a good shine on his shoes. But its proximity to Bassett's office made it an appealing location today.

Robins was holed up with Proud. He hadn't been arrested yet and officially this was just a follow-up chat. But nobody believed that. Not Campbell, not Bradshaw and certainly not Celia Bassett. She had been excluded from the meeting, kicked out of her own office. A union rep had been requested and was on her way, but that didn't stop Proud pinning Robins down to discuss a few 'preliminaries'.

This was the most decrepit part of the prison, all the money predictably having been spent on the prisoners' wings. The walls here had suffered major water damage over the years and the repair funds that had been promised had never arrived. The mortar was soft and crumbling, the concrete decaying, and if you pressed your ear hard to the wall, you could make out the muffled conversations next door.

The brick was cold, but Campbell didn't care. He had never thought Robins capable of violence – he found him slight, effeminate – and, besides, Campbell had had Grace marked down for these murders from the off. But it now looked as if there was much more to Robins than met the eye. Which is why, despite Bradshaw's protestations, Campbell was going nowhere.

This was his territory, his prison, and if Robins had been making a mug of them all, he needed to know.

101

'That's a nasty-looking injury. Shall I get someone to take a look at it?'

Benjamin Proud was the picture of concern as he nodded at Robins's swollen ankle. Robins said nothing, swinging his good leg around to hide the offending limb from view.

'I'll take that as a no. Out of interest, when did you do it? You seemed fine when we spoke yesterday. Must have been last night . . . ?'

Still Robins remained tight-lipped.

'Look, you can sit here in silence if you like. But I am going to keep asking the same questions and I would appreciate answers.'

Robins had been staring at his shoes, but now looked up long enough to mumble:

'No comment.'

Proud eyeballed him for a moment, then replied:

'You were on the night shift, weren't you? Apparently you knocked off early.'

'Says who?'

Proud consulted his notes, then continued:

'I have the testimony of a colleague who was first person on the scene after Jordi Baines's suicide alarm was activated. You were in charge of B-Wing last night, but when your colleague turned up, you were nowhere to be found. Would you like to tell me where you were?'

'No comment.'

'Is there anyone who can vouch for your movements between the hours of nine p.m. and ten p.m. last night?'

Robins shrugged but said nothing. Proud could feel the anger rising in him, but forced it back down, trying to remain polite and professional.

'Do you like being a prison officer, Mark? Do you enjoy your work?'

'S'all right.'

'Lot of stress though, isn't it? For not much take-home pay. Why do you like it?'

'What I'm used to, I guess.'

'Right. You're an experienced hand, aren't you? You know the ropes.'

A half-nod, half-shrug from Robins.

'I'd go so far as to say you're well-known and well-liked here. By your colleagues, the inmates . . .'

'If you say so.'

'Tell me about the girls.' Proud leant forward in his seat. 'Tell me about your relationship with the girls.'

Proud could sense Robins was tightening up and was not surprised at his 'No comment'.

'Well, then, let *me* comment. You've been a bit of a naughty boy, haven't you? Dipped your fingers in a few ponds that you should have left well alone.'

Robins finally looked up at him and Proud was pleased to see anger in his eyes.

'The baby that Leah Smith was carrying was yours. And the semen found on Jordi Baines's teeth? Yours too.'

Proud let this settle, before pursuing his point:

'It's my belief that you had sex with these women and then when they threatened your position, you killed them.

Were the mutilations a little warning to others? I take it you do have other girls on the go . . . ?'

Robins chewed his fingernail viciously, avoiding Proud's gaze.

'Handsome boy like you could take his pick, right? And I bet those lonely girls were only too happy to play ball. But I've got to say you were a little careless? Have you never heard of condoms? Did Leah tell you she had it covered? You wouldn't be the first to fall for that one, but even so . . .'

Robins refused to engage, but his irritation was clearly growing, his good foot beating out the rhythm of his anger.

'And because of that your child is dead. Did you know Leah was pregnant? Is that what the mutilation was about? Sewing up her vagina so it couldn't come out? Sewing up her mouth so she couldn't spill the beans? Blocking up her nose so she couldn't smell the stench of your cowardice?'

'Fuck you.'

'I could see why you would have an issue with them. They were just dirty little girls. Scum who wanted to feed off you. You wanted affection, but they wanted to squeeze you dry, didn't they?'

Robins looked up, glaring at Proud, so the latter pressed home his advantage.

'Or maybe you did it simply because you enjoyed it? Because you liked watching them die, because you liked mutilating their bodies. Tell me, Mark, what did it feel like? What did it feel like when your needle punctured their skin? When you pulled the thread through? Tell me. Did it feel *good*?'

Robins clasped his hands together. He looked to be in real pain, in the throes of some awful internal battle.

'Tell me,' Proud persisted, louder this time.

He felt that he was getting to Robins at last, as though a dam that had been creaking for months was about to give.

'Tell me, Mark.'

Now Robins finally raised his head. But to Proud's surprise, Robins looked calm. And when he spoke his voice was flat and without emotion:

'No comment.'

102

She didn't know what to say or what to do. Suzanne Baines had experienced more than most in her time and had become inured to many of the indignities that life can throw at you. But nothing had prepared her for this. She was sixteen years old – nearly a woman – but tonight she felt like a child.

Flanked by her sister, Chloe, she stood in Holloway's vast courtyard, shivering with cold despite the thick coat she was wearing. It was too big for her and smelt of perfume – she hadn't wanted to take it, but her own coat was bright pink and Verity had said that it wouldn't be appropriate. As if it made any difference. She could have been wearing a bloody clown's costume and her mum wouldn't have known or cared.

During the course of the day, shock had given way to distress, then later to anger. She had been making apologies for her mum her whole life, defending her against the haters who said she was no good – a slut, a whore, a killer. Suzanne had always fought her corner – literally sometimes – and what had been her reward? Here she was standing in Holloway's courtyard watching her mother's body being carried from the building in a wooden box.

She didn't know the men carrying her – her social worker had called a local firm of undertakers – and she didn't know what the next few days would hold. How did you organize a funeral? Who did you invite? Would any of the press turn up? Or, God help them, relatives of her mum's victim?

Suddenly Suzanne didn't want any part of it. She would look after Chloe of course, but the others could go to Hell. She didn't want the burial, didn't want the sympathy, didn't want people staring at her. They were doing it now – scores of prisoners pressing their faces to the windows to drink in the spectacle and she wanted to scream at them all to fuck off.

Right now, there was not a single part of her life that she wanted.

103

Helen clung on to the bars, refusing to let go, despite the cramp that was ripping through her arms. The bed was too low to act as any kind of platform, so she'd had to jump up and grab the bars, holding on to them like grim death. Only by doing so, could she see the final journey of her friend.

Jordi had been the first person – the only person? – she'd shared a laugh with in this place. She remembered it clearly – prior to that it had been weeks since she'd even cracked a smile. She had been in shock when she was brought to Holloway, still reeling from her sudden downfall. Jordi had taken her under her wing, steering her away from trouble, helping her make the transition to her strange, new life.

She could still remember Jordi's amusement at Helen's first reaction to prison food. Helen had said that she'd tasted better grout, which had set Jordi off. Helen had surprised herself by laughing too. Jordi was like that – her smile, her good humour, was irresistible. Helen realized now that she probably wouldn't have survived those first few weeks without the joy that Jordi naturally generated.

And now it had been snuffed out. All that hope, all that happiness and what was left? Two young girls standing in the December rain, watching their mother's corpse being driven away. With only two weeks to go to Christmas, it was the bitterest of blows.

Helen lowered herself back to the ground. She sat in the corner, massaging her aching arms. A pair of cockroaches had emerged now that night was falling and seemed to be engaging in some kind of foreplay but Helen barely noticed. She was too lost in memories, calling to mind the moment when *she* had seen her mother's body. Her sister, Marianne, had presented their parents to her, thinking Helen would be pleased by the sight of the pair of them lying lifeless on the bed. As later events proved, Helen hadn't been. She was horrified – the image of her mother's swollen, blue face still haunting her dreams – and she was scared. Scared for what their murder meant for Marianne and what it meant for her.

Suzanne and Chloe had each other at least, but other than that they were on their own, with no one to protect them from the worst that life could throw at them. They had lost that most precious of gifts – a mother's undying love – and were now more exposed than they had ever been. They had lost their maker, their guide, their focus. She knew just how they felt. Despite the clamour that still echoed around her, Helen had never felt so alone in her whole life.

104

It was late now and the wing was quiet as the grave. The hooded figure stole cautiously along the gantry, hugging the wall. Step by step, inch by inch, checking and double-checking that the coast was clear. The patrols seemed to be coming round every hour tonight – a belated response from a Governor under severe pressure – making any kind of sortie highly dangerous.

And what of the inmates? Were they asleep? Or were they lying awake, anticipating another attack? The more serious the game got, the more risky it became, but there was no question of stopping now.

Each step was measured and soft, each movement slow and deliberate. Every ten yards, the figure stopped, scanning the different walkways, listening intently for signs of life, before continuing purposefully forward. Cell 45 slid by, then 46 and finally here it was. Cell B47.

Gripping the corner of the Judas slit, the figure eased it open. The inmate within didn't react and appeared to be asleep. But there was no point taking unnecessary risks, so the figure now moved in closer, peering into the gloom beyond.

Immediately, the smell hit you. Sweet, sickening, faecal. It made you want to gag, but there was no question of pulling out now. Faint heart never won fair maid. So tugging the door open gently, the hooded figure quietly slipped inside.

105

Her eyes remained wide open. Despite her best efforts, she couldn't sleep tonight, the same nagging thought spinning round her head. It was a foolish thought, a dangerous thought, but one that she couldn't shake. Not when the rewards on offer were so great.

Kaitlin eased herself up on to her elbows and looked about her. The squat was gloomy and quiet, save for the rasping snores of the blokes, who were whacked out on booze and blow. Kaitlin had had her share too of course, but she was a little more restrained than usual, which had not gone unnoticed. She claimed stomach cramps, blaming her period, which shut them up. The truth was that she did feel sick, but it was nothing to do with her biology.

She had been shoplifting in EasyBuy when she'd seen it. A small A4 poster stuck on to the tobacco cabinet. It was the numbers that drew her eye to it – a reward of £10,000. Then her eyes had drifted up to the mug shot. She had expected to see the face of some mindless thug, but in fact she saw the face of someone she knew. A face she saw every day.

She wasn't sure of his real name – he called himself 'Jack' – nor where he came from. He kept himself to himself, selling a little weed when he had it, but otherwise using the squat as a roof over his head and little more. He made no attempt to engage with them, but then that wasn't unusual. Everyone here had a story they would rather forget or someone they were running from. Kaitlin didn't know a single fact about him, but she did recognize his face on the poster. And she had been thinking about little else all afternoon.

She glanced across the squat. He always slept next to the doorway, as if primed to run, which made her task harder now. Getting to her feet, she debated calling out his name to see if he was really asleep, then thought better of it. Instead, she stepped over her sleeping boyfriend and crept towards the door. If she got this right, then they would both be set up for the year.

The boards were old and creaky. Every step seemed to announce her intentions, so she took it slowly, picking the least noisy boards as she made her way to the door. As she got close, Jack stirred, rolling over in his sleep. Kaitlin froze – she was only a few feet away and if he opened his eyes now, he would be looking straight at her. But he remained asleep and putting a hand to her chest, to calm her breathing, she crept past him and away through the open doorway.

'Going somewhere?'

His cool voice made her jump. For a moment she did nothing, unsure what to say or do. Then she turned slowly and replied:

'Just going for a piss. Cheap lager goes straight through me.'

He looked at her, appraising her response.

'Sorry if I woke you,' Kaitlin said, before turning and heading quickly to the bathroom.

Her heart was beating fast, sweat was breaking out on her forehead and she could feel his eyes on her as she disappeared down the gloomy corridor. Had she got away with it? Had she fooled him?

Or did he *know* what she was thinking?

106

The body on the bed was warm, but still. Her chest no longer rose and fell and her lifeless eyes were closed. This was the moment, the magical moment just after death when it felt like her soul was leaving her body, making its way towards the barred window and out into the night.

This one had been a little trickier than the rest. More suspicious, less compliant and there had been a brief struggle as the cardiac arrest took hold – the victim lashing out with flailing arms, striking her assailant. In some ways this shouldn't have been a surprise – this girl had always been a difficult, troublesome presence in Holloway. But at least there had been no screaming or histrionics, nothing to draw anyone's attention to what was taking place.

Still, it didn't do to take risks, especially not with the extra patrols out tonight, so the figure now pulled out a needle and thread. It was gloomy in the dirty cell, but there was enough moonlight to see by and after a number of failed attempts the thread finally slipped into the eye of the needle. The figure now pulled the thread through, so it hung evenly on both sides, then paused for a moment. The silver needle was shining in the moonlight – it looked magical and beguiling tonight.

The victim's lips were now pinched together, edging up slightly at the ends to form a half-smile. This was always the trickiest bit – the skin was much tougher here than on the eyelids or vagina. It required a bit of force to push the needle through the thick, fleshy lips and the figure drove it in now, pushing sharply upwards. The needle exited the top lip cleanly and pulled clear, before turning in the air and descending once more. Five minutes later and the first stage was complete – the killer's victim grinning lifelessly up at the moon above.

107

Mark Robins slouched in his chair, ignoring the breakfast that had been placed in front of him. He looked as if he hadn't slept a wink – his eyes looked hollow and he had large, dark rings beneath them. Benjamin Proud was glad that Robins was in bad shape – they had made little progress last night, his questions constantly rebuffed or avoided. He was pinning his hopes on grinding the surly prison officer down. Experience had taught him that you stood a much greater chance of making a deal or getting a confession when the suspect was worn out.

'How are we feeling this morning?'

Robins didn't dignify this with a response, but Proud was not deterred.

'You've had some time to think about the situation, to process what's happening. So I'm hoping you'll be a little more cooperative today.'

Robins said nothing, stealing a look at the union rep who sat next to him instead.

'You'll no doubt be aware by now that your career as a prison officer is finished. That's nobody's fault but your own. Those women were supposed to be in your care and you took advantage of them. You've disgraced your profession and betrayed your colleagues. You could have been a good officer – you *were* a good officer – but your track record, your many commendations, count for nothing now.'

Robins fidgeted in his seat. He looked ill at ease today,

perhaps even a little ashamed. Unwashed, with thick black stubble on his chin now, he looked the definition of a sleazy sexual predator.

'Now, I know you have parents. Mum and Dad live in Dunstable, don't they?' Proud plucked the detail from the file in front of him. 'I'm sure they are proud of you, your career –'

'Don't you dare bring them into this,' Robins said, suddenly coming to life.

'I've got no choice, Mark. *You've* brought them into this by your actions.'

Proud tossed a copy of last night's *Standard* on to the table. The front page was dominated by a picture of Holloway Prison under the screaming headline 'Double Murder'. Robins gave it a cursory glance, then returned his gaze to Proud.

'Now, I know you killed those girls. You know you killed those girls. So let's not make this any harder than it needs to be.'

'I didn't kill them.'

'Think of your parents. They don't deserve this.'

'I didn't bloody kill them.'

'I bet they raised you to front up to things. When you've messed up, you stick your hand up and take your punishment, right? That's what you should do now.'

'You're not listening to me –'

'No, you're not listening to *me*, Mark. If you continue to hold out on me, if you continue to deny your involvement in these murders, then you will leave me with little choice. I will arrest you, the CPS will charge you and a very long, very public trial will ensue. Your parents will no doubt stick by you. They will attend every day of the trial –'

'Go to Hell.'

'And they will hear every sickening detail of what you got up to. The sex, the murder, the mutilation. They will hear how their little boy became a monster, how he murdered his own unborn child. Is that what you want, Mark?'

Robins stared at the table, shaking his head. He looked deeply miserable, like a man staring destruction in the face.

'You can go that route if you want,' Proud continued quickly. 'Or you can show them, show the world, that you still have some decency left in you. Tell me what happened, tell me how you killed those girls and all that unpleasantness can be avoided. No trial, no publicity. It's in your power to make this happen, Mark.'

Robins looked like he wanted to speak, but couldn't find the words, so Proud spoke again instead:

'Do the right thing. It's not only what your parents would expect of you, it's the only play you've got left.'

'Is that right?' Robins said quickly, looking up now at his interrogator.

Proud had expected Robins to look beaten, but to his surprise there was a defiance in his expression now.

'You know, I came here this morning intending to help you. I thought we could settle this man-to-man –'

'We still can, mate –'

'Shut up. I'm talking now.'

Shocked by the vehemence in Robins's voice, Proud did as he was told.

'But I'm fucked if I'm going to help someone who's prepared to drag my folks into this. They've done nothing wrong.'

'I never said they had –'

'And neither have I. You've not a shred of evidence that

I hurt these girls – no forensics, no witnesses, nothing. So you can keep chipping away, keep asking your questions, but you'll get nowhere with me. I've said all I'm going to say, so now you need to make a decision, *mate*.'

Robins's eyes locked on to Proud's:

'Arrest me now or let me go.'

108

'What have I done to deserve this life?'

Campbell muttered the words to himself as he crossed the gantry. Resources were stretched thin at the best of times, but a couple of officers had called in sick and Robins was still being quizzed, which meant that he and Bradshaw were the only two on B-Wing today. Bradshaw had taken herself off to the Segregation unit to release Grace, so he'd been left alone as he tried to corral the inmates down to breakfast.

They were in truculent mood this morning. Morale had always been shaky, but had taken a massive hit in the last few days. Campbell had heard about the prisoners' delegation to the Governor and Bassett's calamitous handling of the situation. The inmates no longer felt supported, no longer felt safe, and the strict rules of engagement that facilitated prison life were slowly breaking down. The natives were restless, which made Campbell uneasy. A mutiny in this place would be disastrous.

There had been issues before, but never such open defiance. He had been greeted with a constant refrain of 'Fuck you' as he did his rounds. Normally they trotted out, dozy and docile, but he'd had to physically drag a handful of them out of their beds this morning. A task that should have taken ten minutes had taken the best part of half an hour, which made him very angry indeed.

Punctuality was his watch word, order the creed by which he lived and died.

'Get up, Simons, or you will feel my hairy hands upon you,' he bellowed towards the last cell in the line.

Finally, there was movement from within and Campbell now turned to see if the rest of the malingerers had fallen into line. To his dismay, they were only just emerging and one – the reliably troublesome Lucy Kirk – had not put in an appearance at all.

'Lucy . . . Michael . . . whichever half of your tiny brain is working today, perhaps it could tell your arse to get moving.'

Campbell was already striding over to the east side of the wing, slipping his baton from its holster in expectation of trouble. When Lucy resisted, she resisted big time. Could he really tackle her alone, leaving the rest of the inmates unsupervised?

'I am not in the mood for games, cupcake. So unless you want me to break your very manly bones, get yourself in line.'

He was marching fast towards her cell, ignoring the fearful glances that the inmates gave him. They weren't scared of him – that was for sure – there was something else alarming them this morning, which only served to unnerve him further.

'This is your last chance or . . .'

But Campbell didn't have the energy to finish his threat. This was his manor, but now he felt as if his authority had been replaced by something darker, something stronger. He could tell that the inmates were watching him, he could hear them whispering behind his back.

Suddenly he didn't want to go into her cell. For some reason he knew what he would find there and he didn't want any part of it. But the eyes of the prison were on him, it would be fatal to let the inmates think he'd lost his nerve. So, taking a deep breath, he hauled open the cell door and marched inside.

109

The door swung open, jolting Helen awake. Instinctively, she scrambled to her feet, but immediately her head started to spin and she had to steady herself against the wall. She had meant to stay awake all night, ready to snap into action as soon as she was released. But the exhaustion that had been creeping up on her for days had finally taken its toll.

She looked up to see Sarah Bradshaw approaching. The prison officer looked tense, but was trying to hide this behind a forced smile.

'You're not supposed to be out until ten, but I thought I'd do you a favour. If you want any breakfast, you'd best go now.'

But if Sarah was hoping for a friendly reception, she was disappointed. Helen was immediately upon her.

'Where is he?'

'Who?' the startled prison officer replied, backing off.

'Robins.'

'He . . . he's in with the PPS.'

'Where?'

'Bassett's office.'

'Have they charged him?'

'No, course not. They haven't got a thing on him. Not really –'

'What happens when they finish with him?'

'Why do you want to –'

But Sarah didn't get to finish her sentence. Helen grabbed her by the collar and pulled her in close.

'Where can I find him?'

They were practically nose-to-nose now and Helen was gratified to see that the prison officer looked scared.

'The locker rooms, I guess,' Sarah stuttered in reply. 'He's been suspended so he'll get his things and go home until the smoke clears . . .'

Until the smoke clears. Helen could have slapped Sarah for her comical understatement, but instead she pushed past her.

'You can't go there.'

'Try and stop me.'

'We're not finished here.'

'I'm sorry?'

'We had a deal. I scratch your back, you scra—'

The whining prison officer was now pulling her smartphone from her pocket. But even she seemed to lack the necessary conviction today.

'Our deal's over.'

'But I need a photo. I told Garanita I'd get another photo.'

Helen paused in the doorway, smiling ruefully.

'Ok, then . . .'

Surprised, Sarah held up her phone. Helen turned back to her and just before Sarah hit the button, Helen raised her middle finger to the camera.

'. . . there's your picture.'

And with that, she was gone.

110

She walked fast along the street, casting nervous looks over her shoulder. Kaitlin hadn't slept a wink all night, half expecting 'Jack' to round on her at any moment. Had he smelt her deceit, sensed what she was planning? If so, he was keeping it to himself. He hadn't appeared to notice when she'd slipped out of the squat this morning.

She was making straight for the Lamb and Flag on Argyle Street. It was a grim old man's pub in Holloway, with very cheap beer and extremely flexible opening hours. You could get a pint there any time of day or night, though if you visited after midnight, you had to serve yourself – the corpulent Latvian who owned the joint was usually found slumbering under the bar in the small hours.

But Kaitlin wasn't after a drink and walked swiftly past the bar towards the toilets. The handful of serious alcoholics who were enjoying their breakfast pint barely looked up. They were used to the flotsam and jetsam of London washing up here to use the loos or shoot up in the tiny beer garden. Kaitlin was glad of their lack of interest, but still checked behind her as she came to a halt by the payphone. Nobody had followed her, so pulling a pound from her pocket she fed it into the machine. Payphones were relics of a different time, but this archaic, ramshackle pub still possessed one and Kaitlin was glad it did.

This was it then. Decision time. What she did in the next few seconds could make or break her life. Again she cast a look over her shoulder, but satisfied she was alone, she began to dial.

III

Helen was stunned by the sight that greeted her. She had never seen so many bodies in B-Wing, nor such chaos. Prisoners hung over the railings on every level, banging the metal barriers with enamel cups, throwing streamers of toilet roll down into the packed canteen below. Prison officers were trying to enforce the lockdown, but the women were resisting, fighting tooth and nail to avoid being forced back into their cells. Things had already turned nasty. Helen could see one female prison officer being treated for minor injuries, while nearby a protesting prisoner was being dragged back to her cell by her hair.

Down below, amid the tumult, Helen spotted Celia Bassett. This insubstantial woman had always seemed out of her depth, but never more so than today. Her hands were raised above her head as she appealed to be heard, but her charges seemed in no mood to listen. To Helen's surprise, Cameron Campbell seemed to be supporting her. He had always derided his superiors, but there he was, threatening to crack heads unless the inmates returned to their cells. Perhaps he was doing the right thing for once – trying to restore order before someone got badly hurt. Or perhaps he just wanted to be in the thick of it when it really kicked off.

Helen could see Noelle and Babs in the middle of it, backed up by the questionable might of the Golden Girls. In normal circumstances, Helen would have dived in to protect them, but not today. She *had* to catch Robins before he had a chance to escape.

Quickening her pace, Helen dropped down on to Level One, taking the steps two at a time. She was moving fast towards the doors to C-Wing, but as she neared them a familiar figure suddenly came into view. Alexis, her damaged but persistent adversary, barred the way.

'Going somewhere, Grace?' the giant woman lisped, moving steadily forward.

Alexis had been in a bad way following their last encounter, but looked even worse now. She had two nasty gashes on her face, blood oozing from her injuries and running down her face. She had clearly been in the action, but had now spotted a better prize. She wanted revenge and wasn't minded to hang about, so launched herself at Helen.

Helen only had a split second to react if she was to save herself. So as Alexis flew towards her, Helen darted forward, slamming her fist into her attacker's voice box. There was a nasty crunch and even as the burly woman cannoned into her, Helen could see that she was going down. Alexis hit the deck with a horrible clunk and for a moment Helen feared the worst. Alexis was lying still, hardly making a noise, but, bending down, Helen was relieved to see her chest rising and falling. She was not in a good way, but she would live, so without hesitation Helen now sprinted the last few yards to the access doors. If she wanted to catch Robins before he left, she would have to move fast.

The doors remained firmly locked, despite the chaos within the wing, so Helen cast around her for other alternatives. It might be possible to make it to the staff wing via another route if she retraced her steps, but she'd risk running into Bradshaw. Besides she could see Campbell blowing his whistle now, summoning reinforcements, so acting on instinct Helen slunk back into the cell doorway adjacent to the main access doors.

Moments later the doors burst open and four officers in riot gear came running into the wing. Quick as a flash, Helen nipped out of her hiding place and through the open doorway. The doors now came together, slamming shut with a deafening crash.

But Helen was already gone.

112

The corridor in front of her was empty. Usually C-Wing was packed with inmates, mopping floors, cleaning cells, chatting, dealing, fighting. But this morning they had vanished – presumably having gathered elsewhere to confront the authorities. This would further stretch prison resources, which made Helen's task a little easier. A prisoner in the wrong wing would normally attract attention, but there was no one around to ask her awkward questions today, as she made her way along the deserted corridor.

She didn't linger, walking the length of the wing until she came to the access door to the staff quarters. Her plan had been to punch the nearest suicide alarm and hope that one of the harassed officers would hear it, but as she neared the doors she saw that this would be unnecessary. One of the reinforced doors was still in place, but the other hung off its hinges. It was bent double in the middle and the hinges had been almost pulled from the wall. The prison officers had presumably locked the doors to keep the inmates in, but even the strongest barriers couldn't withstand the concerted pressure of a whole wing of inmates. Helen squeezed past the mangled door and into the staff quarters on the other side.

Now she heard it. A terrible noise was coming from the staff recreation area – voices raised in anger, objects crashing against the wall – but Helen decided not to investigate further. If Robins had any sense, he would steer well clear of large groups and make a break for the back of the prison.

It was accessed from a corridor near the staff locker room and Helen bent her steps there now.

This was strictly out of bounds and Helen knew she would find herself back in the Seg if discovered. But she didn't even think of turning back now. Before long, she had reached the locker room door. It too would be locked and there was no point trying to force it on her own. She suddenly felt idiotic and strangely vulnerable loitering in the corridor outside, and thought about lying in wait at the rear exit. But that might bring her into contact with the auxiliary officers who'd been drafted in to deal with the morning's disturbances. They would presumably be brought in via the back exit to avoid the attention of the press, who already had Holloway in their sights.

Helen was still debating what to do when the locker room door swung open. Mark Robins, coat on and rucksack on his back, took a step out into the corridor, but, on seeing Helen, immediately retreated. He pulled the door firmly towards him, but to his horror it wouldn't close. Looking down he saw Helen's foot wedged in the door and seconds later felt her hands on his collar. Still he tried to back away, beating violently at her arms, but, shouldering the door open, Helen yanked him hard towards her. Caught off guard, he stumbled and Helen was quick to take advantage, slamming him hard into the wall opposite. Winded, Robins tried once more to escape her grip, but now found himself spinning round. In a moment, his face was pressed hard up against the wall, his arm secured in a half-nelson.

'Going somewhere?'

Still Robins struggled. Helen allowed him to move a few inches away from the wall, then rammed him back into it again.

'Answer the question,' she continued.

'Home. I'm going home,' Robins gasped.

'Your work here is done, is it?'

Robins didn't respond, wincing in agony as Helen gripped his arm.

'Why did you do it, Mark? What had they done to you?'

'I haven't done *anything*.'

'You don't need to lie to me. I've seen the path reports. I know what you did to Leah and Jordi.'

'I've fessed up to that,' Robins whined. 'What I did was wrong and I'm going to pay for it. But I would never harm them.'

'That's what most murderers and rapists say.'

'I didn't hurt anyone. I didn't *rape* anyone. They were willing, for God's sake.'

'Yeah, right . . .'

'They were lonely. They didn't have anyone. They didn't have a single person who loved them, who cared about them . . .'

It was hard to tell whether Robins was talking about the women or himself here. He suddenly looked a pathetic creature, whining and twisting in her grip.

'Is that why you targeted them?'

'I didn't *target* them,' Robins insisted. 'I liked them and they liked me. I knew it couldn't last, but the moments we had together were special –'

Helen couldn't stomach any more, twisting his arm higher up his back. Robins yelped in agony.

'Don't you dare try and justify yourself,' Helen hissed. 'You took advantage of those women, which makes you nothing more than a rapist.'

'Call me what you will, but I didn't harm them, I swear.'

And now he started to weep. Hanging his head, he sobbed bitterly, his tears staining the wall. For a moment, Helen relaxed her grip. In spite of herself, she saw something in Robins's demeanour that struck her as genuine.

'Why were you in Jordi's cell that night? The night I chased you?'

'I went to see her,' Robins continued, gulping down his distress. 'I used to visit her once or twice a week . . .'

'Blowjob for drugs, was it?'

'No, I gave her stamps and cash. For her company . . .'

'Call it what you want. What happened?'

'I went to her cell as usual. Let myself in and found her. She was already dead . . .'

'So instead of raising the alarm, you ran.'

'I couldn't be found there. They would have had my job, so I left. But then I saw you.'

Helen swore violently, making Robins jump. He cringed as if expecting a blow, but Helen wasn't in the mood to attack him. She was furious, coming now to the inexorable conclusion that she had been barking up the wrong tree with Robins. He was a worm, no more, no less, who wasn't capable of these elaborate, sadistic crimes.

'Think about it,' Robins urged her in a hoarse whisper. 'I was marched off the site last night and accompanied back in this morning. So how could I have killed again?'

'What do you mean?' Helen snapped back.

'Lucy Kirk . . . Michael . . . whatever you want to call her. She was murdered last night, stitched up like the others . . . I wasn't here, so it couldn't have been me . . .'

Robins started sobbing once more and now Helen released her grip. The distraught prison officer slid to his knees. He was exhausted, spent – Helen wondered if he'd even have the strength to make it to the back door. She was half tempted to drag him there herself – he had been a toxic presence in this prison and they were well shot of him – but she didn't have the time. She had been pursuing a dead-end lead for long enough and there was work to be done. So grabbing his ID from around his neck, Helen sprinted away down the corridor.

A kneeling Robins watched her go, broken and defeated.

113

This was it then. The end of the line.

Charlie ran her eye down the long list again, hoping that there was one that they'd missed, one that had slipped through the net. But they'd been thorough, methodical, organized – collating Stonehill's known haunts into geographical bundles to prevent them having to retrace their steps – and they had visited every one. Every listed establishment now had a line drawn through it.

And yet still Robert Stonehill eluded them. They had gambled everything on being able to bring him in and they had failed. The dedicated hotline had received dozens of calls and the Met had followed up on every one – only to find that the callers were lying, greedy or just plain mistaken. Their manhunt for Helen's nephew had promised so much, but delivered nothing.

Charlie stole a glance at Sanderson, who was taking yet another fag break, mobile phone clamped to her ear. In spite of herself, Charlie felt extremely guilty. She had dragged Sanderson into this and where had it got them? What would they say when they returned to Southampton empty-handed? How would they frame it to Gardam? Whatever they did now, career ruin beckoned. They would be on the scrap heap before they were forty with no references, no prospects, no hope.

'Charlie?'

What the hell would she say to Steve? She could hear

him now, taking her to task while struggling manfully not to say I told you so. He was a thoroughly decent man, even when he was furious with her.

'CHARLIE?'

Now Charlie looked up. She was surprised to see that her boss had abandoned her cigarette. Sanderson now looked happy, even a little excited.

'We've got a location. A squat he's been living at.'

All thoughts of defeat were instantly forgotten. Charlie grasped Sanderson by the arm and tried to speak, but somehow she couldn't find the words. So Sanderson provided them for her.

'I think we've found him, Charlie.'

114

'All prisoners are required to make their way back to their cells. Anyone failing to do so –'

'Fuck that shit,' Noelle retorted, pushing the helpless Governor out of her way and making for the main doors.

'You will go to the Seg. You will all go to the Seg . . .'

Noelle kept on walking. She and a nucleus of B-Wing prisoners had formed a fifty-strong group and were not going to be deterred by Celia Bassett's empty threats. Like many others in Holloway, Noelle had spent sleepless nights worrying about whether she was safe, whether she would be alive come morning. The news that Lucy Kirk had been murdered had tipped her over the edge – she had decided not to spend another night in the crumbling prison.

Campbell and a few other officers had retreated to the main access doors and now stood directly in the prisoners' way. Already their batons were out, while, above, Bradshaw and another officer were readying the high-pressure hoses. Still Noelle didn't waver, marching forward, screaming at the prison officers to step aside. They could take some of the inmates down, but they couldn't take them all.

They were getting closer and closer, but just as Noelle braced her body for the fight, she felt someone tugging her backwards. She turned, ready to smash their face in, but her hand froze in mid-air. It was just Babs, trying to pull her back from the brink.

'Don't do this, Noelle,' her friend urged her. 'You're better than this.'

'Step away, Babs, this isn't your fight.'

'Don't give Campbell the excuse. You'll get your head caved in.'

'Let him fucking try.'

'You're scared, you're not thinking straight. If you do this, you will regret it, I promise you,' Babs insisted.

'I'm not going to tell you again – let go of me,' Noelle spat at Babs, eyeing her with real menace.

Reluctantly, Babs released her grip on Noelle's shirt, but she wasn't finished yet.

'You might get out the wing, but do you really think you'll make it out the building? You'll be rounded up and then what? You'll spend the rest of your life behind bars. Is that what you want?'

'What I *want*,' Noelle said tersely, moving in close to the old woman, 'is for you to get out of my face.'

It was said with such vehemence that Babs stepped back, holding up her arms in surrender.

'See you on the other side,' Noelle muttered darkly, before turning on her heel and rushing to join her fellow prisoners.

Babs watched her go. The prison was in tumult, the system was disintegrating and even old friendships were splintering now.

115

Helen slid Robins's ID card through the reader. The light above the doors flicked from red to green and Helen pushed through into the dimly lit room beyond. She had never liked these places and this one was worse than most – dilapidated, crumbling and dirty. Hardly the ideal conditions to examine a corpse, but, then again, Holloway's mortuary had seldom been used. Only during the last few days had it been put through its paces.

'What the hell do you think you're doing?' An alarmed Dr Khan was already pulling a sheet over Lucy Kirk's corpse. 'Prisoners are not allowed in here, so I must ask –'

'In case you hadn't noticed, there's a riot going on upstairs. So all bets are off this morning.'

Dr Khan looked swiftly at the ceiling, clearly alarmed by this news. But he wasn't finished yet and turned his stern gaze on Helen once more.

'What's your prisoner number? I'm going to have to rep—'

'My name is Detective Inspector Helen Grace. Perhaps you've heard of me?'

Khan clearly had, because now he started backing off.

'It's me that's going to be asking the questions today, Doctor. So why don't you be a good boy and put the scalpel down?'

Khan looked at Helen, then at his hand, seemingly surprised to see the blade still there. He quickly placed it with the other tools of his trade and started pulling off his sterile gloves.

'I can't discuss my work with you,' he said, crossing to the table where his briefcase lay.

Now he was taking off his gown, keen to be away.

'I've read your preliminary findings on Leah Smith and Jordi Baines. Now I want to talk to you about Lucy.'

Khan looked genuinely startled by this and remained rooted to the spot as Helen approached the slab. But as she lifted the sheet to reveal Lucy's body, he rushed forward.

'You can't do that. You'll contaminate the body –'

'Give me some gloves –'

'I'm sorry?'

'Give me some sterile gloves.'

Khan hesitated, then complied. Helen snapped on the gloves and lifted Lucy's arm. Moving in close to the armpit, she was not surprised to find a fresh puncture mark on one of the veins.

'Did you log this in your report?' Helen asked, pointing towards the small red mark.

'Of course,' Khan said, looking aggrieved that his professionalism would be questioned.

'And have you got the preliminary blood results?'

Khan nodded, unsure where this was going.

'Any signs of heroin? Or other injectable drugs?'

'No, not yet,' Khan replied. 'But I'd like to test agai—'

'You won't find any. Lucy was trying to get herself clean. She'd been off it for several weeks.'

'So? She could have relapsed and anyway she wasn't killed by drugs. It's my opinion that all three victims died of –'

'Cardiac arrest, I know. So what was it?'

'What do you mean?'

'Somebody injected these three women with a substance that induced a heart attack. Perhaps their killer said it was drugs, but it most certainly wasn't.'

Khan paused for the first time, as if sensing where Helen was going.

'Did you find any insulin in their blood? That can induce a heart attack if given in sufficient quantities.'

'No, nothing like that.'

'Any heart stimulants? Injectable anaesthetics?'

'No.'

'Then what? Do your job and tell me what the cause of death is.'

'I don't know what it is, but I can tell y—'

Helen didn't bother listening, grabbing Khan's briefcase from him and tugging his notes from his bag. She leafed through the pages until she got to the blood analysis.

'There was nothing there that you wouldn't expect,' Khan blustered, 'given the nature of their deaths. Low levels of glucose, high levels of adrenaline, not to mention signifi—'

Suddenly Helen slumped back against the slab. The answer had been staring her in the face all the time.

'Adrenaline,' she whispered flatly.

'That means nothing. The body produces adrenaline during traumas like a heart atta—'

'But it can also *cause* a heart attack, if injected in sufficient quantities. And of course you wouldn't notice anything odd, because the levels would naturally be high after a heart attack.'

Khan said nothing. His face was ashen.

'It's the only thing that links all three deaths,' Helen

continued. 'Very high levels of adrenaline. I should have seen it and so should you.'

'This is not my fault,' Khan replied. 'None of this is my fault.'

He was already backing away towards the door, but Helen didn't have the energy to stop him. She hadn't seen what was under her nose and as a result another innocent woman had died. She longed to bring the killer to justice, but even now she wasn't sure which direction to go in or where to look. She knew the 'how', but the 'who' and 'why' of these awful crimes remained as hidden as ever.

116

'Three. Two. One. Go!'

Taking his cue from Sanderson, the uniformed officer swung his barrel charge. The front door to the squat was rotten and he cut it in half with one blow. Armed officers now swarmed past him, sprinting into the rooms beyond. Sanderson ran after them, scanning the dingy building for their prize.

'Armed police. On your knees.'

The floor was littered with sleeping figures. The whole place stank of drugs and stale beer. Those who called it home were rising groggily now, alarmed to see sub-machine guns being shoved in their faces. Sanderson did a quick audit of who was in the room, but it was too dark to see properly, so turning sharply she yanked open the heavy curtains behind her. Bright sunlight streamed in, causing yet more discomfort to the half-naked dropouts on parade in front of her.

Her eyes crawled over their features, but none of them fitted the bill, so she moved on. There were two small rooms further back and she burst into those now. One of them was a bedroom of sorts – a young couple had clearly been in the midst of an amorous encounter and the naked girl was now screaming fit to bust. Her bearded boyfriend looked similarly stupefied, but Sanderson didn't linger, moving on to the small utility room at the back. This led on to the garden and had once been a laundry room, but it was a dirty hovel now. The washing machine had been torn out, water dripped from cracked pipes and syringes littered the floor. Worse still, it was empty.

'Clear!'

Sanderson bellowed it confidently but her voice sounded reedy and tight. She moved towards the front of the house once more, but, as she did so, she heard a chorus of 'clear' from above. She carried on to the main staircase, but as she reached it, a Met colleague appeared at the top of the stairs. He shook his head, looking as disappointed as Sanderson felt. Clearly Stonehill was not upstairs.

Sanderson swore violently. They had made it to the squat in under twenty minutes. He had been in the house when the young woman had left. Had he suspected something? Had he fled?

And now Sanderson found herself moving towards the utility room once more. Stonehill was an agile and resourceful criminal and Sanderson remembered Helen's description of him falling gracefully from the warehouse window at the Western Docks. She hadn't believed Helen's account then but now she had reason to revise her opinion, and hurrying into the back room, she wrenched the door open and dashed outside.

And there he was. Shinning down a sturdy drainpipe at the back of the house. Sensing movement, he leapt from the house now, landing deftly on his feet. Sanderson was on him in a flash, grabbing him by his T-shirt and spinning him round.

She reached for her cuffs, but too late realized the stupidity of her move. She left herself with only one hand to defend herself and couldn't move it fast enough. Stonehill launched himself forward, his forehead crunching into Sanderson's face, just above the bridge of her nose.

Now she was falling backwards. For a moment, she wasn't sure which way was up. Her ears were ringing and she was seeing stars. She tried to stumble to her feet, but fell to her knees instead. Clamping her eyes shut, she inhaled and exhaled deeply, trying to recover her composure. Now the dizziness was receding and she opened her eyes once more.

Stonehill was clambering over the back wall of the garden. Armed officers rushed past Sanderson but it was already too late. Stonehill had dropped down on the other side and was making his escape. They had gambled all on capturing him, but he had evaded their grasp and the beaten Sanderson had nothing to show for her pains but a broken nose and the fragments of a promising career.

117

Helen stood alone, looking at the corpse in front of her. The modesty sheet lay discarded on the floor now, revealing Lucy in all her glory. She was a curious specimen, born with a slender waist and generous curves but these aspects of her femininity were increasingly under attack. Firstly, from the large amounts of male hormones she was taking, adding muscle bulk and hair, and secondly from the damage visited on her by her own hand. The long, thin cuts on her thighs, arms and breasts were a depressing testament to the latter.

But the damage wreaked by Lucy was nothing compared to the injuries she'd sustained at the hands of her killer. As with Leah and Jordi, Lucy's mouth, eyes and vagina had been sewn up, her nose, ears and anus filled in. Helen tentatively touched the opaque, gelatinous substance that hung from Lucy's left ear and held it up to examine it closer. As expected, it was Vaseline. This could have been found anywhere – you could even buy it from the prison shop – so unless the killer had been careless enough to deposit their DNA on it, it would be useless to investigators.

Helen was about to resume her examination of the body, when she sensed movement out of the corner of her eye. Instinctively she snatched up the scalpel from the tray and spun to defend herself. But no sooner had she done so than her 'assailant' disappeared, vanishing into the brickwork with lightning speed. Helen shook her head at her stupidity – it was just a mouse. Nowhere in this place was sacred.

Returning to the body, Helen took in the stitching. It was efficiently done, so whoever did this was a practised hand. This time the killer had chosen a nice violet thread. Was the different colouring significant or just done to taunt the hapless investigators? Swallowing her revulsion, she moved up close to the wounds, looking particularly keenly at Lucy's sewn-up vagina. She was looking for signs of excessive mutilation – for signs of hate – but the sewing had been carefully executed. There were no bruising, no signs of violence and no traces of blood. In fact, not a single drop of blood had been spilt at any point.

Helen knew she should leave. No doubt Khan would report her intrusion and armed officers would arrive to detain her. But a thought was forming in her mind and she knew she had to stay. She had come across very few bloodless murders in her time, very few acts of brutality in which the bodies exhibited such a complete absence of defensive wounds. She was sure this was significant, so returned to the body.

Taking up Lucy's hands, Helen examined her long fingers for signs of a struggle, of a woman fighting for her life. But there were none. And now, staring down at the lily-white hands, it struck her. Lucy was a woman who hated herself, who hated life and more than anything hated being in Holloway. She had mounted numerous dirty protests, smearing excrement over herself and the walls as each attempt to get herself transferred came to naught. She had attempted suicide twice, gone on hunger strikes and had categorically refused to groom herself. She had insisted that this was because she didn't want to appear 'girly' but everyone knew it was because she had given up. Her hair was lank and greasy, her armpits were stale and her short fingernails always had a thick line of black dirt beneath them.

But not now. The Lucy that lay on the slab in front of Helen was Lucy as she perhaps was supposed to be. Her hair was still greasy, but it was parted and combed. Her normally chapped lips seemed plump and every one of her fingernails was spotlessly clean. Khan might have taken samples from one or two of them, but he would never have cleaned them so thoroughly. Khan wouldn't have noticed these changes, not being a resident and knowing little of Lucy's life, but to Helen these changes were obvious and striking.

And now a handful of images flashed through Helen's reeling mind. The mouse that had just darted across the mortuary. The cockroaches rutting in the Segregation unit. The bluebottles circling the cells, looking for somewhere moist to lay their eggs. And the thought that had been nagging away at her took hold. The killer was trying to *protect* his victims from these intruders, sealing every orifice so their neatly presented bodies couldn't be defiled by the prison's legion of unregistered inhabitants. It should have been obvious to Helen from the start. That rat that had run across her on her very first night here had given her the biggest clue of all.

For a long time she had laboured under the misapprehension that these murders were acts of hate, but they were nothing of the kind. This calculating killer had no desire to abuse the victims – quite the opposite, in fact. He wanted to *cleanse* them.

118

They were inches away from him now. He could smell their vile breath as they railed at him, insulting his manhood, his heritage, even his mother. Flecks of their dirty spittle landed on his shirt, but he made no attempt to wipe them off. He wouldn't demean himself by doing so and would burn his uniform as soon as today's fun was over.

'You heard the Governor, return to your cells NOW.'

Campbell bellowed the final word, but it had no effect. The inmates were spoiling for a fight now and nothing he or anyone else could do would prevent a full-scale riot.

'Get out of our way or I will take your head off.'

Noelle James was leading the rabble of crazed women, all of whom seemed intent on carnage. Campbell stared at her, then, looking up, gave the nod to Bradshaw.

Moments later, a powerful jet of water shot down from above, knocking two inmates clean off their feet. And now pandemonium broke out. There was screaming, shouting, and Campbell suddenly caught sight of a plastic chair somersaulting through the air towards him.

'Heads!'

They ducked in unison, the chair striking the doors just behind the besieged prison officers. Shrieking obscenities, the prisoners now charged forward, but Campbell was ready for them. As he straightened up, he swung his baton freely. It connected sharply with Noelle's chin, sending her flying sideways. Campbell heard the harsh click his baton made and couldn't help smiling. After a couple of hours of phony war, the fun had finally started.

This was the moment he'd been waiting for. And now he didn't hold back. Brandishing his baton above his head and howling like a wolf, he dived into the tumult in front of him.

119

His lungs were burning, his muscles protesting, but still he drove himself on. He had a good lead on his pursuers and was determined to make it count. His senses were in riot, his brain processing furiously, but for the first time the white-hot panic was starting to recede.

Robert Stonehill had been half asleep when the front door had flown off its hinges. The heavy tread of the armed police was instantly recognizable and he was on his feet even before they began to shout their familiar warnings. He was sleeping on the first floor and as the crumbling house only possessed one staircase, there was no way down. The top floor wasn't that appealing either – the floorboards were rotten and unstable and he didn't fancy a rooftop chase anyway. So he'd had to think on the move, charging into the dirty bathroom and wrenching open the window. From there it was a short slide down the drainpipe to the garden.

He had nearly been intercepted by Grace's replacement, but instinct had saved him yet again. He could taste blood dripping into his mouth as he ran and wondered if it was hers or his own. There was no time to check now, but he would need to attend to it, once he'd escaped the immediate vicinity of the squat. An obvious facial wound would attract unwanted attention. And if there was one thing he had been good at during the past few months, it was being invisible.

A long passageway bordered the back of this row of Victorian houses and he raced along it now. It would bring him out on to the main road and from there he could branch off in any number of directions. Tempting though it was to find an alleyway and hide out there, his best bet was to get as far away from the scene as possible. Another carjacking would be too risky – he had to assume there were police vehicles present, even a helicopter perhaps; he would fare better by darting into the warren of suburban streets nearby.

He darted an eye up to the sky now – there was no chopper in sight – then chanced a look behind him. A couple of armed officers had made it into the passageway, but they were nearly two hundred yards away and were weighed down by their battle rattle. They would never chance a shot in the direction of a busy street, so if he could just keep this speed up, he would soon be safely away.

He was breathless and sweating profusely now. The end of the passageway was only twenty feet away. He could see normal life there – mums with prams, pensioners with shopping bags – plenty of ordinary cover to blend in with as he slipped away. Once again, luck was on his side.

Then suddenly there she was. He recognized Brooks instantly, as she came to a halt at the top of the alleyway. He could see the flash of recognition on her face too, could sense her tensing herself for a fight, but he didn't pause for a second. He upped his speed and launched himself at her. He was going to smash her into the middle of next week. He was going to destroy her.

He was seconds from impact, when all at once she ducked. He hit her crouched form hard and then he was spinning in the air, his heels flipping over his head before he came to the ground, his chin jarring nastily on the pavement. Instantly he was scrambling to his feet, but Brooks was on to him quickly. He shrugged her off, buying himself a couple of seconds to slip his hand into his jacket pocket. And now, when she came at him a second time, he was ready. The blade was out of his pocket in a flash and as she bore down on him, he spun and drove it hard into her chest.

Brooks looked stunned, even a little confused. But no more so than Robert himself. For his knife hadn't broken skin – it hadn't gone in. And now he spotted the tell-tale bulk under her shirt – she was wearing a stab vest. Now he lashed at her face, but her strong arm batted the knife from his grasp. He turned in a flash to retrieve it, but instantly felt a brutal blow to the kidneys. Gasping, he fell to the ground, Brooks falling upon him.

He struggled for all he was worth, but it was too little, too late. She had him right where she wanted him and Robert could see the relieved smile on her face when she bent down to him and said:

'Nice to see you again, Robert.'

120

Helen burst through the chapel doors and marched inside. She'd expected to find the place deserted, but Andrew Holmes was kneeling in front of the altar. He had obviously been praying, but disturbed by Helen's dramatic entrance he now looked up. As she approached him she was astonished to see that his cheeks were stained with tears.

'Helen, what a nice surprise,' he said, clambering to his feet. 'We don't usually see you in here.'

Helen stared at him, but said nothing. There was something different about Holmes today. His cheery optimism had evaporated, he seemed hollow and sad. As if sensing her thoughts, Holmes brushed his tears away with his sleeve.

'I apologize for the state you find me in. Even men of faith have moments of weakness.'

It was said lightly, but Helen wasn't fooled.

'There's no need to apologize,' she replied calmly. 'I suspect you knew this day would come.'

Holmes looked at Helen. There was genuine surprise in his expression but then his features softened into a smile and he nodded.

'You're wiser than all the rest of us put together, aren't you? I thought that the very first time I met you.'

'That's very flattering, but it doesn't change anything, does it?'

'No, I suppose it doesn't. Though I'm amazed you care.'

Helen was so shocked by the casual way he said it that for a moment she wanted to strike him.

'Why would I not care?' she spat back bitterly. 'Jordi was my friend. And Leah and Lucy . . . they were decent human beings.'

'I couldn't agree more, though I'm not sure how that's relevant.'

'I beg your pardon?' Helen countered, taking another step towards him. It needed every ounce of her professionalism not to beat him to the floor.

'Is everything ok, Helen?' Holmes replied, stepping back. 'You seem upset.'

'Wouldn't you be in my position?'

'I suppose so, though I don't know what that's got to do with me. I've tried to help you, but you wouldn't resp—'

'Like you *helped* the others?'

Holmes said nothing, looking at her curiously.

'They all had their problems, Jordi, Leah, Lucy, and they were looking for guidance, for someone to help them. And they turned to you, didn't they?'

Still Holmes said nothing.

'Jordi was a regular here, as were Leah and Lucy. I should have noticed that the first two victims had crosses round their neck. I saw Lucy's in an evidence bag this morning. Did you want to save them, is that what this is about?'

'I did what I could,' Holmes replied, dropping his eyes to the floor. 'But it was never enough. Nothing I did or said had any effect.'

'Oh, I wouldn't say that. I suppose you think they are in a better place now?'

'Well, I hope so, but I still don't see wha—'

'You cleansed them, didn't you? Made them clean, whole. Kept them safe from the vermin, free of the filth –'

'Helen, I'm sorry but you're not making any sense –'

'I had to watch Jordi's body being delivered to her family. Leah's too. Was that the point? Sending them home for Christmas –'

'For God's sake, Helen, will you just shut up for a minute!'

He bellowed it, taking Helen by surprise. His face was red, he seemed suddenly angry. No, he seemed distraught.

'You don't seriously think that *I* killed them, do you?'

'That's exactly what I think. They were under your spell, you had easy access to their cells, could pass back and forth without arousing suspicion –'

'This is crazy.'

'I think you love saving these bad girls. They are pretty far gone – drugs, sex, violence even – but you can make things right, send them to their maker as they should have been.'

'Is that what you think of me?' Holmes asked her, for the first time looking genuinely affronted by Helen's accusations.

'I could see how that might have been tempting. Having that control over them, the power of life and death. And I can also see that it was not without its cost. You're not a monster and what you've done hurts. I'm sure that will be taken into account, so why don't we end this now?'

Helen held out her hand, but Holmes made no move to join her. Instead, he smiled a sad smile, shaking his head ruefully.

'I think you rather overestimate my effectiveness, Helen. I did like those women and I wanted to help them. But I couldn't. I talked to them, counselled them, tried to get them off drugs, but nothing I did worked. I'm sad not because of what I've done, but because of what I *haven't* done. I'm a failure, Helen.'

Helen stood her ground. He looked genuine, but it had to be him, didn't it?

'I've worked in this place nearly ten years and how many souls have I saved? How many people have I *actually* helped? People say they're grateful for my counsel and they promise to change. But then they give in to despair and self-hatred, go back to the drugs, cut themselves. This moment has been coming for a while but today it hit home. I have wasted my time here. I have achieved nothing. And do you know why?'

Helen didn't know what to say. She had always found Holmes an uncomfortable presence and his role in the murders seemed to fit so neatly. But unless he was a very good actor, he was speaking from the heart now.

'Because they have nothing to live for,' he continued, hardly pausing for breath. 'The women that come here are on a downward spiral. Leah, Jordi, Lucy – they all maintain the fiction that they might leave here one day, get a second chance. But they're lifers and they know in their heart of hearts that they're not going anywhere. And that's why I couldn't touch them. Why I'm so useless, so ineffective. Because they lack the one thing that you have *always* had, Helen.'

He looked her square in the eye, before concluding:

'Hope.'

121

'This is Jonathan Gardam. Please leave a message.'

Emilia Garanita ended the call, swearing violently as she did so. She had texted Gardam three times, called him twice, but had had nothing in response. It was perfectly possible that he was tied up with genuine police work and had a legitimate reason for not taking her calls. But something told Emilia that he was avoiding her today.

Robert Stonehill had been arrested. And was now closeted away in an interrogation suite in a North London police station. Emilia desperately needed to talk to Gardam, to find out what was going on. Was it possible that Stonehill was guilty after all? Helen had always sworn blind that she had been open with Gardam about her personal knowledge of the S&M victims. She had said in her statement that she had told her superior about this side of her life early on in proceedings and had offered to step away from the case. Gardam, when asked, flatly denied that this conversation had ever taken place. And Emilia had believed him.

Emilia was happy to take him at face value because it helped convict Grace. But had he been lying all along? Did he have some reason for wanting to destroy Grace? Emilia suddenly felt very exposed, as if all her allies were deserting her, as if the certainties that had sustained her version of the Helen Grace story thus far were unravelling.

The day had started badly – a curt text from Bradshaw

ending their deal — and was getting worse. Emilia felt herself being pushed out into the cold, as if the axis of her world was slipping. Perhaps the image Sarah Bradshaw had sent her this morning had more meaning than she had at first realized. She didn't want to, but Emilia couldn't resist looking at it again. But as she pulled it up, she found no hidden messages, nothing meaningful, just an act of open defiance.

Helen Grace staring at the camera, her raised middle finger pointing in Emilia's direction.

122

Helen ran along the corridor until she came to the infirmary. Swiping Robins's ID card through the reader, she pushed inside. Normally it would have been full – whenever there was a spare bed it was always grabbed, by an inmate with a genuine medical need or a prisoner with a healthy imagination. This morning, however, it was deserted, the staff and patients having presumably been evacuated now that a prison riot was in full swing.

Helen had bent her steps here almost by instinct. She may have been a prisoner for several months now, but she was still an investigator at heart. Robbed of her usual resources she had been floundering in the dark, guessing wildly and inaccurately, but she still had one vital clue. The killer had injected the victims with adrenaline. And there was one obvious place to find that.

Did this mean the prison's nursing staff were involved in these murders? Helen suspected not – she wasn't a big believer in conspiracy theories and, besides, she had the feeling this killer was working alone. The crimes were too peculiar and unusual to suggest otherwise. But there were others who had access to the infirmary's registered drugs and Helen had an instinct she would find one of them here today.

The treatment rooms were empty, so Helen tried the large medical storeroom at the back. This was kept locked at all times, but employing Robins's card once more, she unlocked the door and peered inside. It was dark and everything appeared still and for a moment Helen was tempted to move on. But then a tiny noise made her pause and snapping on the lights she discovered Wheelchair Annie.

She was cowering behind cardboard boxes towards the rear of the room. And she was alone. Helen had never seen her like this and now, bereft of her thugs and bodyguards, she cut a rather pitiful figure. She looked somehow smaller, weaker. More than that, she looked scared.

'What do *you* want?'

Annie was trying to sound authoritative, but it was all bluster. Helen couldn't suppress a smile – beyond her own beating, Annie was responsible for much of the misery that haunted Holloway, ensuring that many of the vulnerable women who passed through here remained dangerously hooked on drugs. Saying nothing, Helen walked slowly towards her.

'If you touch me, you'll regret it.'

Annie was trying to wheel herself backwards, but she was boxed in. Still Helen advanced upon her.

'For God's sake, I've got MS. You're a police officer. You wouldn't hit a defenceless –'

'I *was* a police officer,' Helen corrected her. 'And I've got a score to settle with you.'

'Look at me. I'm begging you . . .'

Annie held up her shaking hands. She wanted to use her condition as a bargaining chip, but Helen wasn't interested. Her beating at the hands of Annie's thugs was still fresh in her memory and Helen knew that Annie would be utterly ruthless if their positions were reversed.

She leant in close. As Annie craned away from her, Helen said quietly:

'I'm feeling generous, Annie. So I'm going to give you a choice. Tell me what I need to know or take what's coming to you.'

Annie nodded cautiously. Information was a valuable commodity in prison.

'You supply everybody in here, right? There's no one you won't sell to, nothing you can't source?'

'I do what I can.'

'I know you do. And I'm not interested in the usual stuff, I want to know about one of your more specialist clients.'

Annie nodded obediently, so Helen continued.

'Adrenaline. Can you get hold of pure adrenaline in here?'

'Of course. They need it for the girls with allergies, plus it's in all the resuscitation packs. They use them on the code blacks, if they're too far gone.'

'And have you ever lifted some for a customer?'

'It's not a common request.'

'Answer the question, Annie.'

'I may have acquired a few batches but it was months ago now.'

'Who did you give it to?'

'Why are you so interested? It was a few hundred centilitres at best . . .'

'WHO?'

'Listen, Grace, I want to help you, but I can't go giving up my clients like tha—'

Helen cut her off short, grabbing her by the collar.

'That adrenaline was used to kill three innocent women. Which means *you* are an accessory to murder.'

Annie stared at Helen, genuinely shocked by this revelation.

'So I'm going to ask you again and this time you had better answer me.'

Helen released her grip round Annie's throat.

'Who did you give the adrenaline to?'

123

'She's long gone.'

Khan looked up as Benjamin Proud emerged from the robing room at the rear of the mortuary. He had had no luck finding a prison officer who was interested in Grace's intrusion, but had eventually located Proud, hard at work in Bassett's office. The pair of them had hurried back to the mortuary and Proud had conducted a thorough search. But there was no sign of the former police officer.

'Has she taken anything?'

Khan looked over the body, the tray, the nearby desk.

'Not that I can see.'

'Has the body been tampered with in any way?'

Khan snapped on his sterile gloves and ran his eyes over Lucy's naked body.

'Don't think so. The stitching is as it was, likewise the petroleum jelly. The body hasn't been moved . . .'

He lifted one arm up to check the underside, then laid it down to check the other.

'. . . or marked in any way.'

'And she didn't harm you?'

'No, she just wanted to talk. Somehow she'd managed to get hold of the pathology reports on Smith and Baines and wanted to compare them with Lucy Kirk's death. I couldn't tell her much. I was halfway through the PM . . .'

'But she was interested in the adrenaline, right?' Proud pressed. 'Does her theory stack up?'

Khan hesitated before replying:

'Yes. I think it does. If you inject enough of it, it causes a surge of activity that basically short-circuits the heart. Fast-acting and very effective.'

Proud nodded – finally this difficult case was beginning to make sense.

'But you'd have to be able to source pure adrenaline in order to do it,' Khan continued.

'The infirmary?'

'That would be my guess.'

Proud was already on his way. This new lead didn't narrow down the potential suspects, but it might provide an important piece of the jigsaw.

'Hold on a second.'

Proud had reached the exit but now turned to face the pathologist once more.

'Before you go, you might want to see this.'

Something in Khan's tone intrigued Proud, so he walked quickly back to the slab. As he did so, Khan extracted something from the body.

'This was caught in her watchstrap. Might be a trace of your killer. If there was a struggle perhaps . . .'

Khan held his prize up to the light, examining it intently. Proud moved in closer and was stunned by what he now saw.

Clamped in the teeth of the tweezers was a single white hair.

124

Helen was rocked by the noise as soon as she set foot in the wing. Down in the canteen, riot police had come to the aid of the overwhelmed prison staff, beating their plastic shields with their truncheons, as they advanced upon the rioters. But their heavy-handed intervention was having little effect – chairs, tables, even blocks of concrete rained down on their shields with a savage clatter. The very fabric of the building was being torn apart, the rioting inmates cannibalizing whatever they could to protect themselves, screaming abuse at their attackers all the while. It was a deafening cacophony, as if the entire prison was suddenly howling in agony.

To this brutal din was now added a new, more sinister sound. Helen was shocked to see teargas canisters hitting the floor, hissing ominously while pumping their noxious fumes into the air. Still the enraged inmates refused to give up, clamping T-shirts over their mouths and noses, before diving back into the fray. The situation was swiftly descending into all-out war and normally Helen would have intervened, but she was a woman on a mission today, so pushed past a terrified Sarah Bradshaw in the direction of the cells. They had been unlocked since roll call and the doors now lolled open. Helen had walked this route many times before and did it almost on autopilot now, making her way quickly to cell B25. Without bothering to check that the coast was clear, Helen hurried inside.

Babs's cell looked no different from normal. Neat, tidy and clean. Scrupulously clean in fact and Helen wondered now why she had never noticed this before. There was no sign of the woman herself, however. Normally she would never have abandoned her cell like this, open and unprotected, but today was not a normal day. Was she involved in the violence below? Or was she using the pandemonium below to make her escape?

Suddenly Helen was tearing the place apart, pulling off blankets, lifting mattresses, ripping pillows open. There were very few hiding places in these cells, but Helen was thorough, pulling Babs's beloved novels from the shelves and ripping them down the spine, opening up her picture frames, even running her fingers over the brickwork. The evidence had to be here somehow – Babs wasn't going to stop, not now that she'd got a taste for killing.

But there was nothing incriminating. Just the modest possessions of an elderly inmate seeing out her time. Helen kicked the bed viciously in frustration and as she did so her eyes fell on the cuttings books that Babs kept in a cardboard box. A thought now occurred to her and she snatched them up, pulling the books out until she found the one she wanted. Now she was racing through the pages, past the murderers, thieves and dealers, until she came across the small clipping on Barbara Sarrington, better known in Holloway as Babs.

In deference to her friend, Helen had skipped over this while doing her initial sweep for possible suspects, but now she devoured the details. And as she did so, she was gripped by a sudden feeling of nausea, a sickening coldness that crept over her soul. For everything Babs had told her was a lie.

She *was* serving a life sentence, but not for the crime she had 'confessed' to in this very cell. She was no battered wife. Indeed, the paper called her an 'Angel of Death'. Barbara Sarrington was a nurse who'd murdered several of her patients by injecting them with insulin and later epinephrine, also known as adrenaline. Reading on, Helen was shocked to find that police also suspected foul play in the death of her parents and later her husband. But as these unfortunate 'victims' had been quickly cremated after their deaths, this had been impossible to prove.

Dropping the book, Helen put her head in her hands. She had been so close to the solution early in her investigation and she marvelled now at how calmly Babs had sat there reading her book, as Helen leafed through her clippings. How cold she'd been, how confident that she wouldn't be caught. No wonder she had cultivated Helen – she had used their friendship wisely to shield herself at the critical moment.

Helen now felt a tear sliding down her face. Her trusting nature had blinded her to what was under her nose. And because of that Jordi and now Lucy were dead. She had taken Babs at face value – the warm-hearted spokeswoman for the prison's Golden Girls. The mother hen, the good egg, everyone's friend. But in fact she was nothing of the sort.

In reality, this little old lady was a monster.

125

The phone rang and rang, but still no one answered. Charlie had been trying to get hold of the authorities at Holloway for half an hour now, wanting to make use of a brief break in questioning to give Helen the good news. She had tried the main switchboard, the visitors' centre, even the media liaison office. But every time her call rang out. What the hell was going on?

Hanging up, Charlie fired up her laptop. She googled Holloway and a host of entries sprang into view, most of them from news outlets. Sitting down, she opened the first one and was immediately alarmed by the headline.

'Riot police called in to deal with "major incident".'

She read the details, then double-checked it against the next entry. But both reports said the same. A serious riot was taking place within the old prison and the authorities were struggling to contain its overcrowded prison population. Details were sketchy but the third report alarmed Charlie even more. According to the latest information, the centre of the violence was B-Wing.

'We're back on.'

Charlie looked up to see her Met colleague gesturing her back to the interrogation suite. For a moment, Charlie froze, unsure what to do for the best. Then, rising, she followed her colleague from the room. She was worried about her old friend but until she had a confession from

Stonehill she had no concrete news to give her. So loath though she was to do so, she would have to swallow her concerns about the unfolding situation at Holloway.

Helen would have to fend for herself for the time being.

126

The door clanked shut behind her, the eerie sound echoing around the cell. Pulling her chain from her pocket, she slipped the key in the lock and turned it twice clockwise. Then moving away from the door, she made her way to the corner and slumped down in a heap.

Celia Bassett usually avoided the Segregation unit like the plague – she had no desire to spend her time with the vomit-drenched, shit-stained crazies who spent their time here. Life was hard enough without having to deal with *that*. But today it seemed like a haven. Things had spiralled out of control so quickly this morning. At 7 a.m. the situation had been tense but calm. At 8 a.m. Lucy Kirk's body had been found. By nine o'clock the first outbreaks of violence had begun and a mere two hours later the prison had officially been put in Special Measures.

And, like that, Celia's career had gone up in smoke. There would be no way back from a debacle like this. Three murders and now a full-scale riot. Celia had felt her life slipping away from her for months, but right now it was in free fall. She was an irrelevance, a footnote in Holloway's chequered history.

In one last bid to restore her authority, she had descended into the melee to reason with the rioters, but had barely escaped with her life and wasn't going to attempt anything so foolish again. The inmates wanted blood today.

So she was going to sit it out in the hated Seg, soaking up

the misery of all those who'd passed through here before her. This was what it had come to. The Governor segregated for her own safety. It would have made her laugh if it wasn't so tragic. But then wasn't her whole life a joke? And this was the bitter punchline.

127

The clippings lay discarded on the bed and Helen now stood by the bedside table. In pride of place was a stack of letters from Babs's daughter, Jeannie, who wrote to her mother regularly. Babs had made great play of this, saying how lucky she was to have such an attentive daughter. But another surprise lay in store for Helen now, as she leafed through the letters. Not a single one of them had been opened.

Helen, however, didn't hesitate, ripping open the first one that came to hand. Her eyes quickly took in the words, assimilating their unpleasant content:

Dear Mum,

I hope this letter finds you unwell. I hope that you hate your life and that it causes you pain. Many times in my dreams I've seen you die, but life doesn't seem that kind, so all I can hope is that you continue to suffer.

Helen finished the letter and moved on to the next one. The sentiment in this one was similar – Jeannie clearly believed her mother had murdered her father and got away with it. There was no way she was going to let her forget this, so while she refused to visit her, she wrote regularly, pouring all her bitterness and bile on to her heartless mother.

The last letter, written only a week ago, was even more unpleasant than usual:

If I could ask Father Christmas for one thing, it would be you, swinging from a rope in your cell. That would make me the happiest girl alive. But I suppose that's too much to hope for. They say Christmas is the toughest time of year for prisoners, so I'm sending you my season's greetings. I hope you have a bleak Christmas full of pain, regret and despair. God knows, you deserve it.

Fuck you, bitch. I trusted you.

Jeannie

And there it was in a nutshell. They had *all* trusted nice, friendly Babs and she had betrayed them. Suddenly so many things slotted into place for Helen. There was no struggle during the murders because each victim had woken to find a friend in their cell. Babs had offered them something – a shot of heroin? – presumably telling them to leave their doors accessible so she could slip inside to give it to them. Was it possible that Babs herself had taught Noelle and Jordi how to use the cotton wool? They had said it was an old Holloway trick.

Leah, Jordi and Lucy all had a weakness for drugs. Babs's offer must have looked like a gift from a good friend, a little something to banish their cravings, but in reality the unfortunate women were injecting pure adrenaline. And now another image flashed through Helen's mind – her friends visiting her in the infirmary. They had all given her gifts and treats, but Helen now recollected Babs pressing a bottle of Ribena into her hand. This was why Helen had failed the drugs test. Babs must have spiked the drink. Had Annie provided her with those drugs too?

Babs had wanted Helen out of the way and with good reason. No one had got closer to working out the truth than she had. But even now Helen lacked the primary evidence that would convict this callous serial killer. Everything she had, even Annie's testimony, was circumstantial.

Helen tried to focus. The sound outside was deafening and her emotions were in riot, as she took in the full extent of her betrayal. But she had to keep a clear head – there was no way she could let a multiple murderer remain at large.

Annie said that Babs had got hold of the adrenaline some months ago. Given her history there was no way they would let Babs near the medical stores, hence her need for the drug dealer's assistance. She could hardly have gone back for a 'top-up' after the murders started, so she must have stored the adrenaline somewhere between killings. But where? Each cell had been searched, torn apart as the prison officers hunted for the killer. But they'd found nothing, which was not surprising. After all there were just four walls, a toilet, a bed, a table . . .

Suddenly Helen was on her knees. Crawling across the floor, she came to a halt by the bedstead. As she'd expected the screws that secured the bed to the floor were worn, the paint on the top chiselled away. Pulling Robins's ID card from her pocket, Helen inserted the corner of it in the screw head and began to turn. Slowly at first then, as the screw started to rise, faster and faster. One screw out, she tried the next. Once she'd unscrewed all four, she moved on to the adjacent leg, quickly removing all its screws.

Gently she raised the end of the bed. To her disappointment, there was nothing in the first hollow leg, but in the second one she now found a see-through plastic bag. Easing it out of its hiding place, she opened it to reveal a syringe and a vial of clear liquid. The label on the bottle confirmed that it was adrenaline.

There it was. Final proof of Babs's guilt. Her audacity took Helen's breath away – she remembered now how Babs had advised her to remove the screws from her own bed. This woman had no conscience, no scruples.

And she had been toying with Helen from the very start.

128

Robert Stonehill sat slumped at the table, resting his badly gashed chin on his elbow. He had refused medical attention and, though the bleeding had stopped, he still looked in a bad way. Stonehill had also waived his right to legal counsel and seemed to be receding into himself. Occasionally he would cast a look around him during questioning, as if trying to take in what was happening. He looked a little stunned, as if he never believed he would end up here. Charlie hoped to profit from his disorientation.

Sanderson was still in hospital. Her nose had been cleanly broken, which was something, but the doctors at the Royal Free wanted to keep her in overnight, in case she exhibited any signs of concussion. Charlie had considered holding off questioning until she was discharged, but then had decided against it. There was too much riding on this.

Charlie had laid out the evidence regarding his presence in Southampton during the time of the murders, his flight from Helen and, perhaps most tellingly of all, the footprint found at his nerve centre at the Western Docks. Stonehill sat in front of her in a sterile suit and slippers – a mould of his Vans trainer was currently being produced and Charlie was confident that his soles would match the footprint. Factor in his two attempts to escape arrest and his recent attacks on Sanderson and Charlie, and Robert Stonehill had some questions to answer.

But he refused to engage. He either looked away,

pretending not to hear, or mumbled 'No comment' – the latter used to silence Charlie when she refused to give up on a specific line of questioning. Charlie swallowed her frustration. She knew that the case against Robert was not open and shut, but she had to ask the questions, to lay the case out in front of him, so that there could be no doubt about her conduct when – if – his case came to court.

She had suspected he would dead-bat her, so having completed her initial questions, she changed tack suddenly.

'Look, Robert,' she said, using his Christian name for the first time. 'We can spend all day doing this, asking the same questions, going round and round in circles, but who wants that? I know *I've* got better things to be doing.'

Robert briefly raised his eyes to hers – checking to see if she was taunting him – then lowered them again.

'So why don't we get down to the nitty-gritty? You are going to prison for a long time. Let's forget for a moment the three vile murders you committed earlier this year. We'll put them to one side and concentrate on the last few days. And I'm not going to bother with your rich history of identity theft, financial fraud and your ghoulish habit of looting dead pensioners' accounts. Let's focus instead on . . . resisting arrest, assaulting a police officer and, my personal favourite, attempted murder. I have a hunch here – and correct me if I'm wrong – but I have a hunch that a jury will take a dim view of a sadistic fuck like you trying to plunge a knife into the heart of a serving police officer. A police officer with an exemplary record of service. A police officer who has a partner and a little girl. How do you think that will play, Robert?'

She let the question hang in the air. Stonehill was staring intently at his fingernails, refusing to engage, but Charlie knew she had his attention now.

'Put all that together and I'd say we're looking at . . . twenty years? And for what? For running away. For running away like a coward and trying to stab a police officer. Not very impressive, is it?'

Stonehill said nothing, but he appeared more focused than before, as if the reality of the situation was at last sinking in.

'Is that how you want to be remembered? Is that how you want history to judge you? Let me tell you now, Helen is going to walk. Your arrest creates more than enough doubt, raises more than enough questions, for a jury to exonerate a decorated police officer. So where does that leave you? A petty criminal behind bars, a minor footnote in Helen's story. Unless . . .' Charlie let the word roll on her tongue. '. . . you take ownership of what you've done. Your crimes were brilliant. Though I hate to admit it, they exhibited a kind of . . . genius. *You* did all that. Not Helen. Now maybe you're happy to keep quiet about that, let events control you. You can watch Helen walk, bide your time in prison, hoping for another chance at life, when you're what? Fifty? Or maybe you want to take the lead. To tell the world what you've done. Go down in history.'

Charlie now looked directly at Stonehill and on cue he raised his eyes to meet hers.

'After all, nobody will forget your mother's name. So why should they forget yours?'

129

Gardam's eyes were glued to the exchange. He'd made great play of wanting to be involved and had insisted on watching the questioning through the two-way mirror. But in reality he just wanted to find out what Stonehill was going to say.

Initially he'd been encouraged by Stonehill's silence, by his refusal to react to Brooks. The latter had always been suspicious of Gardam's motives during this investigation and he had never liked her, had wanted rid of her months ago, and now every part of him wanted her to fail.

Except now Stonehill seemed to be talking. He wasn't confessing to anything *yet*, but he did seem to be engaging with Brooks. He seemed keen to find out how things would be framed if he did provide some important information. He clearly had a high opinion of himself and wanted to be sure that he would be presented in the right light. Experienced officer that she was, Brooks was playing it perfectly, pretending to sympathize with his concerns, as she slowly drew information from him.

And now Gardam could only watch on as his career unravelled before his eyes. He had never truly believed that Helen might be released. The case against her had seemed so compelling, despite a few anomalies. But if Robert confessed, if he told Brooks how he'd done it, then her release would be instantaneous. Which would have some profound consequences for him. Helen *had* told him about her connections to the victims. And he had lied to the investigating officers who'd questioned him about this. He'd done more than just lie – he had hung Helen Grace out to dry.

'You have to hand it to Brooks, she knows what she's doing.'

The Chief Constable had also insisted on being present. Gardam turned to Alan Peters now, trying his best to look pleased.

'She's an experienced officer, she knows how to get the testimony she wants,' he replied carefully.

'Amazing, isn't it?' Peters continued, keeping his eyes fixed on Stonehill, who appeared to be in full flow now. 'Amazing how he managed to fool so many people . . .'

'Garanita helped him. Unwittingly, of course, but she'd always had it in for DI Grace . . .'

Peters said nothing, nodding slowly to himself, as if another thought was taking hold.

'Is there anything *you'd* like to tell me, Jonathan?' he replied, turning to face Gardam directly.

Gardam held his gaze, but could feel sweat beginning to pool in his armpits and the small of his back.

'Because if you have,' Peters continued, 'now would be a very good time to do so.'

130

The doors swung open to reveal a scene from Hell. Chairs, benches, even kitchen utensils were now flying through the air, as the inmates engaged riot police in a pitched battle. Odds on the prisoners had by now forgotten what they'd been anxious about in the first place. Years of pent-up anger, frustration and despair were being released and it was a terrifying sight to behold.

Benjamin Proud stood on the threshold, his hand clamped over his mouth and nose. The air was thick with teargas. This made it hard for Proud to see, but even harder for him to breathe, the bitter, pungent vapours crawling up his nostrils. Each breath increased his agony – it felt as if someone were holding a naked flame to his larynx – and for a moment he considered retreating. He had the safety of his staff to consider and, besides, what use could he be here, when his head was spinning and his eyes streaming with tears? But even as the thought presented itself, he dismissed it. The chaos was all-consuming in B-Wing – if ever a prisoner was going to attempt an escape, now was the time.

As soon as he'd left the mortuary, he'd gone to the Governor's office. Bassett was nowhere to be found of course, but her loyal PA had opened up their systems. There were only a handful of elderly prisoners – the so-called Golden Girls – and only one whose charge sheet specifically mentioned adrenaline. Proud had silently cursed Dr Khan – he had missed the injection marks on Leah Smith and it was only thanks to Helen Grace's endeavours that they had realized the importance of the high adrenaline readings. Still, it was pretty much an open-and-shut case now – so long as they could find Sarrington.

But where to look? The whole wing was in tumult, inmates on all levels battling those who sought to contain them. The situation looked hopeless, with no sign of an end in sight, but Proud had no choice. Swallowing down his agony and clamping his jacket over his mouth and nose, he moved forward. Amid the chaos and bloodshed playing out in front of him, he was hoping to find a killer.

131

Helen emerged on to the landing and slammed the door shut behind her. She had decided against leaving the evidence behind – there was every chance that Babs might return to dispose of it – so picking them up carefully, Helen had pocketed the syringe and vial.

What now? It would be hard to hunt down Babs in this chaos. And there was no chance of getting a prison officer's attention right now – every man and woman was now involved in trying to contain the prisoners' mutiny. Her only option was the Governor's office. Maybe Celia Bassett was still in charge, maybe she wasn't. Whatever the situation, Helen would make someone listen to her. Three lives had been lost and it was imperative that Babs be apprehended as quickly as possible. At the very least, Helen hoped to get a call out – to Charlie, to the Met – alerting them to the very real danger that the prison's inmates were now in.

Darting left she hurried along the walkway. Two inmates had decided that now was a good time to settle old scores and were engaged in a vicious fight. They were swinging backwards and forwards, clamped on to one another, blocking Helen's way. But taking advantage of a sudden lurch towards the balcony, she sidestepped them and carried on her way.

The scene before her was insane – it was as if everyone in the place had suddenly succumbed to a crazed blood-lust. There was a mass brawl ahead, blocking the corner junction of the walkway, but still she kept moving. Climbing over the metal railing, she stood on the ledge and without hesitating leapt across the void towards the railing on the other side. For a moment she felt sure she wasn't going to make it – she could see herself plunging down on to the suicide net below – but at the last second she managed to grasp the rail with two fingers. Pulling herself up, she vaulted the railing and carried on her way.

She was soon at the access doors and hurried through them, hoping against hope that C-Wing might be a bit quieter. But, as she did so, she suddenly felt her legs give way beneath her. And as she tumbled to the ground, she realized that she had been hit by something. Her wrists hit the floor hard and she scrambled ahead, but now she felt another heavy blow to her kidneys and she pitched forward, smashing her head on the floor.

Now she felt herself being hauled back into B-Wing. Someone was pulling her by her hair, dragging her along the floor. She flailed her arms wildly to slow her progress and succeeded in grabbing hold of the railings, but her fist was instantly stamped upon by a large black boot. Campbell's ugly face now came into view, moving close to hers. He was sweating hard and there was fire in his eyes.

'Oh no, you don't . . .'

With savage glee, he kicked her hand away and continued to haul her along the walkway.

'Please,' Helen begged, but she was breathless and her voice was weak.

Campbell kept moving and Helen now found herself in familiar surroundings. He had dragged her back into her cell. Releasing her hair, he now picked her up and tossed her on to the bed.

'Please,' Helen repeated, more loudly this time. 'I need to speak to the Governor.'

But a savage baton blow to her stomach was Campbell's only response. Helen doubled up in agony, as vomit crept up her windpipe.

'What you *need* to do is stay in your cell, like a good little prisoner. I will not let you – or anyone else – tear this place apart.'

And now the cuffs were out. Helen tried to speak, but she could only gag and was powerless to resist as Campbell cuffed one hand, then the other, while securing them to the head of the bed. She was now chained to the bedstead and utterly at his mercy.

But Campbell was already retreating. He was a sadist and a bully, but he knew his duty. He would not be found wanting in a crisis and would return as many prisoners to their cells as possible.

Finding her voice, Helen cried out to him once more, but Campbell was gone. She watched in despair as he disappeared from view, leaving her alone.

132

Charlie sped through the streets, bullying the cars out of her way. She was unfamiliar with London, so even with the blues and twos on she kept finding herself blocked by the rush hour traffic. Motorists in the capital moved over begrudgingly, as if an unfolding emergency was merely an irritating inconvenience. Add to that the danger posed by cyclists and couriers who flashed by without warning and you had a particularly challenging driving environment. Charlie was glad this was going to be a one-off.

She had questioned Stonehill for another hour, before deciding to call time on it. The excitement of the morning had dissipated and Stonehill was exhausted, stumbling over the details of his past crimes. Charlie was happy, however, that he had given them *enough* – he had confessed to the murders and added sufficient detail to exonerate Helen Grace.

She should have been cheered by this news. It had been a long and arduous journey to this point, but still she felt no satisfaction. She had been trying to get hold of the authorities at Holloway all day, but had hit a brick wall. They were in the midst of a full-scale riot, so an element of distraction was forgivable, but their continued silence made Charlie uneasy. Helen was alone in that prison, without a protector and with few friends, while a serial killer was at large.

Charlie knew instinctively that Helen wouldn't sit idle while innocent women were being murdered, which would inevitably put her own life in danger. Now something told Charlie she needed to get to Holloway fast.

Suddenly there was a break in the traffic and Charlie stamped on the accelerator. The car leapt forward and she shot into the gap, but no sooner had she done so than a lorry pulled out abruptly right in front of her. Charlie slammed on the brakes, the car skidding to a halt less than half a yard from the lorry's side. The startled foreign driver looked terrified, raising his hands in abject apology, but Charlie was already reversing.

'Move back. Move back,' she shouted at the cars behind that were boxing her in.

They started to move, but all too slowly and suddenly Charlie felt tearful – fear, tension and sheer exhaustion finally getting the better of her. She had a terrible foreboding that something dreadful was about to happen, a final twist in the tale. She had come so far. She had helped prove Helen's innocence. Surely she wouldn't be robbed of her victory at the eleventh hour?

133

It was time to retreat. They had fought a good fight, dodging chairs, ducking batons and facing down a number of enraged inmates, but still there was no sign of Sarrington. One of Proud's colleagues had received a nasty blow to the jaw – she looked to be in serious pain and he suspected a fracture. There was no way he could continue to put them at risk in such an unpredictable and violent arena.

'Pull back,' Proud shouted to his team and immediately they obeyed, only too happy to depart.

Still Proud lingered, however, loath to give up on his prize, and as he scanned the melee one last time, he spotted her. Through the dispersing teargas haze, he could just make out Sarrington at the far end of the hall, creeping towards the kitchen. From there she might access the association yard and after that who knows?

Proud now abandoned his team and sprinted across the canteen. It was in the lap of the gods whether he would make it in time – at any moment he could be smashed sideways by a sudden lurch in the pitched battle – but he kept his head down and made good progress, dodging and weaving through the throng. Sarrington was approaching the door to the kitchen now and it was very possible he would lose her in its cavernous interior, especially if she realized that he was after her. So he urged himself forward, stumbling slightly as he hurdled a broken chair, but staying on his feet.

Now he was only a few feet from her and with a final burst of speed, he fell on her. He spun her round, cuffs at the ready, relieved beyond measure to have intercepted her in time.

But the 'killer' he'd apprehended was not Sarrington at all. Similar height, with a shock of white hair, but it was just one of the Golden Girls and a pretty startled one at that. Already Proud was apologizing and backing off – the terrified pensioner was clearly just seeking sanctuary in the kitchen.

He turned to peer round the canteen once more, but there was no sign of his prize. He had failed and the real killer was still at large.

134

A sound made Helen look up and instantly her blood ran cold. Babs hung in the doorway, breathless but calm. Helen screamed, long and loud, but Babs appeared unconcerned, stepping into the cell and pulling the door firmly shut behind her.

'We shouldn't be disturbed now,' she said, as she approached the foot of the bed.

Again, Helen shrieked – a long, desperate cry that bounced off the brick walls, then faded to nothing. Babs regarded her with something close to amusement.

'Shall we give that a rest? I was hoping we might talk.'

'I've got nothing to say to you,' Helen spat back.

'Oh I think you do.' She sat herself at the far end of the bed. 'After all, you've been a busy girl.'

Helen kicked out at her, but her blows fell agonizingly short. Campbell's handcuffs still tethered her to the bed, severely limiting her range of movement. She tugged at them viciously now, desperately trying to free herself from her restraints, but to no avail. All the while, Babs sat impassively on the bed, coolly staring at her captive.

'So are you going to tell me what you know? You were in my cell for a long time and I'm guessing you weren't there for a nap.'

'I was just trying to find somewhere to hi—'

But Helen didn't finish her sentence – Babs suddenly lunged forward and drove her elbow hard into Helen's ribs.

It took Helen completely by surprise and she howled in agony. She had no strength to resist now, as Babs thrust her hand into Helen's jacket pockets. After a brief search, Babs withdrew the syringe and the vial of adrenaline, a look of triumph on her face.

'Have you told anyone about this?'

'Campbell,' Helen wheezed back, lying.

'I don't think so. He wouldn't have believed you and he wasn't in here long enough. Noelle's been a bit busy, as have I. As for Jordi –'

'How could you?' Helen interrupted, finding her voice once more. 'She was your friend –'

'She was a soul in torment, as was Leah. And Lucy. That's the thing about lifers. At first you think there's hope, but when you realize there isn't . . .'

'You murdered her.'

'I *released* her. Back to her family. Family's important, don't you think, Helen?'

'Like you'd know,' Helen said bitterly.

'Your sister certainly thought so and I'd agree with her. Jordi is back with her girls for Christmas and now they can be with her whenever they want. No walls keeping them out, no arbitrary visiting hours, they're *together*. That's all Jordi really wanted.'

'And what gives you the right to play God? To decide if someone lives or dies?'

'Don't you dare judge me,' Babs snarled. 'You're just a tourist. You have no idea what it's like to rot in here, month on month, year on year . . .'

It was said with such vehemence that Helen said nothing in response.

'Your life stretches out in front of you, long and bleak.

Every part of you wants to be elsewhere, but that is your punishment, that is how they *torture* you. You die a little bit every day, becoming a little less hopeful, a little less human, until all you're left with is despair. Sometimes you feel the entire world hates you. But not as much as you *hate yourself.* Leah would have killed herself in time, Jordi and Lucy too –'

'You don't know that –'

'Yes I do,' Babs replied with certainty. 'Lifers are the walking dead. But I saved them from that. And they weren't *alone* when they died. I comforted them, stroked their hair. I think I even sung Jordi a lullaby.'

'Go to Hell.'

'I'm already there, honey, haven't you realized that yet?'

Babs stared at Helen unflinchingly. She seemed utterly unrepentant and now Helen realized just how far gone she was. What the years of incarceration had done to her.

'How many of these have you done?' Helen said suddenly, a horrible thought forming in her mind.

'What do you mean?'

'You say you don't want to hurt these women, that you want to help them. And yet you mutilate them –'

'I wouldn't call it that –'

'You were trying . . . to protect them, weren't you? From this place . . .'

'Perhaps.'

'You're not the type who wants to get caught. You're on a mission. So why advertise your actions with these mutilations? If you just injected them, you might get away with natural causes . . .'

Babs now broke into a smile, genuinely impressed by Helen's insight.

'Which makes me wonder,' Helen continued, 'if you were refining your technique.'

'Once a copper, always a copper,' Babs replied.

'Answer the quest—'

'You know about my work in the hospitals already. I promised to be good while I was here, but it's my calling, I suppose. When you see someone in terrible pain and you have the power to do something about it . . .'

Helen stared at her. She seemed so convinced of the wisdom of her actions. She seemed totally sure that she had done the *right* thing.

'There were two other girls – Suselie Myers and Deborah Jones. Suselie worked out fine, but Deborah was under twenty-four-hour lock-up, with no one checking on her. I don't know how long she lay in her cell unattended. But when they did finally go in . . . well, it wasn't a pretty sight. The vermin in this place are starving too.'

Helen closed her eyes, horrified by the thought.

'Bluebottles laying their filthy eggs in her waxy ears, cockroaches scuttling all over her, but that wasn't the worst of it. They say that the rats had had both her eyes.' Babs paused for a moment. 'I couldn't let that happen to my girls. They were my *friends*.'

'Keep telling yourself that. You don't have a single real friend in this place. Nor anyone waiting for you outside –'

'Jeannie will come round. In time.'

'Have you read her letters?' Helen asked incredulously.

'I don't need to.'

'You should. Everybody needs to look in the mirror once in a while.'

Babs considered her. Helen thought she saw a flash of anger in her eyes, before she replied:

'I'm not sure you're in any position to be handing out advice.'

It was said calmly, but underlined the desperation of Helen's situation. She yanked hard at her cuffs once more, absorbing the pain as they bit into her wrists, but still the bedstead held firm.

'Don't exhaust yourself, Helen. There's no point.'

'It's over, Barbara.'

'It's not over until I say it is.'

Babs pulled the vial of adrenaline from the plastic bag.

'Don't you ever ask yourself why that is? Why you keep doing this?'

'I've told you why –'

'You're not helping people. You're not on a mercy mission. You do it because you *like* it.'

'That's not true.'

'Don't kid yourself. You may think you're still wearing your nurse's uniform. But you're not. You're a common killer, pure and simple. That's how people will judge you.'

'I don't think so –'

'Look me in the eye and tell me you don't enjoy it.'

For the first time, Babs seemed to hesitate.

'Go on,' Helen insisted. 'Look me in the –'

'Ok, you've made your point, Helen,' Babs said testily.

'What you're doing is wrong. Deep down, you must know that. And it's not too late to stop.'

'Oh I think we're well past that . . .'

As she said this, Babs slipped the syringe into the vial. Helen watched in horror as she started to draw up the clear liquid.

'Though I'll admit there might be a grain of truth in what you're saying,' she continued, withdrawing the syringe and firing a few drops of liquid into the air. 'But then you've been there too, haven't you? You've taken a life. Several in fact.'

'Not like this. This is cold-blooded murder –'

'Call it what you will. I do it because it's the right thing to do, but I do take *some* satisfaction from it.'

Babs rose and moved towards Helen.

Helen was struggling for all she was worth now, but was getting nowhere. Babs was in complete control and smiled as she crouched down to Helen's level. She moved in close, her lips brushing Helen's ear as she concluded:

'After all, there's nothing more intimate than being with someone at the moment of their death.'

135

'Let me in!'

Charlie had tried being reasonable, she had tried begging, but now she resorted to shouting.

'Believe me, you don't want to go in there,' the G4S guard retorted. 'Much safer out here, love.'

'As I've already explained to you, I am a Detective Sergeant with Hampshire Police –'

'I don't care if you're the bloody Commissioner. There is a major incident going on in there and until the situation is resolved I can't admit anyone.'

'I can take care of myself.'

'I'm sure you can. But I need this job and I'm not getting fired for you or anybody else. So I suggest you get back in your car –'

Charlie turned away from him, eyes seeking left and right for some other means of entry. But the perimeter fences were high and strong and she had already tried the back entrance. It was surrounded by armoured vehicles and riot police, meaning the main entrance was the only way in or out. But the barrier was down and her adversary seemed intent on barring her entrance.

'Please,' she said, adopting a softer tone. 'I think my friend's life is in danger. So, please, one law enforcement officer to another, can't you cut me some slack here?'

'Not for all the tea in China. Now get on your way before I rep—'

Charlie was already walking away. Wrenching open the car door, she climbed inside and started the engine. Slipping the gears into reverse, she drove backwards at high speed, her mind spinning all the while. There had to be another way in. There had to be another way . . .

Gradually she slowed to a stop. She thought of Helen. She looked at what lay in front of her. Then she made a decision.

Slamming the accelerator down as hard as she could, she muttered a silent prayer and sped towards the barrier.

136

Helen wrenched her body up off the bed, kicking out viciously at her attacker. But Babs straightened quickly, avoiding the intended blows. Then she moved around the head of the bed, so that she was standing directly behind Helen.

'Now then, the best thing is for you to remain calm,' Babs said soothingly.

But Helen was already twisting round, determined not to be blindsided. The metal cuffs dug deep into her skin as she manoeuvred herself, but she ignored the pain, swinging her legs off the bed. They made contact with the floor and now she pushed off, trying to pivot round the head of the bed and unleash another kick at her enemy.

But before she'd got halfway round, she felt Babs's foot connecting sharply with her left knee, stopping her dead. She roared in pain, and as she did so, she felt Babs grab her roughly by the hair. Now Babs was pinning her head down hard on the bed, exposing her neck. Helen knew what was coming and scrabbled to get some purchase on the floor, but her left leg wouldn't move and her right foot slithered hopelessly over the smooth concrete floor.

'Normally I go for the armpit, but a change is as good as a rest . . .'

Helen's whole body jolted as the needle punctured her skin. She grunted in pain and tried once again to move, but her body wouldn't obey her. And now she felt pressure as

Babs pushed down on the stopper, pumping the adrenaline into her system.

'Goodbye, Helen.'

Helen tried to scream at her, but she choked on the words, fear robbing her of the power to speak.

'There is nothing to be scared of. It will be quick and I will be by your side the whole time. In spite of everything, I've actually grown rather fond of you.'

Helen grunted once more, a long string of saliva falling from her mouth. She tried again to get some purchase on the ground with her one good leg, but her body seemed to be fighting her. Already her heart was beating out a furious rhythm. Her head was aching, her vision becoming blurred and a terrible pain was building in the centre of her chest.

'Hush now, Helen, don't you cry. Mama's going to sing you a lullaby . . .'

She could feel Babs stroking her hair as she sang and she shook her head angrily to dislodge her. Immediately she regretted it, a wave of nausea sweeping over her. For a moment, she thought she was going to faint, but the agonizing pain taking hold inside her brought her to her senses again.

'And if that lullaby don't work . . .'

Helen could feel moisture running off her cheeks and wondered if she was crying.

'. . . Mama's going to buy you a mocking bi—'

And now from nowhere, Helen felt her foot find a rut on the hard floor and acting on instinct she thrust upwards with all her force. The cuffs bit once more, dragging her backwards, but not before the top of her head had connected sharply with Babs's chin. There was a nasty crunch, then Helen felt herself falling back on to the bed. She was barely conscious now and had no idea what had happened to her attacker, but at least her macabre singing had stopped.

The pressure on her chest was unrelenting, it felt like she had a ten-ton weight sitting on it, but she knew she had to turn. Had to find out what had happened to her adversary. But as she did so her heart finally gave out and she crumpled face downwards on to the bed.

A second later, everything went black.

137

Charlie sprinted along the gantry, searching for Helen. But B-Wing was a war zone and there was no one who could help her. Dozens of inmates were staging a last desperate stand in the canteen, penned into a corner now by a phalanx of riot police who showed no restraint as they attempted to batter the rioters into submission. The walkways above were littered with injured prisoners and officers – some shackled to the railings, others curled into a ball, all of them desperate to avoid more punishment.

Charlie hurdled these prone forms, her eyes darting desperately this way and that. She knew Helen was housed in B-Wing but had no idea of her cell number nor even what level she was on. Even if she had known, she wondered how easy it would have been to orientate herself through the fug of teargas that hung in the air.

Movement close by made Charlie turn. A prisoner was crawling along the gantry on her hands and knees. Charlie hurried towards her, helping her up off the ground.

'Can you tell me which one is Helen Grace's –'

But the sentence died on her lips. The prisoner's eyes were dull and there was a bloody mess where her mouth ought to have been. If she had ever had any teeth, she certainly didn't now.

'I'll get help for you. I'll get help . . .' Charlie said, laying her back down and hurrying on.

Thirty yards ahead she could see a prison officer, crouched down by the rail, clutching his arm. He was an intimidating figure, tall, muscular, but he looked beaten today. His arm was badly broken and he cradled it carefully, wincing as he did so.

'Can you tell me where Helen Grace's cell is?'

'Why do you want to know?' the moustached officer snapped back, his Glaswegian accent punching through his pain.

'Because I do,' Charlie replied, holding up her warrant card.

The officer looked at it, at her, then seemed to crumble.

'B32,' he muttered before collapsing back on to the ground.

Charlie was away in a flash, counting down the numbers as she sprinted past the open cell doorways. B36, B35, B34, B33 . . .

Wrenching open the door, she ran inside. She wasn't quite sure what she was expecting, but the sight that greeted her stopped her dead in her tracks. In the far corner an elderly inmate was lying on the floor moaning, while closer by Helen lay face down on the narrow bed.

Charlie hurried to her, turning her gently over on to her back. To her horror, Helen's face was waxy and grey. Her eyes stared straight up and she seemed totally unaware of Charlie's presence.

'Helen, it's me.'

Helen didn't respond. Her body felt like a dead weight in Charlie's arms.

'Please, Helen. Say something.'

Still nothing. And now Charlie noticed the syringe lying on the bed close by. What the hell was going on?

She slapped Helen gently, then harder, but her old friend refused to respond. So slipping her hand under her neck, Charlie pressed down on the carotid artery, searching desperately for a pulse. But there was none.

She was too late.

138

Dying is strange. You think it's going to be painful. Or sudden. Or both. Helen had never anticipated that it might feel . . . nice. She had left her body far behind her now and was somewhere strange, but not unpleasant. It wasn't Heaven, nor was it Hell, which cheered her, as Marianne was standing beside her. She'd always said that her sister had goodness within her and this seemed to prove it.

Marianne took Helen's hand and smiled at her. Helen realized how long it had been since she'd seen her sister smile. In life, Marianne had rejected her, but here they were together again and it felt totally right. Their lives had been shorter than most and marred by terrible suffering, but the one constant over the years had been the strength of their love for each other.

They had been peas in a pod when they were young and later, after life soured things, their bond had still been a powerful one, Marianne's sense of betrayal fostering a fierce, passionate hatred for her younger sister. This had cost Marianne her life, and Helen her soul, but perhaps in the end it was just one stage of their story. For here they were again, united in love. Maybe this had always been the promised end.

Helen wanted to say something, but wasn't sure where to start. She opened her mouth, but couldn't shape the words. She wanted to say she was sorry, that she loved her Marianne, but all that came out was a groan. A long agonized groan. She tried again, but suddenly her whole world seemed to shake, the fabric of her surroundings becoming unstable and blurred. She could hear distant voices now, though their words were indecipherable. She turned to Marianne to ask if she could understand what they were saying and was surprised to see that Marianne wasn't smiling any more.

'Clear.'

Helen's world lurched again. Now Marianne seemed to be shouting at her, but agonizingly all she produced was a mocking silence. She seemed angry now, even hurt. Helen tried to reach out to her, but Marianne's face was no longer clear, and she wasn't even sure she was the same person.

More noises intruded on her consciousness now. A kind of shrieking, and the steady mechanical pulse of a machine.

'Clear.'

The shock ran right through her and this time Helen's eyes shot open. She gasped for breath as her eyes swivelled in their sockets. She had no idea where she was or what was happening. She was confused, breathless and very scared.

'We've got a pulse.'

Helen closed her eyes and tried to breathe. She felt like she was going to be sick, like she was spinning round and round. Nothing seemed real. But even now images started to punch back into her consciousness. Babs, Campbell, the bed in her cell . . .

And now finally Helen opened her eyes, realizing to her surprise that she was alive. And as she did so, it was not Marianne's face that she saw looking down at her.

It was Charlie's.

139

Sunlight streamed in through the window, illuminating the large room. Jonathan Gardam had long coveted the Chief Constable's job, not least because of the spacious office that came with the position. He had worked hard to curry favour with his superior, hoping that he might eventually nominate him as his successor. But that seemed like a bad joke now.

A week had passed since Robert Stonehill's capture and he had been busy. He'd given the police everything they needed to be confident of convicting him for the murders of Jake Elder, Maxwell Carter and Amy Fawcett. He had been officially charged with triple murder two days ago and less than twenty-four hours later all charges against Helen Grace had been dropped.

It gave Gardam no satisfaction that Helen had suffered in the interim. Despite everything, he still had feelings for her and was pleased that she was making a good recovery. However, her release from prison brought with it certain complications, which is why he'd spent the last two days being interviewed by the Anti-Corruption unit. They had just delivered their findings and Gardam had been swiftly summoned to the Chief Constable's office as a result.

'Do you have anything to add?' Alan Peters said tersely.

They had already been through the contents of the report, which didn't make for pleasant reading.

'No, sir. I have already given my testimony and my lawyers –'

'In which case, let *me* say something,' Peters replied calmly. 'You have been asked on a number of occasions to explain your actions. Both in relation to DI Grace and more recently to DS Brooks. And at every turn, you have failed to respond in a manner befitting your position. You have ducked questions, refused to give credible explanations and, in my opinion, you have lied. I'm not sure why, that's between you and your conscience, but I have no doubt that you deliberately tried to destroy the careers of two of your fellow officers.'

'As I've said before, I completely refute those allegations. However, it's clear that you and I are never going to see eye to eye on this, so I've brought with me a letter of resignation.'

Gardam reached into his jacket, but Peters beat him to the punch.

'Resignation not accepted.'

Gardam stared at him.

'I know that's often the way of things. Least said, soonest mended and all that. But resignation is too good for you.'

'You can't be serious –'

'I called you here today, Jonathan, to let you know that your employment has been terminated. HR will be in touch, but I fully expect you to lose your pension and your benefits. Though of course I never said that.'

Gardam stared at him – this was far worse than he had envisaged.

'You have twenty minutes to clear your desk, after which time you will be escorted from the building.'

Shaken, Gardam stared at his boss. He wanted to spit something back at him, but couldn't find the words.

'We'll be wanting to talk to you again of course. Maybe as early as next week. We're looking at perverting the course of justice, misconduct in public office, behaviour unbecoming and a few more besides. So don't leave town, eh?'

It was said with a smile, but Gardam could feel the anger that simmered beneath. There was nothing more to say, so turning he walked calmly out of the office and away down the corridor. All the while, he could feel the eyes of Peters' assistants upon him, savouring his misfortune.

Like him, they knew that his disgrace was now complete.

140

They threw themselves at the moving vehicle, desperate for a glimpse of the condemned man. Pressing their camera lenses to the small windows, the journalists shrieked questions, jockeying for position with the local thugs who were simply there to hurl abuse and beat the sides of the van.

The noise inside the vehicle was deafening, but Robert Stonehill kept his head down. He had been the centre of wild media interest ever since his arrest – he'd even had a request from Emilia Garanita for an interview – but he wasn't going to give those vultures anything. Certainly not a picture of him looking broken and cowed in the back of a police van. They would see him in court later today, but even then he would offer them only defiance, as he was formally charged with triple murder.

Once he'd made the decision to confess to Brooks, Robert hadn't held back, explaining in minute detail how he'd killed, then how he'd set Helen up. Typically, this damning testimony had been promptly leaked to the press and he was now the tabloids' favourite bogeyman once more, the serial killer's spawn finally reverting to type. The first time these hacks had smashed into his life, he'd been shaken to the core. Now a little older and a little wiser, he accepted the attention as his due. Better to be a somebody than a nobody.

The sound of the banging was getting louder, the insults becoming ever more graphic. Looking up briefly, Robert caught Rawlings smiling to himself, amused by the chaotic scenes outside. Many of the people Robert had come into contact with this past week shared Rawlings's views, the prison officer having made it abundantly clear that he thought Robert degenerate, evil, beyond redemption. He'd taken every opportunity to make Robert's life uncomfortable, denying him toilet rolls, soiling his food, demeaning him in every small, spiteful way he could think of. This was payback – revenge for Robert's attempt to frame a highly decorated police officer.

Rawlings caught his eye and his smile widened still further. Robert turned away, dropping his eyes to the floor, provoking a throaty chuckle from the prison officer. Perhaps Rawlings thought that despair was finally setting in, that the events of the last week were now taking their toll. But the truth was very different. In fact, Robert was staring at his socks.

Rawlings expected him to buckle, gleefully elaborating on the sort of treatment he could expect from his fellow inmates at HMP Winchester, but Robert would never give in. His mother had fought tooth and nail her whole life, refusing to be beaten by *anyone*. He would do the same, which is why his eye now strayed to the ballpoint pen secreted in his sock. He had stolen it during his interrogation, stowing it away for future use. It wasn't much of a weapon but it could take an eye out.

Raising his head, Robert caught the prison officer's gaze once more, but this time he refused to look away. As soon as the cuffs were off, he would strike, paying Rawlings back for every petty insult. Robert was going to spend the rest of his life behind bars, so what did he care for the consequences? He had lost his war with Helen, lost his liberty, but he had not lost his bite.

This was one prisoner who was not prepared to go quietly.

141

It was a pitiful array of possessions. A mobile phone, now starved of power and credit, a few coins and a half-empty packet of Marlboro Gold. But to Helen they seemed like a treasure trove. It was a long time since she'd been able to smoke a cigarette without begging or bartering for it and even longer since she'd held a mobile phone in her hand. They weren't worth much, but they were hers and no one could take them away from her. Which is why they felt priceless.

Slipping them into her pocket, Helen signed the docket.

'Good luck, ma'am.'

Helen looked up to see the custody officer smiling at her and suddenly felt choked with emotion. It had been a strange week and she was still coming to terms with the change in her fortunes. She had nearly died in this place, but now she was being released and in the pleasant face of the beaming custody officer she recognized something she hadn't seen in a long time. Respect.

Thanking him, Helen departed quickly. The riots had only lasted a day and the situation was now calm. Celia Bassett had resigned and a new governor was in place, as the clock ticked down on the old prison. But now that the charges against her had been dropped, Helen just wanted to be away. She had spent more than enough time behind bars.

Charlie was waiting for her in the courtyard outside and immediately hurried over. Helen had made a good recovery following her cardiac arrest, but was still walking with a stick and needed to take it easy for a while. Charlie had been fussing over her all week and Helen didn't blame her – both knew that it was only because of the skilled work of the paramedics that she was still alive. Nevertheless, she had rejected Charlie's suggestion that she be ferried to the awaiting car in a wheelchair. Helen was determined to walk out of Holloway with her head held high.

Charlie was keen to get her to the car, as a bitter wind was ripping through the prison this morning. But Helen paused as she crossed the courtyard. In her mind's eye she could see Leah and Jordi's coffins once more. Lucy too had left this yard in a box, returned to her devastated father. There were three families out there, recipients of the bitterest possible Christmas presents, who were struggling to cope with their loss. Helen grieved for Leah, Jordi and Lucy, but also for the families too, who had a long road ahead of them. Holloway had played host to many dark deeds over the years, but the old prison had saved its darkest chapter until the very end.

Pulling her coat up around her, Helen turned away from the prison buildings and limped towards the exit. It had been a terrible few months, but at long last justice had been served. Babs was in Segregation, and Robert Stonehill was behind bars. The latter pained her, but it was where he belonged and Helen felt no sympathy for him, just a deep sadness that it should have ended this way.

Charlie had pressed Helen to stay at her house during her recuperation, but she was anxious to get back to her flat. She needed to be alone for a while, to gather her thoughts and regroup. More than anything, she wanted to sleep in her own bed, surrounded by her own things. Her journey forward would not be easy, she knew that, but she was eager to make a start, determined to reclaim her old life.

She would do that best in her own space and, besides, her Kawasaki still idled, unloved and unused, in the basement car park. Helen knew that when the time was right – no doubt way before the doctors allowed it – she would sneak down there and reacquaint herself with her old friend. She knew she should take extended leave, perhaps even consider a career change after everything she'd been through, but she knew there was little chance of that. You are who you are.

And Helen was burning to get back in the saddle.

142

She watched the car until it was no more than a speck on the horizon. Then slowly Babs lowered herself to the floor. The Segregation unit was not a pleasant place to be, but it provided an excellent view of Holloway's main courtyard and she'd been keen to see Helen's departure. It was always moving to watch an inmate go home.

Crossing to the bed, Babs lay down and closed her eyes. She was exhausted and wanted to sleep, if only to block out her filthy surroundings for a few hours. She had been told she would be held in the Seg until her trial, as she was too much of a safety risk to be housed elsewhere. So here she would remain, fighting off boredom by day and the vermin by night.

Many of the inmates had promised that she would never make it to trial, that they would find a way to deal with her first, in revenge for what she'd done to those 'poor girls'. But she rather doubted it. They were all too afraid of her to follow up on their threats. Her reputation would keep her alive – for the time being at least.

Her days now stretched out in front of her, long and lonely, but she would find ways to survive. Christmas was just days away – she could hear the prison choir practising for their annual concert – and that reminded her of the importance of hope. Better things were always just round the corner. Christmas Day would bring a turkey dinner, extra TV allowance and perhaps even a card from Jeannie.

If the latter did arrive, she didn't expect the sentiments to be friendly, given recent events, but she hoped that her daughter would eventually come to understand her calling. She had only ever wanted to help. People would come to see that in time – they would realize that her intentions had always been good. Was it too much to hope that one day she might even be in a position to help people *again*? She dearly hoped so and knew that she would be rewarded for it.

After all, there is always a place in Heaven for a Good Samaritan.

DI HELEN GRACE
WILL RETURN IN . . .

FOLLOW
MY
LEADER

MARCH 2017

THE FIRST DI HELEN GRACE THRILLER

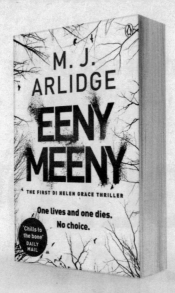

The girl emerged from the woods, barely alive. Her story was beyond belief. But it was true. Every dreadful word of it.

Days later, another desperate escapee is found – and a pattern is emerging. Pairs of victims are being abducted, imprisoned then faced with a terrible choice: kill or be killed.

Would you rather lose your life or lose your mind?

Detective Inspector Helen Grace has faced down her own demons on her rise to the top. As she leads the investigation to hunt down this unseen monster, she learns that it may be the survivors – living calling cards - who hold the key to the case.

And unless she succeeds, more innocents will die . . .

**'Helen Grace is one of the greatest heroes to come along in years'
JEFFERY DEAVER**

Available now from Penguin in paperback and ebook

THE SECOND DI HELEN GRACE THRILLER

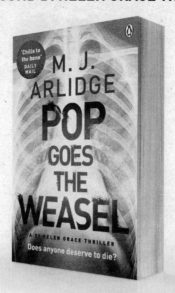

A man's body is found in an empty house. His heart has been cut out and delivered to his wife and children.

He is the first victim, and Detective Inspector Helen Grace knows he will not be the last. But why would a happily married man be this far from home in the dead of night?

The media call it Jack the Ripper in reverse: a serial killer preying on family men who lead hidden double lives.

Helen can sense the fury behind the murders. But what she cannot possibly predict is how volatile this killer is – or what is waiting for her at the end of the chase . . .

'Taut, fast-paced, truly excellent'
SUN

Available now from Penguin in paperback and ebook

THE THIRD DI HELEN GRACE THRILLER

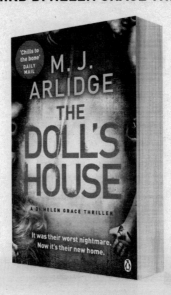

A young woman wakes up in a cold, dark cellar, with no idea how she got there or who her kidnapper is. So begins her terrible nightmare.

Nearby, the body of another young woman is discovered buried on a remote beach. But the dead girl was never reported missing – her estranged family having received regular texts from her over the years. Someone has been keeping her alive from beyond the grave.

For Detective Inspector Helen Grace it's chilling evidence that she's searching for a monster who is not just twisted but also clever and resourceful – a predator who's killed before.

And as Helen struggles to understand the killer's motivation, she begins to realize that she's in a desperate race against time . . .

'This is going to be as big as Jo Nesbo'
JUDY FINNIGAN

Available now from Penguin in paperback and ebook

THE FOURTH DI HELEN GRACE THRILLER

In the dead of night, three raging fires light up the city skies. It's more than a tragic coincidence. For DI Helen Grace the flames announce the arrival of an evil she has never encountered before.

Because this is no firestarter seeking sick thrills, but something more chilling: a series of careful, calculating acts of murder.

But why were the victims chosen?
What's driving the killer? And who will be next?

A powder keg of fear, suspicion and dread has been laid.
Now all it needs is a spark to set it off. . .

'DI Helen Grace is a genuinely fresh heroine . . . Arlidge weaves together a tapestry that chills to the bone'
DAILY MAIL

Available now from Penguin in paperback and ebook

THE FIFTH DI HELEN GRACE THRILLER

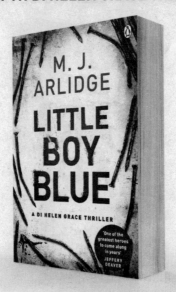

There are some fates worse than death . . .

Called to a Southampton nightclub, Detective Inspector Helen Grace
cuts the duct tape from the asphyxiated victim and discovers
she knows him.

A man from the double life she has concealed from her superiors,
Helen is determined to find his murderer – while keeping their
relationship hidden at all costs.

When a new victim is found, Helen works around the clock to stop
her life unravelling. She'll do anything to solve this case – but dare
she reveal her own darkest secrets and lose everything?

And would even that be enough to stop this killer?

'Page-turningly chilling'
THE TIMES

Available now from Penguin in paperback and ebook

He just wanted a decent book to read ...

Not too much to ask, is it? It was in 1935 when Allen Lane, Managing Director of Bodley Head Publishers, stood on a platform at Exeter railway station looking for something good to read on his journey back to London. His choice was limited to popular magazines and poor-quality paperbacks – the same choice faced every day by the vast majority of readers, few of whom could afford hardbacks. Lane's disappointment and subsequent anger at the range of books generally available led him to found a company – and change the world.

'We believed in the existence in this country of a vast reading public for intelligent books at a low price, and staked everything on it'
Sir Allen Lane, 1902–1970, founder of Penguin Books

The quality paperback had arrived – and not just in bookshops. Lane was adamant that his Penguins should appear in chain stores and tobacconists, and should cost no more than a packet of cigarettes.

Reading habits (and cigarette prices) have changed since 1935, but Penguin still believes in publishing the best books for everybody to enjoy. We still believe that good design costs no more than bad design, and we still believe that quality books published passionately and responsibly make the world a better place.

So wherever you see the little bird – whether it's on a piece of prize-winning literary fiction or a celebrity autobiography, political tour de force or historical masterpiece, a serial-killer thriller, reference book, world classic or a piece of pure escapism – you can bet that it represents the very best that the genre has to offer.

Whatever you like to read – trust Penguin.